WHEN LOVE BREAKS

Kate Squires

ISBN-10: 1533421978
ISBN-13: 9781533421975
Library of Congress Control Number: 2016910269
Createspace Independent Publishing Platform
North Charleston, South Carolina

ACKNOWLEDGEMENTS

It's time to thank the little people again—who really turned out to be big people in the end. So I'll start with God. Without You, none of this would be possible. Thank You so much for giving me the talent and the imagination! To my beta readers: Jody, Toni, Hayley, Steve, Jodie, and Josie. Thank you all for your willingness to read my stories in the raw. I know it's not always convenient, so thanks for that, and for giving me feedback on time (Well, most of you...you know who you are).

Ashlee, what can I say? You're a miracle worker! Thanks for seeing my mistakes and liking me anyway!

Steve, I know you see a little of yourself, and a bit of our conversations in my books, so let me just say how grateful I am that you are the way you are. Without you, my books might not be as captivating. You are truly a blessing to me.

Melinda, you helped me understand how difficult, but still normal, life after an amputation can be. Thanks for all your advice.

Bernadette, Rachelle, and Cindy, my medical trio. Bernadette, I have to give you credit for being so knowledgeable about physical detriments, and for a willingness to guide me in things I would have no other way of knowing. Rachelle, first, thank you for letting me borrow your husband, Steve at all hours of the day. I know he's goofy and a little weird, but he knows a lot so that's worth something. ;)

Also, your nursing info and insight really helped me on my journey in writing this book. I'm so grateful. Cindy, you worked your butt off to get me accurate information, and double checked that I had it all correct. For that, and many other things, I'm in your debt. Thanks to all three of you!

Thelma, I know you don't think you're that important, but I love you (more) and I cherish your feedback and our friendship.

To my family, thanks for not getting mad at me for all those days I don't have dinner ready because I'm on a writing binge. I love you! You're priceless!

Lastly, to my readers and fans: Thank you so much for all your kind words of encouragement, and for letting me know how much you love my stories. Without you, I wouldn't be putting out my fifth book! <3

WHEN LOVE BREAKS

Kate Squires

1

Love is a delicate balance of knowing how tightly to hold on,
and when to let go.
It smells like warm, summer evenings and starlit nights,
yet tastes of salty tears.
It's the sound of infectious laughter, but also gut wrenching
sorrow.
Love deserves respect.
Love is pleasure, and love is pain.
It can seek you out, then turn and walk away.
Love is the greatest antidote, and the most powerful venom.
Love is complicated, yet it's as simple as breathing.
Love heals, but it wounds just as easily.
Love is the most sought after desire,
but there's no foretelling the collateral damage
when love breaks...

ELORA

Nervously, I pull my hair back, and fasten the rubber hair tie around my ponytail. Grabbing two fistfuls at the back of my head, I pull them in opposite directions to tighten its hold on my hair. I look in the mirror and blow out a steadying breath. This job is going to be difficult. Seven caregivers, in as many days, is *not* a good track record. Is this man some sort of sadist? I shake my head at my reflection, and test out my most sincere smile. Will this expression be enough, or will he see right through me, and send me running from the house, never to return…just like the seven before me? I slouch and roll my eyes. Why did I agree to take on this client? Surely, there were others I could've taken that would be a lot less stressful. A frustrated groan passes between my lips. "Well, it's now, or never," I say, resigned to my fate. I walk out on a mission to survive what could be my first, and last, day with this client.

The neighborhood is quiet, as I drive onto his street, although it's still very early in the morning. The lawns are well manicured, and the landscaping looks professionally done. I assume the homeowner's association takes care of most of that. The houses, which line the streets of this picturesque community, are the typical cookie-cutter variety. The only differences between each one are the colors of the shutters. As I glance down at my watch, I realize it's seven o'clock on the nose, and I'm still trying to find the correct address. *Damn it.* The voice of my father pops into my head, uninvited. *If I were you, I'd leave earlier, Elora. I'd rather be half an hour early, than five minutes late.* Well, it's too late for that now.

Finally, I spy Melanie's car in a driveway a few houses down from where I'm stopped, so I speed up and park beside her.

"Sorry I'm not earlier," I say, as I quickly exit the car.

"It's fine. Let's just get in there," she says with a forced smile.

That can't be a good sign.

"Do I need a gait belt to lift him? It's in my car. I can go get it." I begin to turn back in the direction of my vehicle.

"No need," Melanie says. "He's already got one inside. I brought you a box of gloves and the care plan. Once we get inside, I'll do the introductions and go over the basics with you." She smiles again, but the emotions she's so obviously hiding from me, are worrisome. "Hey, don't worry too much, okay? He just got discharged from the hospital a little over a week ago. He's new to home health care…and his condition. It's going to be tough for him, but I'm sure you can make it work."

I nod, unsure of how I feel about all this and insecure about my capability of taking care of someone who's a double amputee.

Melanie opens the door to the home and announces our presence. Apparently, we didn't need to knock.

"Mr. Turner? I'm here with your new aide," she says, as I close the door behind us. While waiting for some sign of an inhabitant, I scan the place for anything that could give me more information about the man I'll be taking care of today. The house is neat and looks as though it could've been a model home at one time. That's not what I expected from someone in his condition. I walk in farther and see a smartly organized kitchen to my right. The open-concept dining room and living room is to my left, with a set of stairs leading to a loft which overlooks the whole area. A noise causes my eyes to look straight ahead, then land on a darkened figure. The hall, which I assume leads to the bedrooms, is dimly lit, and it isn't until he gets closer that I can make out his features.

Wheeling himself down the hallway, Mr. Logan Turner rolls toward us. His hair is a mess, and it looks as if he just got out of bed. His jaw is tense and in desperate need of a shave. The tight, worn t-shirt he's wearing clings to him, and his hardened biceps inform me that he's had to work way too hard for simple, daily functions, which most of us take for granted. I note that his amputations are just below his knees, and I'm relieved to know his knee joints are intact, which might possibly make both of our lives a bit easier. He stops just short of us and looks up. His eyes shifting from Melanie, to me, then back to her. His mood is hard to gauge.

"Hello, Mr. Turner. How are you doing today?" Melanie asks politely.

He looks down at his lap, then up at me.

"Well, I still don't have any legs, so I'd say I'm pretty shitty."

I swallow reflexively, not knowing how to respond.

"Other than that," she continues.

He looks back at her.

"Just peachy." His expression is sarcastic, as if his disability should've warranted a different question.

Out of nowhere, a small, nervous giggle bubbles out from my mouth. I try to cover it with a cough, but his narrowed eyes shoot straight to mine.

Shit.

"Um, sorry, I think I just swallowed a bug," I say quickly while patting my chest.

Still looking at me with a death stare, he turns abruptly, swinging his chair around, and heads for the kitchen table. Melanie walks behind him, and I follow.

"This is Elora Foster. She'll be your new aide. If you need anything, she's more than capable of handling it."

He says nothing as he picks up his newspaper, but I think I hear a quiet grunt.

"Can she cook?" he finally says. His voice is gruff.

I clear my throat and take a step toward him.

"Yes. I can cook," I say, trying to sound confident.

"Well?" he responds coldly.

"Um, *I* think so."

He grunts again and shakes his head slightly.

"We'll see," he mutters quietly, but I'm not sure I was supposed to hear him.

Melanie goes over the care plan with me and points out where everything's kept. She's obviously done this a few times.

"Well, I guess I'm going to go now," she says. "Walk me out, Elora?" I nod. "Have a good day, Mr. Turner." She smiles at him, but he doesn't even acknowledge her. I follow her to the front door.

"Melanie, I'm not sure if—"

"Elora, look, just do the best you can," she whispers. "As you know, we've had a lot of aides come and go from this place, and I just need someone who can tolerate him for the ten-hour shift. After that, his brother comes home and can take over. *Please?* Do this for me. We've been friends a long time, and I need this placement to work." She's practically on her knees begging me to give him a chance. I sigh and roll my eyes.

"Okay, fine. I'll do my best, but you *owe* me," I say and mean it.

"Thank you." She smiles, and gives me a quick hug, then exits, and I'm stuck with *Mr. Happy*.

I take a few seconds to gather my wits before reentering the kitchen. Logan sits in his wheelchair, still reading the newspaper, his back to me. I inhale, then blow out a ragged breath.

"So, what would you like for breakfast, Mr. Turner?"

His head turns slightly in the direction of my voice.

"Eggs," he says gruffly.

"Just eggs?"

"And toast."

"Okay...anything else?"

"Juice."

I nod, although he can't see me, then open the refrigerator to fetch the ingredients.

"Orange juice or apple juice?"

"What kind of question is that?" he says, clearly irritated.

I'm a little shocked at his tone.

"Um...I was just giving you options."

"What am I, four? What grown man drinks apple juice?"

"Uh, sorry. Orange juice it is then," I say apologetically. "*Would you like that in a sippy cup?*" I mutter begrudgingly under my breath. His head turns slightly, and I freeze. God, I hope he didn't hear my last comment. He says nothing then continues to read the paper. I blow out another relieved breath and get to work.

Within a few minutes, I've fried two eggs, toasted two slices of bread, and poured a tall glass of orange juice. I walk over to the table and place the dishes in front of him.

"*Fried* eggs?"

"Yes. Sunny side up," I reply.

"I wanted scrambled," he says petulantly.

"I'm…sorry. I just thought…I assumed that's how you wanted them."

"Well, you didn't *ask* me, did you?" he says acidly, and for the first time since my arrival, he looks directly at me. I shrivel under his scrutiny then open my mouth to say something, but I've got nothing. I'm literally speechless. Then, I watch as his expression changes. It almost softens momentarily. His tensed facial muscles relax, and his brow lifts slightly. But, just as quickly as it appeared, it's gone, and he resumes his seemingly permanent scowl. "It's fine. I'll deal with it," he says, and looks back down at his plate. I nod and make a hasty retreat.

After his breakfast, I clear the dishes and place them in the sink to be washed. Fearing his response, I ask anyway.

"Do you need help with anything else right now?" I try to keep my face passive. The last thing I need is for him to know how much he intimidates me.

"No," he says curtly. "But, if you're bored, you can straighten up a bit after the dishes are done. I'll be in my room." Without so much as a glance in my direction, he wheels himself out of the kitchen and down the hallway, disappearing behind a closed door. I sit in a nearby chair, sagging into it. I'm able to breathe again without him telling me I'm doing it wrong.

An hour or so later, I'm sitting at the kitchen table when Logan wheels himself into the room. I stand abruptly, unsure if I should look as though I was doing something constructive. He eyes me up and down, which makes me uncomfortable.

"Hi," I say. My response sounds breathy.

He frowns.

"I need a pen. They're over there," he says and points to a drawer near me.

"Okay." I walk the two steps it takes to reach the drawer and open it, hoping to find one right away. I rummage through for a few seconds, when my eyes land on one. Taking it out, I hand it to him. "Here you go. Are you writing a letter?" I ask, just to be polite.

His eyes narrow. Is he offended?

"What business of that is yours?"

"I was just trying to make small talk, that's all. I thought we could get to know each other better."

Not that I really want to.

"I'd rather not. I hate small talk. And, I'm sure there's something else you could be doing besides interrogating me."

My eyes brows shoot up. I did not expect that reaction.

"I'm sorry. I didn't think asking about a pen was an offense."

As soon as I finish my sentence, I realize I sounded a bit pissy. Even though I meant every sardonic word, I instantly look at the floor and hear him scoff.

"I don't need to tell you a thing. This is my house, and you were hired to do what I ask you to do. If you'd just stick to doing your *job,* and keep your nose out of my business, we'll get along just fine. Now, if it's all right with you, I'll be in my room." He turns his chair around and starts back down the hallway.

And, I don't know why, but something deep inside begs me to speak up.

"Well, thank God for small miracles," I mutter quietly, knowing full well he might be able to hear me. He stops abruptly and turns back to face me with an angry expression on his face.

"What did you say?"

"Who me?" I say innocently while looking around behind me. "I didn't say a thing." I smile sweetly at him as he stares at me for a few more seconds. It's almost as if he's trying to read my mind. When he's done trying to melt my brain with his heat vision…or whatever, he retreats back into his bedroom.

I slump into the kitchen chair, rest my head in the palms of my hands, and wonder how I'm going to get through the rest of this shift.

Lunchtime comes and goes, and Logan's no different than he was after breakfast. Although I've learned to ask how he wants his food prepared, I feel as though it really doesn't matter. He seems bound and determined to find fault with everything I do.

Before disappearing back into his room, for who knows how long, he stops in front of a fairly large pile of boxes and bags. They're all but blocking the entrance to the living room, and I would imagine that they make it hard for him to get around. He shakes his head in disapproval.

"Dammit, Michael. How the hell am I supposed to get to the thermostat? Why the hell wouldn't he put this shit in his room?" Logan says, clearly irritated.

"I could move the boxes...if you'd like." I'm hoping my offer will cause him to lighten up a bit when it comes to my abilities to be helpful.

He looks back at me, and his eyes sweep over my small frame. Is he assessing my strength? I stand taller, with my shoulders pulled down and back.

"You're really that bored?" I shrug, and he sighs. "Fine. I don't think there's anything heavy in them. Just move them to the bedroom, down the hall from mine, then shut the door. After that, turn the temperature down about five degrees." I nod, and he heads toward his room, closing the door behind him again. I begin the task before me.

He's right. The boxes aren't heavy at all, and I'm glad I have something to do. If I had to guess, I'd say they're probably filled with a bunch of his brother's stuff, since the name 'Michael Turner' appears on most of them. I'm also assuming it's his brother's room I'm placing them in.

As I open the door, I'm shocked. This room looks nothing like the orderly, well-kept rest of the house that I'm used to seeing. No, this place looks like a tornado touched down. There's a bed, which isn't made, a dresser, that has clothes spilling out of it, and more piles of boxes. I find a clutter-free spot on the floor and stack the first two boxes there. I continue this process, until everything is inside. Looking around to ensure no one's watching me, I take a few minutes to snoop a bit. The room is sparsely decorated, but that's probably because his brother just moved in. I see a few trophies, which look as though they're from his high school or college days. I pick up a framed picture and wipe the glass a bit. It's a portrait of a handsome couple. They're most likely in their late fifties or so. I squint to see if I notice a family resemblance, but the picture is too small.

The next one I pick up is a photo of two men. They have their arms slung around each other's shoulders, and both are wearing military uniforms. They have huge grins on their faces and upon further inspection, I recognize one of them—it's Logan. He's tall, and his hair is much shorter than it is right now. His five o'clock shadow is nonexistent, which brings out his amazing eyes. His smile is bright and, for the first time since I met him, I find myself unable to look away. He's stunning. I can't help but feel as though I'm seeing a completely different person, both literally and figuratively. Then, I look lower and notice that his legs are intact. I stare at them, wishing I could go back in time, for just a moment, to see what he was like when this picture was taken. He looks happy. Then, something distracts me, so I look up.

"Are you done rifling through my brother's things?" Logan asks. His face is expressionless. Embarrassed for being caught red handed, I quickly put the picture down.

"I—I'm sorry. I was just looking at this picture," I say, pointing to it. "Is it you and your brother? I didn't mean to—"

"I don't care what you *didn't mean to do*. I asked you to turn down the thermostat. Did you even get to that yet, or were you too busy snooping?"

Sheesh. What's his problem?

"Um…"

He scoffs and shakes his head.

"Can you go do it now?" His tone is patronizing, and I'm getting a little fed up with his bad attitude.

"Sure," I say curtly, then exit the room on my way to my mission. After I pass him, and with his back to me, I show him, with one finger, exactly how I feel about him at this very moment.

After a boring, isolated afternoon, I begin to prepare dinner for Logan and his brother. I look around the kitchen and ultimately decide on baked chicken, green beans, and mashed potatoes. Including prep time, it takes about an hour to cook, in total, which brings me almost to the end of my shift. I'm relieved at the realization that I get a reprieve from this hell for the rest of the evening.

Suddenly, I hear the squeak of a door as Logan exits his room, but he doesn't come out into the kitchen. I listen carefully, then hear him say a few choice words, so I quickly go to investigate.

"Do you need some help?" I ask through the closed bathroom door. Then, I hear a bang and something fall to the floor. "Is everything alright?" I touch the doorknob, ready to rush in, if need be.

"I'm fine. Go away," Logan's muffled voice replies.

"Are you sure? I can help if you can't—"

"*I said I've got this!* What part of that don't you understand?" he snaps. His voice cuts through the door, hitting me directly. He's really angry, more so than any other time today.

"Okay, okay." I roll my eyes and sigh before walking away. This is my job. What does he think I'm here for?

Minutes later, Logan comes into the kitchen, a slight sheen of sweat is on his brow.

"I've cooked dinner for the two of you. It's chicken. I hope that's okay," I say, trying to gauge his mood.

"Fine," he says petulantly and without looking me in the eye.

"It's almost time for me to go. Is there anything else I can do for you, before I leave?" He shakes his head. "Okay then, I'll be on my way." I grab my coat and head for the door. I almost expect him to say good bye, but then, I'm not dealing with the average man here.

I'm right, when I walk out the door without so much as a '*see ya*' from him.

Closing myself inside my car, I rest my head on my hand as I run through the events of today. As much as I don't want to admit it, I'm disappointed by the lack of appreciation for the shit I put up with. I've never been made to feel so stupid, or purposeless, in my life. Clearly, this man has some issues. I'm used to caring for the elderly, not someone who's bitter about the hand he's been dealt, and who's got a giant chip on his shoulder. I rub my face with my hands and sigh. I don't want to go back tomorrow; I can't go back tomorrow. What am I going to tell Melanie?

"What's for dinner?" Daniel asks, lifting the various lids from the pots on the stove. I playfully slap at his hands, scolding him.

"I'm cooking several things, actually, none of which are ready yet."

He smirks at me in the way he's done for most of my life. I fist my hands on my hips, trying to appear angry, but it's no use. I've never been able to stay mad at my one and only brother.

"It smells good. Is it some sort of holiday I don't know about? Why are you cooking for a small army?"

I lift the lid off one pot and stir it.

"No, it's not a holiday. I just figured I'd get ahead with making our meals for the week. I'm going to freeze them, so we can just pull one out as we need them."

"You're stress cooking," he says.

"No, I'm not. Can't a girl just cook to cook? Do I really need to be stressed out to get ahead for the week?"

"Most people don't cook this much when there are only two people living in their house." He knows me well.

"Well, that's not why I'm doing it."

"Okay, Okay. I get it," he says, holding his hands up in surrender. "Feel free to vent about whatever it is when you're ready. Besides, all this preparation will come in handy when your hours change with your new client."

I stop stirring, remembering my earlier encounter with Logan.

"I already started that job, but I think it was a one-day deal." I look up to his puzzled expression, and feel I should elaborate. "He's a tough client, and I just don't think we're a good match."

"Oh?"

I sigh, not really wanting to get into too much detail, and knowing Daniel can be overprotective.

"Yeah. He's had it rough recently. His current health condition has made him a little bitter and hard to please."

"So, he pissed you off?" he asks.

"No. I just think he'd rather have someone else taking care of him, that's all."

He nods his head.

"Well, I'm sure you'll find another moldy oldie to take care of."

"Daniel! These people are human beings, and they're usually very sweet. I've told you before, *be nice.*"

"All right. I guess I'll never understand why you love to wipe ass for a living." I reprimand him with my angry glare, so he backs off the subject.

My phone rings. Daniel picks it up, then hands it to me.

"Hello?"

"Hi, Elora. How did it go today at Logan Turner's house?" I excuse myself and walk out of earshot of my nosy brother.

"Hi, Melanie. It went okay, but I don't think—"

"I'm so happy to hear that! I know he can be difficult, but I appreciate all your efforts."

"But I don't think I can go back there."

"Elora, as you can imagine, this case has been particularly difficult to staff. As long as he didn't ask for someone new, I'd like to encourage you to stay on it. Frankly, I'm running out of options for him." The pleading tone to her voice makes me feel a certain obligation to her. Melanie's my friend, as well as my supervisor, so I reluctantly agree.

"Ugh! Fine. I'll just figure out how to stay out of his way as much as possible. But, if you hear about his murder, then have trouble finding me, you'll be able to guess what happened," I say wryly.

She laughs.

"I may help you bury the body," she says.

We finish our call, then hang up. I drop onto the couch, thoroughly exhausted.

Although Melanie and I walked right in yesterday, today I feel I should knock, or ring the doorbell, before gaining entry into Logan's house. I'm apprehensive about what his reaction will be when he sees me standing in the doorway and inwardly hope he's in a better mood. It takes several minutes for him to appear, and it's an obvious struggle to open the door, given his wheelchair is in the way. When our eyes finally meet, I witness a mixture of emotions wash across his face. He goes from shock, to, if I'm not mistaken, relief, but then quickly, and clearly, he shuts down into irritation.

"You're back. You weren't supposed to ring the bell. It's hard for me to open doors. *Remember that,*" he says bitterly then rolls away from the entrance, allowing me to walk in.

I roll my eyes, knowing he can't see me, and close the door.

What an ass.

"My apologies. I'll make a note of that," I say. *For the* next *person who has to deal with your bullshit,* is what I want to say, but I refrain.

He wheels himself up to the kitchen table and begins leafing through the newspaper. "I'll have eggs again this morning," he says gruffly.

"Okay. How would you like them?" My face is an exaggerated grin, complete with fluttering eyelashes and all. If there's one thing I've got going for me today, it's that I can make all the faces I want behind his back. It's not professional, I know, but if it helps me get through the day, then so be it.

"Over easy. Yours weren't horrible yesterday. Just put more pepper on them this time."

I sneer. Not horrible? Is that his idea of a compliment? He really needs to work on his people skills. Then, it occurs to me. If he's going to make me miserable with all of his negativity, I'm going to annoy the shit out of him with my best happy-go-lucky attitude. I smile at my new plan and open the fridge.

"Coming right up."

A little while later, I lay his breakfast in front of him. He seems satisfied and begins to eat.

"It's supposed to be a beautiful day today," I say, trying to make small talk. He just grunts. "Do you ever go outside?" He shakes his head but says nothing. I guess it would be hard for him to get out there. I'm wracking my brain trying to come up with a topic that interests him. "Do you have any hobbies?" There's no reply. He's not much of a conversationalist, which is making this first half hour awkward and difficult. "So, your brother…what does he do for a living?"

Logan turns his head, enough to be able to see me.

"You know, it's really hard to eat and talk at the same time. Would you mind keeping your questions and comments to yourself?" he says.

My brows knit together, involuntarily.

"Sure," I say flatly, not even trying to disguise my frustration.

I start on the kitchen clean up.

An hour has passed. The dishes have been washed, dried, and put away. The kitchen is cleaned up, and the rest of the house has been straightened. As I turn away from the kitchen sink, I'm startled, as Logan has wheeled himself up right behind me. I have to grab onto the counter to keep from falling into his lap.

"When you moved those boxes yesterday, did you see a small wooden box?" he asks, a very angry expression on his face.

"Um, I'm not sure. Why?"

"*Think.* Did you, or did you not, put a small wooden box in my brother's room?"

"I don't remember."

His sigh is one of pure frustration.

"I *need* that box. It has something important in it."

"I'm sorry, I really don't know if I moved it or not. Chances are good, that if it was near the rest of the pile, I did. I can just get it for you." I step around him in an attempt to walk toward his brother's bedroom.

"Forget it. He keeps his door locked, and I don't have a key. *Thanks a lot,*" he says in a condescending tone. He then mutters some swear words and stalks off, back down the hall.

He doesn't have a key? And, what the hell is so important about some stupid box that has his panties in a twist? This job is getting really old, really fast. I'm not sure how much longer I can take his ridiculous behavior. I'm here to help, not to be mistreated. I want to tell him off right now, but I decide to let him cool off a bit, before I rile him up again.

After about fifteen minutes of letting *myself* calm down, I walk gingerly down the hall, toward Logan's bedroom. The door is ajar, so quietly, I peer through. I see him. He's sitting at his desk. The laptop that's in front of him is on, but he's not paying any attention to it. I watch, curiously, as he exercises. With his arms on the arm rests of his wheelchair, he lifts himself up and down repeatedly. His shirtless back is toward me, and I get an uninterrupted view of his truly impressive physique.

Holy hell. He's really ripped.

In awe, I observe him as his muscles contract with each extension of his arms. I expect him to stop after a few minutes, but he continues. A sheen of sweat that has formed, trickles down his back, as he pumps up and down, never once even pausing to rest. I can hear his labored breaths, and I know he's been at this a while.

Suddenly, his hand slips off, no doubt from the perspiration of his palms, and he's knocked off balance, almost falling out of his chair.

"Agh!" he exclaims, as he tries to right himself.

Automatically, I rush in, ready to catch him, or at least soften his fall. I grab him around the chest from behind and pull him back onto the seat. He squirms in my arms, and pries my hands apart.

"*What the hell do you think you're doing?*" he barks. I back off immediately as he turns to face me. "*Why are you in here?*" His face is full of rage, and I know I made yet another mistake.

"I…I'm sorry. I thought you needed my help. You fell…you *almost* fell. I was just trying to help," I say, desperate for some sort of sympathetic look. "I was just doing my job," I say softly out of frustration.

"I don't need your help or your pity. Save it for some frail, old lady!" he spits. "Were you spying on me? How long were you standing there?" His tone is accusatory, as if I was ogling him for fun, which in a way, I suppose I was. Tears threaten, but I hold them at bay.

"Only for a few seconds," I lie. "The dishes are done, and the house has been tidied. I was looking for you to ask what else I can do."

He sighs loudly.

"Nothing. You can go."

"But, I still have most of my shift left."

"I can take it from here."

My puzzled look generates an expression of, *are you stupid?* from him, so I step back and bow my head. I hear another exasperated sigh.

"Look, I'm good. My brother hired your company to come and babysit me while he's at work. I don't really need you here. I'll call and tell them I dismissed you, so you don't get in trouble." I nod without looking at him. "If you want, you can take the garbage out to the street before you go. My brother will practically wet himself with delight," he says sarcastically.

"Okay," I say quietly then back away from his room, until he's out of my line of sight. I turn the corner and lean against the cold, hallway wall, feeling defeated as tears, once again, prick my eyes. I knew this job would be hard. I just didn't think it'd be *this* hard.

LOGAN

*S**hit.* I was too hard on her. Why am I such an asshole? She was just doing her job, like she said. I close my eyes and silently castigate myself for chasing another one off. Only this time, I feel guilty for it. I touch my chest where her warm hands just were and oddly, my skin has never felt so cold. Her touch was an automatic response to her training, yet it seemed different, sincere, kind. I rub my forehead in frustration. I feel bad that she has to put up with me but then, I doubt I'll see her after today. Good. She doesn't need the hassle, and I don't need her help. But, even as I think it, I know it's bullshit.

I throw my shirt back on and wheel myself out of my bedroom toward the kitchen. She's still here, but not for long, as she's putting on her jacket.

"I'll need you to sign this, to say I was here, and that I did the tasks listed here." She points to a line on the paper. Her face is sullen, and she doesn't look me in the eye. I feel terrible for yelling at her. None the less, I take the pen from her hand and scribble my name. Our fingers touch briefly as I hand it back to her, and it's as if an electrical pulse travels up my arm. I pull back immediately. Silence overtakes the room, and my need to fill it is unlike me.

"Thank you, for...um...breakfast, and...everything else." My words come out awkwardly, as though I'm a nervous teenager talking to a pretty girl who's way out of my league.

"You're welcome," she says softly, still not looking directly at me.

I want to see her eyes one more time.

"Hey," I say sharply, and it works. She looks up. "Have a good rest of the day."

The confusion on her face is evident. I'm sure she's wondering why I would summon her attention to say something so random and so...normal. Hell, *I'm* wondering the same thing. She nods and turns to walk out the door. I want to say something else...*anything*, to make her turn back around, but I don't, and my heart sinks as the door latches behind her.

2

LOGAN

"You did *what?*" Michael shouts at me while clenching his fists.

"I dismissed her. I don't need a babysitter, Michael."

"Like hell you don't! You can barely manage to get in and out of the damn bed without falling onto the floor! You need help, Logan. You do. The sooner you admit that, the better. I'm calling the agency back and asking them to send her again tomorrow. Hopefully, she'll come, or you'll be on aide number nine." His voice is strained. He's serious—not that I care.

"Fuck you! If you tell them I still need someone, I'll just have them sit on their ass all day and do nothing. Won't *that* be a great use of money?"

Michael's face is turning a menacing shade of red as he scoffs at me, then he stomps off to his room, slamming the door behind him. I roll my eyes and flip him off. Deep down, I know he's right, though I'd never, in a million years, tell him that.

My thoughts then involuntarily drift to Elora. Will they send her again? Probably not. Surely, by now, she's told them she never wants to step foot in this house again. Hell, who could blame her? I've done nothing but give her a hard time since she walked in. If she's smart, she'll never agree to come back. But, somewhere inside me, hope springs. What is it about her that feels different? She's beautiful.

19

Actually, she's more than beautiful, but she's kind too. She's observant and seems to anticipate my needs before I know what they are. Hell, she even cooked my favorite meal without even knowing it. I bow my head. I can't get too excited about this girl, after all, what would I possibly have to offer her?

Michael struts back into the kitchen and begins to heat up leftovers from yesterday. Thank God she made so much.

"Well, despite you being a giant douchebag today, Elora has agreed to come back and work here. I'm not sure how much extra they offered her, but I'm sure it was well worth it. I know it was worth the groveling I had to do on your behalf to get her. And, you'll apologize and be nice to her, damn it," he says, while taking his plate out of the microwave. He begins to eat while staring at me and smirking.

"What?" I snap.

"If you're so independent, why don't you heat up your own dinner?" He raises his eyebrows in anticipation of my response.

"You know I can't reach the microwave."

"I know. That just proves my point. You need her, Logan. And, to top it off, *I* need her." My brow furrows, and an odd sensation creeps in. "To keep cooking meals like this," he says, then he takes a bite, thoroughly enjoying his dinner, and the fact that he's right.

"Fine. Whatever. I'll just eat cereal." I roll toward the cabinet to grab a box.

"Dude, shut up. I was just messing with you. I'll do it for you."

And, that last, little, five-word sentence, is the crux of my problem. I hate my life.

ELORA

I reach for the doorbell, then I remember my scolding from yesterday. Instead, I grasp the knob, twist, and push. The door creaks slightly as I open it.

"Hello? It's me, Elora," I say, as I step inside. There's no response, but soon I hear him rolling down the hallway.

"Morning," he says, his voice is monotone, and his expression, as always, is hard to read.

"Morning," I say, keeping my voice void of any emotion. "Eggs again today?" I take off my coat, lay it over a nearby chair, and walk to the fridge. I'm trying hard to ignore my instant urge to leave.

"Yes, please."

Yes, please? Well, that's something.

"Fried?" He nods, and I nod in return.

In silence, I begin to make his breakfast, when I notice he's not reading the paper, as he usually does. He's sighing a bit and looks fidgety. What's he up to? Suddenly, he turns his chair to face me.

"I'm sorry about yesterday...being gruff with you and asking you to leave, I mean. It wasn't very nice of me, and...I apologize." His sincere eyes meet mine, and it occurs to me, that this is the first time he's ever spoken to me in a normal tone of voice. I nod my head slightly.

"Thank you. Apology accepted. Shall we start over?" I walk over to him and extend my hand. "Hi. I'm Elora," I say with a genuine smile. He smirks slightly.

He has a great smirk.

"Logan," he simply says as he shakes my hand.

"It's very nice to meet you, Logan. If there's anything I can do for you, please don't hesitate to ask.

His face turns sullen, and he nods gravely.

Did I say something wrong?

Slowly, he turns back to the table and picks up the paper.

After setting his breakfast in front of him, I begin the kitchen clean up.

"This is good," he says without prompting, and I'm taken by surprise.

"Uh, thank you. I hope I put the right amount of pepper on it this time."

"Yes, it's fine. Thank you." He opens his mouth, as if to say more, but closes it again without another word.

Looking for a topic of conversation, I open the pantry.

"You know, you're getting low on some of your groceries. Does Michael do the shopping?"

"Who else would do it?" he says, sarcastically, then seems to recover his manners. "He has been, but he hates it and rarely finds the time."

"I could do it for you," I say without thinking. "I mean, I *am* doing most of the cooking anyway. I could go, if it would help."

He thinks for a moment.

"I guess that'd be fine. When do you want to go?"

"I'll go after my shift here. I'll wait until your brother gets home and—"

"No, do it during the day," he says in a rush, as he interrupts me. "I can manage without you for an hour or so."

"I'm not sure I'm supposed to—"

"It's fine," he interrupts again. "I'll be fine. I'm not an infant." His tone is chastising. Even though I didn't mean to imply he's helpless, I bow my head anyway, knowing I've struck a nerve. Then, his face suddenly softens. "I'll get my credit card." He wheels himself out of the kitchen and toward the bedroom. He's gone only a few minutes, when he returns with the plastic card and hands it to me. "Get whatever you think you'll use in a week." I nod.

"Okay," I say, then grab a pen and paper in an attempt to make a basic list of items. It's also to keep from making eye contact with him. I quickly jot down milk, bread, and coffee. Then, it occurs to me. I don't know if he drinks coffee. My curious face must be cause for him to inquire.

"What is it?" he says.

"Um, do you drink coffee?" My voice sounds timid.

"Not usually, but sometimes. If we're almost out, get some." I nod again. "Michael mostly drinks it and trust me when I say, we're *all* better off if he doesn't run out." He chuckles at his own little dig at his brother's expense, and I automatically look at him. The faintest of smiles graces his lips and for the first time, I see a tiny glimpse of the man in the picture.

"Okay then, I think I wrote down everything you're low on. I have an idea for a couple dishes I'm going to make for you, so I'll pick those items up too. I won't be gone long."

"Take your time. I'm not going anywhere," he says, then he rolls back down the hall.

The grocery store isn't busy, so I breeze down each aisle with ease. The fact that I know the layout like the back of my hand gives me a lot of time to think about things. Logan's moods have been all over the place today, going from angry to smirking in the blink of an eye. I can't say I've seen him actually happy yet, but the small hints of a different Logan lead me to believe there's a more pleasant part of him in there somewhere. I wonder what it'll take to bring the rest out.

LOGAN

"Forty-seven, forty-eight, forty-nine, fifty." I grunt, as I finish the last rep of my make-shift push-ups from the arms of my wheelchair. I heave a heavy sigh, as I realize it's time to get onto the floor. I hate the floor. Well, it's not so much the floor as trying to get my ass *off* the floor. It's something I've yet to master. There doesn't seem to be an easy way to hoist myself back up. Never the less, I reach downward and clumsily plop down onto the carpet.

After a few too many floor exercises, I grab my water bottle and rest. I figure I've got about fifteen more minutes or so, before Elora comes back from her shopping excursion. I'll be in my chair before then. I no sooner think it, when I hear the front door open and close, then hear the rustle of grocery bags.

Shit.

I hurriedly recap my drink and reach up for my chair. Grasping the front of it, I pull as hard as I can, all the while knowing she could come in and find me like this. *I don't want her to find me like this.* Unexpectedly, the chair begins to tip forward, which forces me to let go.

Shit.

Shit.

Shit!

I try again, as I hear her trundling toward my room.

"Logan? I'm back. Are you in there?"

I see the doorknob turn slightly.

"I'm here, but…I'm not decent. Don't come in." My voice is breathy from the exertion, and I know she won't leave it alone.

"Do you need help?"

Do I need help? I need more than help.

"*No!*" I say, a little too harshly. God, why do I do that? "Just finish putting the food away. I'll be out in a minute," I say, frustrated with myself.

"Okay." Her answer is quiet, and I hear her footsteps fade as they get farther from my door. I sag with relief but realize what a jerk I sounded like.

Finally, after what seems like an eternity, I manage to get back into my wheelchair. It wasn't pretty, but I'm up. I slide my shirt on, slather on some more deodorant, and blow out a steady breath. I look at my reflection. "Be nice. Don't be an asshole." Then, I wheel myself to the kitchen.

She's there, and I watch as she removes the items from the bags and tucks them away, where they belong. She doesn't make eye contact with me, and I've come to learn that she does this when I've snapped at her.

Asshole.

"I bought you some more orange juice," she says, still not looking at me. "I got the kind without pulp. I wasn't sure if that's what you prefer, but I figured I'd err on the side of caution."

"That's fine. Thank you."

"And, I bought some coconut oil to cook with. It's good for all kinds of things. It's a bit more expense, but you told me to get whatever I needed, so I did."

"Good. That's fine too."

She puts the last item away and immediately starts on lunch.

"Elora."

"Hmm?"

What am I trying to say?

I hesitate a little too long, and I catch her attention.

"You know, that's the second time you've done that today," she says boldly.

"Second time I did what?"

"Started to say something but stopped. You should say what you're thinking. I can't get to know your needs if you keep things from me."

I'm taken aback by her words.

"I just don't always think it's appropriate to say what I'm thinking without filtering things first. I'm not great at choosing the right verbiage."

She lets out a small giggle which dances playfully into my ears.

"Did you just use the word *verbiage?*"

I'm confused as to why that's funny.

"Um, I guess. Why?"

Did I use it wrong?

"It just sounded strange coming from your mouth."

"And, why is that?"

She shrugs.

"I don't know. You just don't seem to be the type who uses those sort of words. Not many people even know that word exists."

"Are you suggesting I'm uneducated?" My stern expression causes her face to fall immediately.

"No! Not at all. I didn't mean anything by it. I just..." She's flustered.

"I read. A lot. I don't have anything better to do, so that's my hobby, I guess." My tone is unnecessarily brusque.

"I absolutely understand. Forgive me if you thought otherwise," she says, then turns her attention to making lunch again. Silence lays thick like a blanket covering the room.

I sigh. Why does every conversation seem to end with me making her upset? Of course, she didn't mean anything by her comment. I feel the need to make amends.

"Would you like to eat lunch with me?"

Her jaw goes slack as she turns her head in my direction. I think I've shocked her.

"W—what?"

"Now that I know we have a fully stocked pantry, I'm asking if you'd like to eat with me." *Seal the deal, Logan.* "Please?"

She smiles politely at my offer and sets down the butter knife she's holding.

"Thank you for the offer, but I was planning on studying while you ate lunch."

"Oh? What are you going to school for?"

"Nursing."

"Really. You like taking care of grumpy old men that much?"

She smiles broadly, and it's as if the sun has suddenly entered the room. Then, a giggle escapes. I could get used to that sound.

"Some are grumpier than others," she says, still smiling, and I know she's referring to me. I shrug.

"Some have a good reason to be grumpy."

"And some should look at what they still have, instead of stewing on what they've lost."

My instinct is to lash out at her. How the hell does she know what my life is like now without the most basic of functions? She has no idea what I've lost, aside from my legs. My life is crap now, and there's not a thing anyone can do about it. Her smug expression remains, so I take a deep breath and choose my words wisely, implementing every filter I have.

"You're right. Maybe some men would find the good in even the most tragic situations, but some, would-be nurses, might want to be a little more understanding too." I smile smugly right back at her, and her mouth twists.

"Touché. I hope those grumpy men and would-be nurses come to an understanding someday and learn that things aren't always black or white."

I raise my glass.

"Here's to that hope."

ELORA

It's one o'clock in the afternoon, and Logan has just eaten the last of his turkey sandwich. He rolls away from the table and toward the hallway.

"Do you need any help?" I ask as I look up from my books.

"No. I'm just going to wash my hands. The bathroom sink is a bit easier to reach for me."

I nod, understanding how much more complicated his life must be now.

He wheels himself down the hall and into the bathroom, closing the door behind him. I'm just putting away the last of my papers when I hear a loud thump. I inhale sharply and sprint toward the sound.

"Everything okay in there?" I ask through the door.

"I'm fine," he says, but his voice is strained.

"Are you sure? I can help you."

"I said I'm fine. You can go!" His voice sounds as though he's trying to reign in his temper. "I meant you can go in another room, not go home," he adds.

I smirk. It's a small triumph, but I'll take it.

"Okay," I simply say, then I move away from the door. I know he's a proud man but really, what am I here for, if not to help him?

When he emerges back into the kitchen, he looks flustered. A silent conversation takes place between us where I ask him what's wrong, and he tells me he's fine. I don't buy it though. Boldly, I speak up.

"You know, it's not unheard of to ask your home health aide to help you in the bathroom." His expression is one of horror.

"Absolutely not."

"Why not? It's not like you have anything I haven't seen before."

"You're not helping me in there."

"Modest, are we?" I flutter my eyelashes, imitating shyness.

"Not modest, just proud."

"And in need of a hand or two, wouldn't you say?"

"No, I wouldn't say," he says, adamantly.

"Okay, but you've got to be tired of struggling every time you're in there."

I hear his frustrated sigh.

"Look, while it's true that I still haven't mastered certain things yet, you can be damn sure I won't ask *you* for help." His irritated tone tells me I've struck another nerve, and I need to change the subject. I hold up my hands in surrender.

"I get it. It's fine. I'll stick to cooking and cleaning." I stand and walk toward the sink.

"Elora ," he starts, then stops, seemingly grasping for the right words. "I'll be in my room if you need me."

If *I* need *him*? I almost giggle at his wording, but nod.

The end of my day has arrived sooner than it did yesterday. Well, it hasn't really. I guess it just seems that way because it went a little better. I'm putting the finishing touches on the lasagna I made, when Logan rolls back into the kitchen.

"All right, the lasagna is done and keeping warm in the oven. Just have Michael take it out when he gets home. Is there anything else you need before I leave?" He shakes his head sort of sadly. "Well then, I should go." He nods, and I eye him suspiciously.

Something's wrong, but I just don't know him well enough to pry, so I let it go.

"Elora?" he says as I'm about to open the front door. I turn and look at him.

"Yes?"

"…Be careful going home."

I grin appreciatively.

"Thank you, I will. See you tomorrow."

"I'll be here," he says, then smiles very contently.

"There's a spring in your step. Did you have a better day at work?" Daniel asks.

"Yes. I got an apology from my client, and I think we're starting to bond, which is a good thing."

"Good. Let's hope it lasts."

"Tell me about it," I say, rolling my eyes.

"So, he's a double amputee? Was he injured in the war?"

"Yes and yes. Well, at least I think so. He doesn't talk about it," I say, curious myself.

"I guess I don't blame him. War isn't pretty, and I'd hate to think about all he's seen on his tours of duty."

"Yeah." Then, I remember something. "Ugh! I have a test coming up that I didn't study very much for," I say as I move away from him. "I'll be in my room, with my nose in a book, if you need me." I stalk off toward my bedroom.

"What about dinner?" Daniel shouts at my retreating back.

"Just microwave something from the freezer," I call out, before closing the door to my room and sinking into nursing student mode.

3

Logan is eating the breakfast I prepared. He made an effort today. He shaved, combed his unruly, brown mop, and put on fresh, clean clothes. I noticed immediately, and was sure to compliment him on looking more human. When the unintentional joke at his expensive came across my lips, I wasn't sure what his reaction would be, but his mood is great today and so was his ability to laugh at himself. It's so nice to see him smile.

"Earth to Elora," Logan says to get my attention. I perk up immediately.

"Huh? Oh, sorry. I guess I was day dreaming. Do you need something?" I walk around the counter and come to stand in front of him.

"Yes, actually. Why don't you have a seat and eat breakfast with me? I know the chef personally, and she wouldn't mind." He smirks, as he refers to me.

I smile at his thoughtfulness.

"I don't know. I'm not very hungry," I say.

"Did you eat before you came?"

"A little. I had a piece of toast." He frowns.

"That wouldn't keep a bird alive. There are more eggs in the fridge. I'd offer to make them for you, but I'm not sure you're into eating charcoal briquettes."

I laugh.

"No, I'm not, and thank you, but no. I'll be fine."

"Okay, maybe lunch then," he says.

"Why are you always trying to feed me? Do I look like I need to eat more?" I chuckle at my own words, hoping not to sound as though I'm offended.

"Not at all. I'm just trying to get to know you. Besides, don't most people converse over a meal? It just feels natural."

"I suppose." I rub my chin, thinking about his proposal. "Okay. I'll have a little breakfast with you, but don't think this'll become a habit."

"I wouldn't dream of it. Besides, I'm sure you have terrible table manners," he says in jest.

"I totally do. Elbows on the table, slurping soup—the whole nine yards. You should see me eat spaghetti."

He makes a face of disgust, and we're both smiling. It's really nice.

An hour or so goes by, and we're still at the table talking. I'm telling him about my life, or lack thereof, as a nursing student, and he's explaining to me how the simplest movements are so much harder for him now. I could've guessed that already, but he's talking, so I let him.

"So, why didn't you do occupational and physical therapy while you were still in the hospital?"

"They wanted me to, but I was so bitter about my situation, and I was the furthest thing from cooperative. Without my legs, all I wanted to do was die. I had no interest in learning how to get along in a world that I no longer wanted to be a part of. It was all or nothing for me. It still is in a lot of ways."

"But why? Lots of people lose limbs and function just fine in society."

"I know. It's hard to explain. My brother's been amazing though. He moved here from California, just to help me adjust to everything.

Luckily, he has a job that allows him the freedom to travel, so his company just let him transfer to their Ohio hub. I don't know where I'd be without him."

"Wow, he sounds great."

"Yeah. We have our moments, but I can never repay him for all he's done."

I nod, and a weird silence hangs in the air. I feel the need to break it.

"Well, it sounds to me like you need some lessons on how to modify your behavior to accommodate your new lifestyle." I stand and begin to clear the table.

"Huh?"

I laugh.

"You need to go back to therapy."

"No," he says, and I get the feeling that he's not going to budge.

"Why not? It can only help you. What are you afraid of?"

"I'm not afraid of anything. I just don't want to do it. I'll figure it out on my own."

"That's stupid." His brow furrows at my audacity. "What? I'm serious. They have methods that could enhance your day to day life. You wouldn't have to struggle as much."

He scoffs, as if that's not possible.

"I'm a smart man; I'll do it on my own."

He's so damned stubborn. I'm aggravated at the notion that he won't take help from anyone. I wish I knew more about the types of things a therapist could teach him. Then, maybe, I could guide him, until he's more comfortable with it. What the hell is he so afraid of?

"And, will you build yourself a new set of prosthetic legs too?" I cross my arms in a defiant stance. I'm irritated.

He glares at me.

"I don't need plastic and metal holding me up in some vain attempt to make me appear normal. And, don't stand there lecturing me about what I should and shouldn't be doing. You have legs. You can walk and run, if you want to. You can jump and for God's sake, you can walk up those stairs right there!" He points toward the living room. "I can do none of that. So, no, nothing you say, nor anything a therapist can do for me, would bring my legs back, which is the only thing that could give me back my life. Until you lose a limb or two, you have no right to say a fucking word!"

His face is red from his angry outburst, and I feel terrible. He's right. I don't understand, and I probably never will, but he's wrong too. His life can get better. He does have the chance to walk and run again. He could most definitely walk up a flight of stairs, and do everything anyone else with their natural legs can do. He just has to believe it's possible and put in the work. I bow my head in defeat, and I don't stop him from leaving the room. He needs space, and so do I.

While sitting alone in the kitchen, self-doubt about my care giving capabilities creeps in again, and I wonder if I'm the best home health care worker for this man. I'm agitating him more than I'm helping him. Maybe, I should cut my losses and get out before I get too attached to him. But, deep down, I realize I already am. I know the man from the picture is still inside him somewhere. I have yet to meet him, but he has to exist. I feel like maybe, just maybe, if I can get him to see how his life can improve, I might coax out the old Logan. I've got to try, and I know what I have to do.

Lunch time comes and goes, and Logan refuses to come out of his room. I knock several times, announcing that his lunch is ready, but he says he's not hungry. I wrap up the sandwich and place it in the fridge. Then, I occupy my time with menial tasks, such as laundry and dusting, but still, Logan stays hidden. It's nearly five o'clock, and I've just finished dinner. Placing it in the oven to keep it warm, I walk toward his room. Tentatively, I raise my fist and knock gently.

"Logan? It's time for me to go. Do you need anything?"

I wait anxiously for his reply.

"No," is all he says.

A strange urgency fills me, and I realize I need him to say more than that. I don't want to leave it like this, so I try again.

"Are you sure?"

"Yes." His tone is clipped.

My heart sinks. Is he that upset with me? Did I go too far this time? I feel tears start to well up, but I dash them away quickly.

"Okay then. I'll see you tomorrow."

Knowing that he's not about to open the door, I let the floodgates open. Although I don't make a sound, my tears run down my face and onto my scrub top. I wipe them again, and walk away.

"Elora?"

I turn to see Logan's face. It's riddled with concern. I'm suddenly embarrassed to be crying over something so stupid, but I can't seem to stop them. I can see the apology written on his face.

"Elora, I'm sorry. I didn't mean to…" He sighs.

"It's nothing. I'll see you tomorrow," I say, then turn back around, desperate to be out in the fresh air. He says nothing more, and I leave without another word.

"Where does he live?" Daniel says angrily. "I don't care if he's got legs or not, he has no right to be such an asshole!"

I touch his chest, holding him at bay.

"Stop it. I'm fine. I just had a rough day—*we* had a rough day. It'll be better tomorrow."

"It had better be," he says, then placing his hands on my shoulders, he bids me to look at him. "Are you sure this is what you want to do? Taking care of people who couldn't care less about your feelings?"

I push away.

"That's not how it is. There's a nice person inside him somewhere. I just have to help him find himself."

"Elora, that's not your job. Your job is to take care of his physical needs, not be his shrink."

"That's part of it though. Look, I'm the only aide who's come back. All the others stayed only for the day. He's tried chasing me off too, but—"

"But, you're too stubborn," he interrupts.

I smile.

"Yes. I am."

LOGAN

"Mmm. Something smells good," Michael says as he puts his jacket on the chair. "What delicious concoction did she make for us today?" He opens the oven door to discover some sort of casserole. It does smell good. "Dude, you should be having sex with this girl. Imagine what she'd cook for us then."

"Fuck off, asshole! Don't talk about her like that!" I spit. God, he's such a pig.

Michael holds up his hands in surrender.

"Okay, okay. Relax. I was just being funny. But, really dude, if she's as good in bed as she is in the kitchen..." His eyes widen.

"If you want to keep your *middle* leg, you'll shut your mouth right now," I warn.

He laughs loudly.

"Calm down. I'm not planning on banging your girl."

"Michael, I've told you, she's not *my* girl. She's *a* girl who works for me. That's all." I wheel myself up to the table.

"So, she's fair game then?" I shoot virtual daggers at him, and he backs off the subject.

Michael scoops two portions of Elora's casserole onto our plates, and we dig in.

"When am I going to meet this girl whose virtue you're protecting from me?" he asks as he chews.

"Hopefully never," I mutter petulantly.

"Oh, come on. I'll behave."

I snort.

"When has *that* ever happened?"

"While it's true it's a rare occasion, I *can* be good when I want to be. Just ask Mom. By the way, she said she called here today, but no one answered."

"I wasn't in the mood to talk. I'll call her back later."

"You always say that, and never do."

"I don't want to hear a lecture from her," I say. "I'll call her another day."

"She's just worried about you, you know."

I nod sadly.

"I know."

The rest of dinner is eaten in relative silence. Afterward, I resign myself to the fact that I must call my mother, before she gets too concerned and pays me a visit. I go to my room and grab my cell phone. She answers on the second ring.

"Logan! How are you? I called you earlier today but got no answer. Were you in therapy?"

I sigh. Here we go.

"Hello, mother. I'm fine. How are you?" I recite the standard greeting and brace myself for the barrage of motherly advice.

"I'm fine, darling. How's the recovery going?"

"It's going fine."

"Did you get to speak with someone in the prosthetics department?"

"Mom, you know I'm not ready to do that yet." I say *yet* as though I'll *ever* be ready for fake legs.

"Oh, sweetie, please reconsider. You're so young. You have a whole lifetime ahead of you."

I roll my eyes and think, *this is why I don't call her more often.*

"Yes, I know."

"So, Michael tells me he's hired someone to come and help you during the day, when he's at work."

"Yeah, he did."

"And?"

"And what? She's very helpful. What more do you want me to tell you?"

"Well, there's no need to be cross. I was just wondering. Does she help you with therapy too?"

"Mom…" I hate that every subject seems to turn back to therapy and artificial legs.

"Oh, all right, darling. I'll stop bothering you, for now. But, I do hope you'll think about getting back on your feet, both literally and figuratively."

I agree to think about it, and she goes on to talk about my stepfather, and how he bought a new yacht. She babbles on for who knows how long as my mind drifts to what happened earlier today, with Elora. I made her cry. I was an asshole, and I actually made her cry. Even still, she said she'd see me tomorrow. Who does that? I should ask the agency for someone else. I should relieve her of her obligation to me and let her find another client to take care of—one who deserves her. She's kind, caring, and determined to help me, and I just keep fighting her. What if I gave in? What if I said I'd try therapy? Would it make her smile? I'm guessing it would. I'd love to be the reason she smiles. I sigh into the phone. Don't get ahead of yourself, Logan. She might not come back.

"So, darling, that's where the name of the yacht came from."

"That's nice, mother," I say, not having a clue what she's talking about.

"Nice? Were you listening to me at all?"

"Hey, I've got to go. I have another call coming in that I have to take. We'll talk again soon?"

"Um, okay. Give Michael a hug for me," she says. We say our good-byes, and I promise to take good care of myself.

She said she'd be back today, but a little voice in my head tells me she's through trying to help me get better. It taunts me and tells me she's not coming. I give that voice a virtual punch in the throat, when I see her apprehensive face walk through my front door. She's shocked to see me already in the kitchen but smiles politely.

"Good morning," I say before she has the chance to.

"Good morning," she repeats. "You sure are bright eyed and bushy tailed today."

"Yes, I suppose I am."

"The usual?" she asks, and starts to pull out the pan.

"No," I say, and she stops. "How about if I try cooking with you today?"

Her eyebrows shoot up in surprise, and her head tilts to the side, making sure she heard me correctly.

"Oh. Okay. What do you want to make?" She tries, but she can't hide her small smile from me.

"How about pancakes?"

"That sounds good. How should we do this?"

"Well, if you get the ingredients down from the cabinets, along with a mixing bowl, I'll measure everything out and stir it. I'll let you pour it onto the griddle and do the flipping."

She smiles again and gathers everything. Holding the bowl in my lap, I add the water into the mix. Stirring vigorously, she sits and watches me. Her amused expression is way different than yesterday. Before handing it over, she adds just a touch of cinnamon and a bit of vanilla. Puzzled, I look up at her.

"It just makes it taste better," she says, then takes the bowl.

The batter sizzles slightly, as she pours it onto the hot surface. Then, within a few minutes, she flips the first batch.

"How do you know when to flip them?" I ask, completely clueless as to how to cook anything.

"You'll see bubbles form on the surface of the pancake. You can also do a test lift with the spatula. Next time, I'll put the griddle on the table, so you can see what I mean."

I nod and continue to watch her. Before too long, there's a stack of pancakes, buttered and ready for consumption.

"Are you eating with me again?" I say, hopeful.

"Do you want me to?" she replies.

"Yes."

"Then, I will."

I smile at her, and she back at me, and suddenly, it feels like a new day.

"These are really good," I say, because they are. "Everything you cook is good. I'm sorry I never gave you enough compliments."

"Thank you. I try to add my own touches to everything I cook. Sometimes it works out and sometimes, it's a disaster. But, I learn what I like and don't like that way."

I finish my bite and clear my throat.

"I'm sorry about yesterday. I shouldn't have yelled at you like that."

"I deserved it," she says. "I pushed too hard. I'm sorry about that."

"No, don't be sorry. I need to be pushed. I've been feeling really sorry for myself, and I need someone to call me out on my shit. It's fine. You're doing the right thing by saying those things."

"Yeah, but sometimes I have a habit of going too far. Clearly, you're still reeling from the amputation. That's something I'll never be able to understand. I should be respecting your boundaries. Instead, I'm expecting you to just snap out of it. I'll be more considerate from now on."

Then, without thinking, I place my hand on her forearm. Her warm skin makes my hand tingle, but I don't pull it away.

"Just keep doing what you've been doing. I'll adjust," I say softly.

Our breaths are shallow as we stare into each other's eyes. I feel my face heat, and an internal energy spreads throughout my body. Her cheeks flush and, for a split second, I think she may be feeling the same way. But, as soon as I think it, the growling voice, in the back of my head, shoots me down, asking, *what on earth would she want with you?* I retract my hand and sit back, trying to recover my wits. My heartbeat continues to race, even after we separate, and I nonchalantly blow out a slow, steady breath, trying to return it to a normal rhythm.

𝒮

Our last day of the week together is almost done. Michael doesn't work on the weekends, so there's no need to have Elora here. The thought is depressing. She's putting the finishing touches on the dinner she's prepared when I come out from my daily workout.

"I'm almost done. Make sure your brother takes the foil off and lets it brown for another five to ten minutes, when he gets home." I nod. She stands stationary in front of me. "Well, it's been an interesting week, hasn't it?"

"Yes, it sure has," I agree. "Are you brave enough to come back again on Monday?"

She rubs her chin. Her expression is blank, and that concerns me. Suddenly, she grins widely.

"I'll see you on Monday."

Relief washes over me. She was teasing me, so I give her a wry smile.

"Good. I'll see you then."

She shuts the door behind her, and I instantly feel lonely, but content, at the same time. The week started out badly, but what we've gone through has given us an understanding, and I know this will work.

It has to.

4

ELORA

I throw myself onto the couch and fling my feet onto the coffee table in front of me, sighing and sagging into my relaxed position as I do.

"Rough week?" Daniel asks as he enters the living room.

"Definitely a rollercoaster ride," I reply.

"Then, I guess you don't feel like going out tonight, do you?"

My lip curls up. "Seriously? I'm exhausted. The only thing I want to do is crawl into a hot bath, then crawl into my nice, warm bed." I close my eyes and lean my head against the back of the couch.

"You can do that later. I want to go out and drink, and I'll look like a pathetic drunk if I do it alone. Come with me."

"Why don't you just call John, or Luke? They're usually all too willing to go out partying with you."

"Well," he says, "John is helping his sister move this weekend, and Luke has some girl on the line. His latest flavor of the month is quickly becoming a habit. You're all I've got, so suck it up, princess. You're coming with me."

I groan, in hopes that it makes me seem more incapable of moving from this spot, but he knows all my tricks and keeps bothering me, until I agree to go.

The bar is crowded. Daniel acts as an icebreaker, as I follow him through the dense crowd. Somehow, we find two seats at the bar, and he gives the bartender our order. Within minutes, I have a beer in front of me.

"Is that kind okay?" he shouts over the pounding beat coming from the speakers.

I nod. "It'll do," I shout back and take a long drink. It's more bitter than I'm used to, but I down it very quickly. After the week I've had, I need to relax.

"To a great night out with my favorite sister!" Daniel toasts. "And, here's hoping at least one of us gets laid—hopefully me." He grins widely from ear to ear, and I laugh.

"I'm your *only* sister, and yes, I can guarantee it'll be you."

We snicker as we enjoy the show that walks past us every few minutes. Some people should really look in a mirror. Suddenly, Daniel jumps up from the stool.

"I'll be back in a minute," he says, and leaves me alone at the bar.
Great.

I sneer at Daniel's retreating back and take another sip of my beer, not noticing the bitterness anymore. As I sit, my mind begins to wander. I wonder if Logan drinks beer.
Where did that come from?

I'm supposed to be out having a good time, and *he* pops into my mind? How odd. Still, I wonder. Does he get out much? I suspect not. He doesn't seem like much of a people person. I begin to daydream about a different Logan Turner. One who likes to go out. One who's the life of the party. A guy who has any number of women hanging on his every word because let's face it, he's hot.
Did I just...

I shake my head to clear it. Where did that thought come from? He's my client. I can't think of him that way.

Then, out of the corner of my eye, I spot the first wave, and what I'm guessing won't be the last, of men scoping out their hopeful conquest for the night. A man winks at me, which makes me want to audibly gag. I roll my eyes and turn my head, in an attempt to discourage him. It doesn't work, and I find my view of the dance floor, blocked by the tall man, dressed almost entirely in denim.

Really? Who on earth wears all denim?

"Hi, there," he says with every tooth on display. "Can I buy you a drink?"

I smile politely at him and shake my head, holding my nearly empty, beer bottle up for him to see.

"I've already got one, but thanks," I say, then turn my head away again, hoping he'll take a hint.

"Okay, can I buy you the next one?"

I shake my head again. "I have a one drink limit, sorry," I say eager to get rid of him.

"Well, how about a dance then?"

Ugh. Why won't this guy go away?

"No, thank you."

"Are you from around here?" He's really trying. I'll give him that, but I'm just not in the mood to be hit on.

"I've got to go to the little girl's room," I say, and I set my beer down, making a beeline for anywhere but here. Thankfully, he doesn't follow. While in the restroom, I stare at my reflection. I look tired, if I'm honest, and I wish I could just go back home. I wonder what Logan's doing right now. I know he said he reads a lot, but is that since the surgery, or was he like that before? Did he frequent bars, like most men his age, or was he always a homebody? I splash some cold water on my face, trying to rid my mind of these strange, wayward thoughts, then exit the bathroom. I look over at my spot. The denim clad man is gone, so I assume it's safe to return to my seat.

"Did you see who's here?" Daniel asks as he approaches. I shake my head. "It's Ashley."

"Who's Ashley?"

"You know..." He winks at me, hoping I'll remember.

"You mean the Ashley you went on and on about six months ago? The one whose acrobatic skills in the bedroom are second to none?" I roll my eyes.

"Shh! Shut up! Yes, *that* Ashley. Do you want her to hear you?"

I shrug.

"I don't care if she hears me."

"Well, I do," he whisper-shouts. "I'm trying to get back with her, and I don't want her thinking I went around telling everybody our business."

"But, you *did* tell everybody your business."

"I know, but she doesn't need to know that," he says.

"You're a pig, you know that?"

He smiles triumphantly. "I know, but I want to get laid, so mum's the word." He holds up a finger to his lips to silence me, and I roll my eyes again.

Three hours later, I find myself leaving the bar with Daniel. I pour him into the cab and step inside after him.

"Pearl Road apartments, please," I tell the driver, and we speed off into the night. Daniel, who is drunk, and now depressed about the prospect of not getting Ashley back, is leaning on me and groaning.

"Ashley, oh, Ashley, wherefore aren't you with me right now, Ashley?"

Oh, brother.

His half-assed attempt at Shakespeare, on her behalf, makes me feel a bit agitated.

"Daniel, she's a whore. Just let her go."

He lifts his head and looks at me, affronted.

"Don't you think I know she's a whore? But, she was *my* whore." He lays his head, back on my shoulder, as we continue our ride.

I pay the driver the fair, and put Daniel's arm over my shoulders. He's quite a bit taller than me, but I manage to get both of us up the flight of stairs to our place. I open the door and shove him onto the couch.

"You're the best sister ever. You know that, right?" he says, cocked sideways in an awkward sitting position.

"Yep, I'm the best," I say in a monotone voice and begin taking off his shoes.

"You save me from very flexible whores. You let me stay at your place to save up money. You cook and…clean…and…"

And, he's out. The limp body of my very drunk, very sad brother is finally unconscious and now, I can go to bed. After tipping him over, so he's lying across the seats, I pick his legs up onto the couch and throw a blanket over him. After the lights are out, I head toward my bedroom and fall into bed.

Morning arrives, and I wake with a pounding headache. I carefully pry my eyelids open to see the bright sunlight streaming in through my window. I didn't have that much to drink last night, but there's little doubt where my pain is stemming from: cheap beer. Gingerly, I sit up, covering my eyes as virtual daggers jab into them. I swing my legs out of bed and stand.

"Agh!" I exclaim, as my left ankle rolls to the side and buckles under my weight. I sit back down on the bed quickly. "Damn it," I say, while taking my sock off and rubbing my ankle gently, trying to ease the pain. After a few minutes, I limp toward the bathroom in search of a bandage to wrap around it.

After wrapping it up, I hobble toward the kitchen and spy the, still sleeping, figure of my brother huddled under the blanket. He stirs as I begin making breakfast.

"Good morning, sunshine," I say only to hear him moan in protest. "How's your head?"

"I hate you," he replies, and I laugh.

"Why do you hate me?"

"Because you didn't get as shit-faced as I did, and you're able to be upright."

I laugh again.

"I'm not exactly upright," I say, lifting my pant leg to reveal the bandage that's tightly wrapped around my ankle.

"How'd you do that?"

"I stepped down on it and twisted it this morning. It's really sore."

"Well, I hope it's broken."

"Nice, Daniel. Really nice."

"Only because you cost me Ashley," he goes on to say.

"What are you talking about?"

"If you were any kind of *good* sister, you would've encouraged me to keep pursuing her."

"Yeah, if I wanted you to catch something." I snicker at my statement.

"Whatever. If you liked your amputee, I'd encourage *you*."

"Daniel, he's my client! That's all. I can't like him like that, even if I wanted to. And, I don't." I say the words, then sigh. I'm not sure why the thought of that barrier makes me sad. It's not like anything would ever come of me and Logan Turner anyway.

I grab the two plates of food I just made and walk slowly toward the kitchen table.

"Breakfast ready?" he asks.

"Yes, and come get it while it's hot."

I'm almost to the table, when my ankle rolls once again. I cry out and stumble, spilling the food onto the floor.

"Are you okay?" he asks, shaking his head and chuckling quietly.

"Damn it. I just twisted it again. I'm okay," I say, irritated with myself.

"Are you sure?" He walks over and pulls out the chair nearest to me, so I sit.

"Yeah, I'm sure." We both look down at my carefully cooked meal now strewn all over the floor. "I guess I'll have to start over again."

"I didn't feel like eating eggs anyway," he says with a shrug.

I sit down on the floor to clean up my mess, and Daniel joins me there. We pick up what we can, then the small carpet scrubber does the rest. When we're just about done, I look up at the chair beside me.

"Huh."

Daniel looks at me curiously.

"What?"

"I wonder how hard it is to get up in that chair from this position on the floor." Without using my legs to propel me, I grasp the edges and begin to pull up. Almost immediately, the chair tilts forward, halting me. I try again, this time grabbing the table too. I manage to get halfway up, before the chair decides to tip. "How can I do this?" I try one more time but ultimately, I'm forced to use my feet to push me upward. "This is harder than I thought it would be."

"What are you doing?"

"Trying to put myself in Logan's shoes, so to speak."

"Nice pun."

"Not intended." I smirk.

"Here, let's try this," Daniel says, and he opens up his laptop. He searches the internet for, *ways to transfer into a chair from the floor.* Dozens of videos pop onto the screen, so we watch some of them.

"Let's search some more transfers," I say, excited and teeming with new ideas.

We spend hours typing phrases into the search engine, and experimenting with them. It's a bit harder to try them out, with our legs in the way, and our brains, telling us to use them.

"Good morning," I say, as I enter Logan's house. It doesn't take long before he appears with a smile on his face.

Well, that's a good start.

"Good morning. How was your weekend?" he asks.

"Revelationary," I say. "Yours?"

He smirks. "Mine was uneventful, and revelationary is not a word."

"Maybe not, but it should be. Some new ideas have come to light and I've brought you something."

"Oh? What is it?"

"It's what I'm hiding behind my back." I gesture over my shoulder with my head. "You can't see it until you've eaten all your breakfast though."

He smiles. It's nice to see.

"Well, we better get cooking then."

I grin at him and nod. He wheels himself into the kitchen, and I hide my surprise behind a potted plant in the foyer.

"What are we making today?" I ask.

"I think you should show me how to make scrambled eggs."

"Really? Are you *that* culinarily challenged?"

He laughs. It's the first time I've heard him laugh. It's a great laugh. I want to make him laugh again.

"That's not a word either," he scolds playfully.

"I don't care. I'm going to contact Mr. Webster and request that it become one."

He shakes his head, smiling again.

Logan helps me gather the ingredients, and we set the griddle on the table, within his reach. I beat the eggs; he chops up the rest of the items.

"So, my brother approves of your cooking. I meant to tell you that earlier," he says.

"Oh?"

"Yeah. He basically told me to not to let you get away, or we'll be back to eating cereal for dinner."

I laugh.

"Seriously?" He nods. "Well, I'll have to make sure to teach you everything I know, in case something happens."

His face falls. I watch his throat as he swallows reflexively.

"I hope nothing happens." His voice is serious. We stare at each other for longer than is necessary, when I finally look away and break the silence.

"Well, I'm not planning on dying anytime soon, so…" I let out a schoolgirl giggle, and the corners of his mouth reluctantly lift.

We eat the breakfast we made together: scrambled eggs with bits of bacon, onion, peppers, and a bit of cheese, buttered toast, and fresh squeezed, orange juice.

"Can I help you dry the dishes?" Logan asks.

"That's very diplomatic of you, but no, thank you. If I let you get too independent, you might not need me anymore."

We laugh, but his is somehow...off.

"So, what's this surprise you've brought me?" he asks. I can tell his curiosity is piqued.

"I'm so happy you asked." I move toward the front door and reveal a thin box. "This was part of my revelation, which you so wonderfully pointed out was not a word."

"Revelation is a word, revelationary, is not."

I wave him off and continue. "After an incident that happened over the weekend, I got to thinking about your mobility, or lack thereof. I watched several videos on the internet and discovered ways to enhance your life."

He sighs, looks down, and rubs his forehead.

"Elora—"

"Now, I know what you're thinking," I interrupt, "but, you don't have to go anywhere. I'm going to be your in-house therapist." I smile broadly. I can tell he's not impressed, so I open the box and pull out the contents. "It's a transfer board!"

"I see that," he says, solemnly.

"Oh, come on. It's not that bad. I'll show you what I've learned, and we'll practice together." His expression is unsure. "Okay, I'll go first." I drag a kitchen chair to the middle of the living room, then position another next to the first. I sit on one, and place the board between the two. Trying not to use my legs, I gently slide across the board onto the other chair. "There! Now, it's your turn," I say. He doesn't move. "Come on, Logan. You have to at least try it."

"I really don't want to. I'm fine just sitting in *this* chair." He gestures toward the wheelchair.

"But, you can't stay in that your whole life. What if you want to go to a restaurant? How will you get yourself into their dining chair?"

"I won't, because I don't go out."

"I've noticed. Why is that?"

He sighs again, rubbing his forehead even harder.

"I just don't like to, okay? Can we just stop this now?" His voice is irritated, and I can tell he's trying to reign in his temper. He turns abruptly, wheeling himself away from the chairs, and down the hallway, toward his bedroom. Closing the door behind him, I soon hear something being thrown against a wall. It makes me jump. I guess I pushed too hard. Defeated, I place the board back in its box and put it in the front closet.

It's nearly lunchtime, but I haven't seen Logan since he stormed out after my attempt to teach him transfers. I raise my fist and knock gently on the door.

"Logan? Lunch is ready," I say quietly. I hear silence. Should I knock again? Will he get mad if I do? I lean against the wall, next to the entrance to his room. I'm contemplating what I should do, when the door opens. His face is apologetic, so I give him a small smile. "Are you hungry?" Again, my voice is small. He says nothing, just nods, then begins to roll in the direction of the kitchen.

We eat in relative silence, which feels awkward. I want to tell him I'm sorry, but the truth is, I'm not. He needs to be pushed. He told me that himself, and if he's going to get along in this world, he has to try. I open my mouth to tell him just that, when he speaks up.

"I'm sorry I got upset with you. I know I told you to push me, and I'm sorry I was so resistant to that. You did nothing wrong, yet I got angry with you, and you didn't deserve that." He finally looks at me. His expression is bleak. "I apologize. Please, stay."

I try to keep my face as neutral as possible, but it's hard to hide my triumphant grin.

"Well, you know you're getting extra homework for your lack of enthusiasm for today's lesson."

"Am I?" he responds cheekily.

"Yes. I'll expect you to perform extra transfers from chair to chair before tomorrow morning. If you don't, and I'll know if you're faking it, you'll get detention. Are we clear, Mr. Turner?"

He smirks. "Yes, Miss Foster."

"That's better. Now, let's finish our lunch. We have work to do."

After the dishes are washed, I drag one kitchen chair back into the living room. He pulls up the arm of his wheelchair, and begins to practice. He's shaky at first, a bit afraid of falling, I think, but soon, he's got the hang of it, as I knew he would.

"Woo hoo!" I cheer him on, and he bows gracefully in turn. Logan holds his hand up for me to high five, but when I step forward to slap it, I step crooked, twisting my ankle again, and fall onto my hands and knees.

"Elora!" Logan shouts and reaches out toward me. "Are you okay?"

I'm holding my ankle. The pain is excruciating, and it takes me a few seconds to be able to speak.

"Yeah. I'm fine," I squeak out. "I rolled my ankle this weekend, and I'm afraid I just did it again."

"Do you need a doctor?" he says; his voice is urgent.

"No, no. I'll be okay. I've done this a couple times since the original incident. I'll be fine."

"Why don't you sit on this chair and let me have a look at it?"

"Logan, it's okay, really. It'll be fine," I say.

"Stop being stubborn. You might've broken it. Let me take a look, please." I look up at him as if to ask, *what do you know about broken ankles*, when he continues. "I was a medic in the military," he explains.

"Oh."

He holds his hand out to help me up, so I take it and get to my feet...well, I get to my foot. I sit on the practice chair and gingerly take off my shoe. He gestures to give him my foot, so I carefully place it in his lap.

"You have it wrapped. Mind if I take it off?" I shake my head, and he slowly unwinds the bandage. His hands are warm, and the heat from them radiates through my foot, up my calf, past my thighs, and settles awkwardly a bit higher. It's getting hot in here, and I realize I'm becoming flushed. My heart races, as his deft fingers glide across my instep. He holds my foot by the heel and turns it slightly from side to side.

"Does this hurt?" I shake my head as he presses against different parts of my foot. "How about now?"

"No," I say. Finally, he turns my foot just the right way, and I wince. "That hurts." I tug my foot away, out of instinct.

"Hm. It could be broken. It's hard to tell. Most likely, it's just sprained, but I think you should have it looked at. You're weight bearing though, so that's good."

"Well, I *was,* until now."

"See if you can stand on it."

I retract my foot and step down. I don't put my full weight on it at first, but slowly, I stand equally on both feet, with little discomfort.

"How's that feel?"

I shrug.

"It's a little uncomfortable, but nothing I can't deal with."

"Can you walk on it?"

I take a step with my left foot, then my right, but it's a quick step.

"You're favoring it. You should play it safe and stay off of it. Let me wrap it back up."

"You don't have to. I'm more than capable of—"

"I know. Just let me do it," he interrupts. Then, our eyes meet, and I notice the sincerity in his offer. His eyes, God, his eyes, they're mesmerizing. I could easily get lost in them. His small smile lets me know he really wants to help, so I nod my head slightly and replace my foot in his lap. With slow tenderness, he wraps the bandage around and around. I watch as his fingers graze my skin, and I'm hoping he doesn't notice the shivers he creates. I'm embarrassed at my body's reaction to his touch and ashamed that I feel this way toward someone I work for. I look away, hoping to distract myself from my wayward thoughts, but it does nothing to ease my traitorous body.

Then, he says something that I don't hear.

"What?" I'm confused.

He smirks.

"I said, I think that'll do, don't you?"

"Oh, um… yes," I say, glowing bright red, I'm sure. I pull my foot from his reach and wipe the sheen of sweat from my brow. "Thank you." The spell is broken, as I try to calm my heartbeat.

"You're welcome. Please take it easy today. Don't put much weight on it. In fact, you should keep it up for the rest of today."

I laugh.

"And just how am I supposed to do my job?"

"What's left to do? I hear your boss is a real asshole, but I know for a fact that he'll be very understanding about why you're just sitting around with your feet up." He winks.

"Really. Well, I hope this boss of mine likes to make his own dinner. If not, he and his brother will be eating cereal again."

He shrugs.

"They'll live with it."

I shake my head in disbelief at the completely different man who sits before me. One week ago, I was ready to walk out on this job. Today, nothing short of a hurricane could drag me away.

5

LOGAN

The next few days go smoothly. Elora seems excited to see the progress I've made with the transfer board and without it. I've really been working hard at being more independent, and I'm glad she's noticed. The day after she brought the board over, I worked well into the night on transferring myself, not just to and from a chair, but onto the bed, and in the bathroom too. I don't know why I refused this instruction while in the hospital. It really isn't that hard, and it's a necessity to get along in life. I've chucked the board since then and can now do without it, which makes her smile. It feels good to be responsible for her smile.

The door opens, and I grin when she walks into the house.

"Good morning," I say from my seat at the table.

She gasps and covers her mouth.

"Logan, what did you do?" she says, in shock, I think.

"You like it?" I say, gesturing to the breakfast laid out before me. "I got up extra early and wanted to surprise you."

"Well, you've definitely done that. How did you reach everything?"

"Last night, I asked my brother to take out anything I might need that I couldn't reach."

He shook his head at me the whole time, calling me whipped, but I'll keep that part to myself.

"And, you cooked this, all of this, all by yourself? But, how?"

"I happen to know a great chef." I wink at her, giving her all the credit she deserves. She walks in farther, astonishment still gracing her face.

"This is incredible. It smells good too."

"Take off your coat and have a seat. I have orange juice, or there's coffee, if you prefer."

She pulls out the chair and sits, then notices I'm in a regular, kitchen chair.

"Nice touch. I can see I've been a good influence on you," she gloats.

"Yeah, well, a little birdie told me to basically suck it up, and start living."

"I didn't say it like that," she says.

"I know. Your words are gentler than that, but it's pretty much the same thing."

She beams with pride, and so do I. The truth is, I like making her happy—probably way more than I should.

"So, what do we have here?"

"Well, I made scrambled eggs, toast, and sausage links. I wanted to make bacon, but I thought it would splatter all over me, and the microwave is too high up to reach. If you notice, I added ingredients to the eggs. I improvised. I hope it tastes all right."

She takes in a forkful and hums her approval.

"Logan, this is delicious. I think you should make breakfast every day."

"Whoa now. I may know how to do it, but yours is still much better."

Her grin is broad, and I realize just how much I love that I put it there.

After we're done, we start on the dishes…together.

"I think I know what we should do today," she says.

"What?"

"I think we should make your kitchen more accessible to you."

"How so?"

"Well, we could take the items you might use the most and put them on lower shelves. The pantry can also be arranged in this fashion. The only problem is the microwave. It's hardwired underneath the cabinet, and I don't know how to remove it."

"My brother can do it, or maybe, I can just buy a new one that sits on the counter. I think it's a great idea. Let's do it," I say with a grin.

We get right to work. Elora begins the arduous task of pulling everything onto the countertop, while I do what I can from my wheelchair.

"Why don't you sit on the floor and do that? It'll make it easier and faster, I would think," she says, and my heart sinks. I haven't practiced floor-to-chair transfers very much, and I don't want her to see me fail.

"I'm good. I'll stay in my chair."

"Really?" she says, eyeing my suspiciously. "It's obvious you can't get low enough to the ground while staying in your chair."

I sigh.

"Okay," I say, reluctantly. I just pray I can get back into it easily. Reaching down, I grab the floor with my left hand while holding on to the chair with my right. The descent to the floor is smooth enough, so she goes back to the task at hand.

"Tell me about your experience in the military. Was it hard to be away from home?"

I freeze, while in the middle of pulling out a box of garbage bags, then swallow. She's making small talk, I'm sure, but this is not a subject I like to discuss.

"I don't really like to talk about it." I try to divert the conversation, but she continues.

"I know you don't, but you also didn't want to try transferring, and look how well that turned out." Her smug grin makes me a bit irritated, and I have the urge to storm out of this room, but it seems that she has me at a disadvantage here on the floor. I endeavor to keep the information at a minimum.

"Um, I don't know. It was interesting to say the least."

"Care to elaborate?"

"Not really." I look up to see disappointment on her face. I sigh again. "It's a tough place to be. I was a medic. I saw things no one should see. Guys with shrapnel plugged into all parts of their bodies, grown men begging for their mommies. You name it, I've seen it. I've tried hard to forget about it all, so you'll forgive me if I don't go into detail."

"I'm so sorry. I just thought…" She stops and bites her thumb nail. "We don't have to talk about it." She turns back to the upper cabinets. I know she regrets asking me, but she's still curious, so I decide to give her a bit more.

"Losing my legs wasn't the worst thing to happen to me." She looks at me again, a puzzled expression mars her beautiful face. "Seeing what was happening to the guys in my platoon and wondering if, or *when,* it would happen to me, was terrifying. Each day I woke up in that hell, was an exhausting effort to stay focused on what I had waiting for me at home."

"Oh," she says, sadly. Then, my words penetrate. "What did you have waiting for you at home?"

I look down at the floor and wipe the sweat that's started to form on my brow. *God, I hate talking about this shit.*

"My ex. Well, she wasn't back then. She left me."

"Oh," she says. I hear the regret Elora has in asking me that question, and I don't want to see the pity in her eyes, so I continue looking at the floor in front of me.

"It's not something I prefer to talk about, but—"

"It's okay. It's none of my business."

"No, it's fine," I interrupt. "It's history. It doesn't matter anymore anyway."

Silence lays thick in the room, as neither of us knows what to say next.

"How long were you with her?" she asks softly.

"Since high school. We met in our sophomore year." I smile and shake my head, as an image of her as a teen surfaces. "She was pretty and popular. I didn't know why she was interested in me." I snort, still not understanding her logic.

"It's not hard to figure out," she says, as she climbs off the countertop. I look at her sincere face then quickly back at my hands. She folds her legs in and sits across from me on the floor.

"Thanks, but you have no idea what I was like back then. I was this clumsy, wannabe jock. There was nothing special about me, other than the fact that I was Michael's brother." I look at her again. "Michael was a very popular football star. Me, not so much. I tried my hardest, but I was never as good as his reputation."

Her eyebrows lift slightly. I'm sure she doesn't mean it, but I know that look well.

"I'm so sorry, but I'm sure you were good at lots of other things."

I scoff. "Yeah. I was good at being put into the friend zone. *I like you as a friend, Logan. You're such a good friend,*" I say in a faux female voice. "I heard that line dozens of times."

"Your ex didn't do that."

"No. She didn't. Although, I wish she had," I mutter under my breath.

She reaches out and covers my hand with hers. I stiffen, taken by surprise, and immediately, look at her again. She's much more beautiful at eye level. Her sweet smile is warm and inviting. It calls to me to continue, though I'm not sure why she'd want to hear any of this. But, before I can, the phone rings, breaking the spell, and I'm relieved to halt this conversation.

"Would you mind getting that? You'll be quicker than I would," I say, pointing out the obvious.

She nods and goes off to grab the phone. When she comes back, she hands it to me.

"Hello?"

"Hey, douchebag," Michael says. "Was that Elora who answered the phone?" I can almost hear his cheesy grin.

"None of your business. What do you want?" I look up to see a look of concern on Elora's face, so I tone down my irritation. "I mean, do you need something?"

"Sheesh! She must be standing close enough to overhear you, eh?" He laughs, and I want to reach through the phone and punch him.

"What can I do for you, Michael?"

"Nothing. I just wanted to let you know I'm getting off early today. I should be home around four o'clock, so I'll finally get to meet the elusive Elora."

I almost audibly snarl at him.

"Great. Thanks for letting me know. I'll talk to you later."

I don't even give him the chance to respond before hanging up on him and reach up to place the phone on the counter. I look up at her, and she abruptly looks away, pretending she wasn't watching me. I clear my throat.

"That was my brother," I say.

"Oh," she says.

"He'll be home earlier than usual tonight, so you can leave early too."

"Um, okay...although, I could stay if you'd like."

"No," I say a bit too quickly. "It's fine. We have plenty of food left over from yesterday's dinner. You can go as early as three o'clock, if that's okay."

She nods, but her expression tells me I need to lighten the mood, so I say the first random thing I can think of.

"When my brother and I were kids, we had a cat we named Dammit. My mother and stepfather didn't approve, but to spite her, my father let us do it. We'd go around the neighborhood yelling, 'Dammit' everywhere we went. When another parent would question us, we'd just say we were calling our cat."

She giggles.

"You're kidding?"

"Nope, I'm not."

"Boys will be boys, I guess," she says, shaking her head slightly.

"Yeah," I chuckle.

"Well, you'll be pleased to hear that my cat's name was Tornado... for the same reason." She smirks at me, but it takes me a few seconds to catch on.

"Was it really?" She smiles and nods. "So, you'd go around yelling '*Tornado*' when you were looking for your cat?"

"Yep. At first, my neighbors looked at me weird, but they got used to it. It was great fun to watch the expressions on the faces of new neighbors."

I'm really beginning to like this girl.

"So, innocent Elora, isn't so innocent."

"Who said I was in the first place?" she says with a coy smile.

Within an hour or so, we're done with the cabinets. We've made most everything wheelchair accessible, which will make my life that much easier.

"Now what?" she asks.

"Now, I guess I get up off the floor and make sure I can reach everything." As soon as I say it, I realize that means she'll witness my awkward ascent back into my chair. It's the one thing I haven't found a good way of doing yet. I close my eyes and bite my bottom lip.

"What's wrong?" she asks. I find it interesting that she is so perceptive of my moods. I decide to go for honesty.

"I…have trouble getting up from the floor." I instantly look anywhere, but at her, as I wait for her reply, which I already know the contents of.

"I'll help you. But, first, show me how you've been doing it."

I nod, and hope she doesn't see me as the clumsy invalid that I am. She wheels my chair toward me, and I turn to face it. Gripping it tightly with both hands, I use every bit of strength and leverage I have and begin to hoist myself up. Even though the chair wants to tip forward, I hold on, trying to shift my weight toward the back, until I can get up high enough to twist my ass around. For the first time ever, I make it on my first attempt. I breathe a sigh of relief.

"Well, that wasn't too bad. Is that always how you've done it?"

"Pretty much. Why?"

"I saw an easier way on the internet. Can I show you?"

I nod. She instructs me to get back onto the floor, then she joins me there. We briefly make eye contact, but she breaks it first.

"Now, you grab here, making sure your wheels are locked, of course, then push off with one hand on the floor like this," she says, as she demonstrates. "The video showed the person facing *away* from the wheelchair, then their head goes down, while their butt goes into the air. You then push your butt back onto the seat and sit up." She makes it into the chair better than I ever have, and I'm amazed. But, can I duplicate it? "The lower your head goes, the higher your butt is. Then, you can just sit."

"Hm. It's that easy, huh?"

"Try it," she says.

Hesitantly, I position myself in the way she just showed me. I feel her behind me. Her hands grasp my hips lightly to spot me in the event I would face plant. I'm distracted, momentarily, by the close proximity to my groin and secretly pray her touch doesn't wake my libido. I'm embarrassed to be putting my ass in the air, but I have to admit, she's right. It works much better this way.

"Hey! Look at you! You made it up there with no problem." Her smile is wide.

"Yeah," I say, genuinely amused. "Who'd have thought?"

"I knew you could do it."

I feel my face heat, and I have a sudden urge to hug her in celebration. I refrain, however, and just thank her. Her warm hand is atop mine again, and I can't ignore my rapid heartbeat.

God, help me.

"Where's Elora?" Michael asks, as he lays his coat over a chair.

"She left early."

"She couldn't stand you anymore?" he says with a snicker.

I snort.

"No. I told her she could leave early. I knew you were on your way home, so I let her go. Why?"

He shrugs.

"Just wondering. I'd like to meet the woman who single handedly gave you a new lease on life."

I laugh.

"A new lease? No." I shake my head, but the more I think about it, the more I think he may be right.

"What's with the shit eating grin on your face, asswipe?"

I ball up a piece of paper and whip it at him. It's a direct hit, in the middle of his forehead. He laughs and pitches it back, missing me entirely.

High school jock, my ass.

"It's nothing. I'm just in a good mood."

"For a change," he adds.

"Yeah, yeah. Whatever." I try to wave the subject off, but he brings it right back around.

"No, really. You've been unusually chipper for a while now. *And,* you haven't sent her running from the house screaming." He rubs his chin in an exaggerated manner. "If I didn't know better, I'd say you like this girl."

My eyes fly to him instantly. Can he see through me? Does he know? I watch his expression go from joking to realization, and I begin to sweat.

"What?" I snap, attempting to dodge the question.

"You *do* like her. I can see it in your eyes." He's pointing at me, taunting me, and it's pissing me off.

"Michael, knock it off." I swivel my chair away from him and start down the hall to my room. He steps into my path before I'm out of the kitchen.

"Oh, no you don't. You're going to tell me what's going on, and I'm not moving until you do."

"Seriously? There's nothing to tell. She works for me, that makes me her boss, in a way, so even if I thought there was a possibility, it would be unethical for her…and me. Just shut up about it." I try to ram through him, but he stops me with his hands.

"Dude, I don't know what this chic looks like, or what she's like, but you've definitely got it bad for her. Why don't you talk to her, feel her out? Maybe, she has feelings for you too."

I roll my eyes and scoff at him.

"The very idea is ridiculous."

"Why is it ridiculous? You're a good guy…most of the time, and she'd be lucky to have you."

I scoff again.

"Right. Yeah, any woman would be lucky to have someone who will never be able to stand up next to her, or open a simple door for her, because this damned chair is always in the way. I have to look up to every person I meet, Michael. Do you know how inferior that makes a person feel? To know that I'll never be equal to anyone ever again because I'm half a man? What the hell do I have to offer her? Huh? What? A life of free wheelchair rides and all the burdens she could ever ask for? Get real. I know what she needs, and it's *not* an invalid."

I'm pissed, and all I want is to get to my room, but he's standing, stock still, in front of me.

"Are you done?" I grit my teeth and exhale sharply, but say nothing. "First of all, you're not *half a man*, you're three quarters of one. Those doctors took *part* of your legs, but now I'm beginning to think they took your brain too." My eyes dart back to him. "Got your attention now, do I?" I look back away from him. "This self-pity thing you've got going on is getting really old. Just because your legs are shorter than the average person does *not* make you less of one. You're still my brother, and you're still stupid no matter what your height is at the moment. You want to be whole again? Then fucking go to therapy. Go get some new legs, and show this girl how much you care about her. Because I've never seen you fight *against* something so hard in my life. And, *that's* how I know you're in love with her."

We both remain still, panting from the words we exchanged. I'm pissed, and all I want to do is get out of here. Now, of all times, I wish I had legs to run far away, but all I can do is roll to my room. A minute passes, maybe two, and Michael finally lets go of my chair. I immediately push myself down the hall to my room, slamming the door behind me.

A book I'd been reading, that lay on my desk, suddenly flies from my hand and hits the wall, as my anger and frustration comes out. I'm so pissed right now. I'm pissed at my situation, I'm pissed at my brother's goading but most of all, I'm pissed that he might be right. Am I in love with her? Does she have feelings for me? What if I pursue this, and I've read her wrong? I'll be mortified, and our relationship, whatever that is, will be changed forever. On the other hand, what if it *does* work out? What if she's waiting on me to make a move? I scoff and immediately dismiss the notion.

6

LOGAN

She bursts through the doorway like a gale force wind, pausing only slightly to close the door behind her. I instantly notice that she's not wearing her usual scrub uniform. Instead, she's wearing a figure flattering, fitted t-shirt and a pair of snug, blue jeans. I've never been able to study her shape before, since the work clothes she wears are anything but tight, but I take this opportunity to do just that. She's perfect.

"We're going out!" she announces, then she continues farther into the house.

"Excuse me, what?" I say, trying to comprehend what just passed between her lips.

"You heard me, and I won't take *no* for an answer." She nods satisfactorily with her hands on her hips, as if it's a done deal.

"Elora…" I whine a bit; I'll admit it.

"Logan, you have to get out. You've been cooped up here for way too long. You need to feel the sun on your face, the wind in your hair, and hear the birds chirping in the trees. You need this," she says, with her hands tucked into her back pockets.

"I don't go out."

"Why not?"

"You know why not."

"No. I know that you tell me you don't like it, but you've never said why. So, give me one good reason I should let you stay at home." She crosses her arms and taps her foot awaiting my reply. I smirk then grin at the sight before me. She looks like a petulant child who's trying to convince her parents to give in to her demands. I snort and roll my eyes.

"You know, you don't fight fair."

"I fight very fair. You're just mad because you know I'm right."

I roll my eyes again.

"How's this going to work? I've never practiced getting in and out of a car."

"Well, you've mastered all the other transfers, chair to car and back again, so it shouldn't be that much different. Besides, I can help you."

"No," I simply say.

"No?"

I shake my head.

"You're saying *no* to what? No helping you, or no car ride at all?"

I stay silent for a moment, letting her twist in the wind. Her brow furrows as she pouts, and I can't hold out anymore.

"No helping me." She squeals and claps rapidly while hopping up and down, in realization of my agreement to go out with her. "I'll go on your little outing, but you're not helping me at all. If I fall onto the ground, it'll be my responsibility to hoist myself back up. Capiche?"

She nods excitedly, and before I know it, her arms are around me. I'm stunned at first, but my arms automatically reciprocate. Her hair smells good—almost flowery. Her cheek brushes against mine, and I can't help but notice how soft it is. I'm not sure if this was planned, or if it was out of instinct, but here we are, hugging. I close my eyes and savor this moment, however brief it might be. She stills slightly, in realization I guess, then pulls back slowly. *No. I don't want it to end.* We stare at each other, our arms still touching. We're both speechless. I watch, seemingly in slow motion, as she licks her bottom lip, then pulls at it with her teeth. I've seen her do this a thousand times but somehow, this time is different. My breath hitches, and her eyes sink to my mouth. Is she thinking about…

Then, she suddenly seems to recover herself and looks anywhere but at me. Smoothing a strand of hair that had escaped from her ponytail, she straightens.

"S—so, I think we should get, um…going then." Her awkward stutter makes me wonder. Did she feel something? Is her heart beating as fast as mine? Can she tell how attracted I am to her? I do a quick mental check to make sure my desire isn't outwardly obvious. It's difficult to talk, but I manage.

"Um, sure. I could use the fresh air—I mean because it's hot in here—not because I'm hot, or you're hot, but because it's a nice day out, and the furnace is still on, and…"

Ugh! Shut the fuck up!

She smiles shyly.

"I know what you mean," she says as our eyes meet briefly, but I can tell she's still avoiding eye contact with me.

Oh, God, please just let this be like one of those dreams where you go to work or school in your underwear.

I wheel myself toward the foyer closet and grab a light jacket. It's unseasonably warm for late winter, but judging by the way my body reacted to her, I won't need more than this.

She opens the door for me and steps to the side to allow me to roll out. The threshold is raised, so I have to pop my front wheels up a bit. She smiles as the cool breeze winds through my hair. I smile back at her for the same reason. Her wind-blown look is just a beautiful as every other look she has.

As I turn the corner from my front walk, I see a shiny, black sedan parked in my driveway.

"Is that your car?" I ask, perplexed. It's funny, I pictured her as more of an SUV type. My suspicions are confirmed a few seconds later.

"No. It's my brother's. Mine is higher off the ground, and I thought you might have trouble getting into it. My brother was kind enough to trade vehicles with me today." She smiles sweetly.

"Well, that was nice of him."

"Yeah. I'm not much for conventional cars. I like to be able to put it in four-wheel drive and go." She giggles, then opens the passenger's side door and motions to me. I take a deep breath and steel myself for the inevitable crash to the ground.

"And, if you think I'm going to help you at all well, then, I guess you don't really know me," she says, feigning disinterest but with a slight smirk.

"But, what if I fall on my face?" I say, teasing her right back.

"Well, I suppose you'd better not. This concrete is very unforgiving. I wouldn't want your pretty-boy face to get injured."

"*Pretty-boy?*" I raise my voice in faux indignation. "I'll have you know that it's anything but pretty to start with, so there's really nothing to worry about." I smirk at her but as I do, I see her shy smile, and a blush washes across her face. I wonder what that's all about.

"Can we stop talking and go, Mr. Procrastination?"

"A pretty-boy and a procrastinator? You really think highly of me, don't you, Miss Sassy Pants."

I grin as her mouth pops open at my comeback. I don't think she was expecting that. Inwardly, I hope I didn't go too far.

"Just for that, I'm not telling you where we're going," she says stubbornly, and she leans against the side of the car.

"Okay, okay, I give," I say, grinning. "I'm going. I'm just trying to size up my obstacle."

She opens the back door and retrieves a transfer board. Then, laying it between my chair and the seat of the car, she watches as I carefully slide over. It isn't as bad as I'd thought. She grins victoriously at me then closes my door.

"So, where are you taking me?" I ask. She glances over at me, while driving, and smiles.

"I'm not sure I should tell you." I give her a sideways glance. "Oh, all right. We're going shopping."

"Shopping? For what?"

I'm alarmed.

"Groceries," she simply says, then turns her focus back to the road.

Not more than ten minutes later, we pull into a spot adorned with a disability sign.

"Not here," I say, adamantly. She looks at me, puzzled.

"But, you're—"

"Not here," I say again, interrupting what I know was about to come from her mouth. She stares at me for a few seconds longer, then puts the car into reverse.

"This one's fine." I point to a parking place farther away from the entrance. She pulls in and parks.

"It's okay to use that space, you know," she says, a little irritated, I think. "You do own the placard to show you deserve it."

"I don't need a special parking spot just because I don't have legs," I snap. "I can make it inside the store just fine. Now, are we going to do this, or not?"

Her face pales momentarily, and I suddenly become aware of my harsh tone. Before I can apologize, she exits the car to retrieve my chair. Setting it out in front of me, she opens it up, crosses her arms at her chest, and leans against the rear door, ignoring me completely. I hesitate, wondering what, if anything, I should say to her. I choose silence.

We walk, well, *she* walks I roll toward the entrance. Her strides are long, and I have to strain a bit to keep up with her. She grabs a shopping cart and begins putting produce into it. One thing after another gets dropped carefully inside. She's said nothing since I snapped at her. I should say something.

"Are you going to ask my opinion on what to get?"

"Nope," she says, then keeps on going. I catch up to her and try again.

"What if I don't like cantaloupes?"

She looks down at me, melon in hand.

"You don't like them?" Her tone is chilled.

"I like them just fine."

"Great," she says with an overly sweet, exaggerated, smile, then looks away and continues on.

Wow. She's really pissed at me. I try another tactic. Moving around a table of bananas, I head her off, essentially blocking her from moving forward. She stops just short of running into me.

"What the…" Her brow furrows, when she's forced to stop abruptly.

I grab onto the front of the cart to ensure I have a captive audience.

"I'm sorry, okay?" I say, although it's not my most sincere apology.

"Are you?"

"Yes, I am. I didn't mean to snap at you back there."

She snorts then rolls her eyes.

"Hey," I say in a gentler tone. "I really am sorry. This is my first time outside of my house. You have to understand, there's a certain mentality you have to adjust to when you're eligible to park in a handicapped spot. Cut me a little slack, okay?"

I see her face soften at the realization of my confession. She then exhales quietly.

"I'm sorry too. I just wanted to make your first outing as easy as possible, but at the same time, I guess I don't think of you as being different than anyone else. I forgot that this is a big adjustment for you. I'll try to be more considerate." She smiles, and I'm relieved.

"Thank you. Next time, I'll try to explain things instead of getting angry."

ELORA

We get back from our outing with groceries in hand. After putting them away, I begin to make him lunch.

"Not eating with me today?" he asks.

"No, I can't. I have an exam coming up, and I haven't studied at all," I say, as I place my books on the table.

"What's the test on?"

"Pharmacology."

"Ah. I remember that. It's nothing but tedious memorization of facts, as I recall."

I snort.

"You've got that right. I don't know how I'm going to remember it all."

He contemplates my predicament.

"How about this. You eat lunch with me, and I'll help you study afterward."

"Why would you want to torture yourself?" I say with another snort.

"Let's just say, I'm a glutton for punishment."

"Clearly."

I agree, then make another ham sandwich.

"Are you ready?" he asks.

"As I'll ever be."

"Oh, come on now. It can't be that bad."

"Yes, it really can, but go ahead. I'm ready."

"Okay. What's a salicylate?"

"Salicylate," I repeat. "Better known as Aspirin, salicylates treat inflammation, reduce fevers, and help relieve pain. It's also good for breaking up blood clots during a heart attack."

"Good, but that one was easy. How about this one. What are nitrates?"

"Nitrates are drugs that treat heart pain, also spasms of the heart vasculature. It works by dilating the blood vessels; basically opening them up to let blood flow through better. It's most commonly known as Nitroglycerin."

"See, you're good at this stuff."

"No, I'm really not. You're just going easy on me to make me feel better."

"What?" he laughs. "I wouldn't do that. Besides, what purpose would that serve? If I went easy on you, you might get cocky and think you know everything."

I giggle.

"Hardly. I feel so overwhelmed with this stuff sometimes that I wonder why I enrolled. It can be really hard," I admit.

"I know how you feel. I was the same way. I thought if I learned about one more thing, I might push other, more basic, knowledge out of my head, and maybe I'd forget how to tie my own shoes."

I laugh at his joke, but then remember his lack of feet, so I stop.

"Sorry," I say.

"What are you sorry for?"

"For laughing. I sometimes forget you don't have feet."

He looks down.

"Oh, my God! You're right!" he says, mocking me. My mouth twists.

"Funny."

74

"It's no big deal. If you can't laugh at yourself, who can you laugh at?"

"I suppose." My mind wanders to his injury. I want to ask him about it, but I don't think he'll tell me.

"So, what made you want to become a nurse?"

Well, that question came out of the blue.

"Um…I don't know. I guess I just wanted to help people."

"Save the world, one patient at a time? Sounds noble."

"Not really," I say.

"Not everyone can do the job that you're studying for. Are you squeamish?" I shake my head. "Good, because you'll see some really nasty stuff."

"Like what?"

"You really want to know?"

"Uh…okay," I say reluctantly.

He scrutinizes my expression.

"You know, maybe I'll save the horror stories for later. There are lots of good things that happen too. It's those times that make you glad you chose to work in the medical field."

I smile, grateful he didn't go into detail.

"Yeah, I'm sure I'm going to like it."

I hope.

Weeks have flown by as if they were days. Logan and I have found a rhythm, and I'm proud to say he's a different man than he was when I first met him. He still gets angry at my gentle nudging, but I now know that's just how he is.

As I walk into Logan's house, it's oddly quiet. He's usually out of bed and dressed by this hour of the morning, not so today.

"Logan?" I call out as I remove one of my shoes. "Are you up yet?"

I no sooner remove the second one, when I hear a garbled scream coming from down the hall.

"Oh, God," I whisper as I drop the shoe onto the floor and sprint toward his bedroom. For a split second, I hesitate going in, but then, I burst through the door anyway. I find a tormented Logan, still in bed, clutching his covers and burying his face in them. I rush to his side, visually sweeping across his body, looking for the source of his agony.

"My leg!" he cries out. "Something's wrong!"

Immediately, I throw back the blanket, not knowing what I might find, and search for anything that could give me clue as to what's going on, but I see nothing.

"Where?" I ask, frantic to relieve his pain.

"My ankle! It's...being crushed!"

Confused, I observe his anguished expression.

"What?"

"*My ankle!*" he screams again, while reaching down trying to grasp it.

"Logan, you don't have an ankle," I say sadly.

Tears threaten as I realize what this is. Logan is experiencing phantom pains. His brain still believes his natural legs are intact, therefore it's tricking him into thinking he feels pain in them.

I cover my mouth, trying to hold it together, when all I really want to do is wail. As if he hasn't been through enough, now he has to endure this. I'm no longer able to hold them back, and they stream down my face, seemingly without end.

"Oh, God, Logan. It's okay," I say, as I sit next to him, cradling him in my arms. "Shh. It'll stop soon." His entire body is tense as he lies against me, allowing me to comfort him. Resting his head against my chest, he rides it out, until the pain relents. I feel his body begin to relax, so I loosen up the hold I have on him. After a few minutes, he lets go of me, rolls onto his back, and lies, panting and breathless, on the mattress. Sweat trickles down his brow as he stares up at the ceiling. I'm not sure what to say, so I wait for him to break the silence.

"That was intense...and real," he says, still winded, then he looks over at me. I wipe the remnants of emotion from my face and nod.

"Are you okay?" I ask softly.

He nods.

"Yeah. I think so." He rubs his face with both hands. "Shit. I don't want to experience *that* again anytime soon."

"I'm sorry."

He sighs heavily as if the weight of the world is on his shoulders.

"They told me about this…" He looks back at the ceiling. "It's like it was happening all over again. I could feel the bones in my ankle being compressed then popping as they—" I gasp, and he looks over. His sincere expression is an apology for saying too much. "Sorry," he says when he realizes he was thinking out loud.

"It's okay. I've just never thought too much about the actual mechanics of what happened to you. It's hard to imagine."

"Yeah. Thankfully, I don't remember much."

I've always wondered, but we've never really discussed the circumstances behind his amputation. That conversation will have to keep for another time, however. I can tell he's relived it enough for today.

"Thank you," he says, taking me by surprise.

"For what?"

"For helping me get through it."

"You're welcome," I say with a small smile, which erupts into a huge grin, the moment I turn my back to him and start walking out of his room.

Yeah. I wasn't entirely selfless.

7

ELORA

Logan heads for the bathroom to take a shower as I clean up from our meal. I reach across the counter for a glass when I bump into, and knock over, a plastic jar of peanuts. They bounce and scatter onto the floor, and I moan in frustration.

"Damn it!" I say, as I drop to my knees and begin to pick them up.

"Everything okay out there?" I hear Logan ask.

"Yeah. Everything's fine." I reassure him.

Standing up, I move toward the hall closet to retrieve the broom and dust pan. As I open the door, several things tumble forward, taking me by surprise, and make me yelp.

"Elora?" Logan's concerned voice calls out again.

"I'm good. I've just been attacked by a broom." I giggle at my luck.

"What?"

"Nothing," I say, realizing he can't hear me. "I'll talk to you when you're done."

"Huh?"

I roll my eyes and laugh.

"I said, *happy showering.*"

"Oh. Thanks."

Smiling and shaking my head, I bend forward to pick up the fallen objects. I'm stuffing things anywhere they'll fit, when I soon discover a crutch. Then, I find a second one, along with a cane. How odd. The crutches hardly seem used and the cane still has a tag on it. Who's are these? Maybe, one of them had broken a leg a while back and never got rid of the assistive devices. I hear the water shut off, so I hurriedly stuff the remainder of the items back into the closet and shut the door.

"Elora?" Logan says through the closed bathroom door.

"Yeah?"

"What were you trying to tell me?"

"Oh, nothing. I spilled some peanuts and was looking for a broom."

"Oh…Oh! Wait, I'll get it for you," he says in a rush.

"It's okay. I found where you keep it." It's then I realize I forgot to get it out, so I open the door, more carefully this time, just as the bathroom door swings open. My head swivels to see Logan in nothing more than a towel, and my jaw goes slack.

"Oh, my God," I whisper unintentionally. I know the polite thing would be to look away, but…I can't seem find the correct muscles to do it. His upper body glistens from the water droplets he has yet to dry. His damp hair is messy…and sexy. My eyes automatically lower to his abs, which are tight and well defined. And then, I look at the towel, which is neatly wrapped around his waist. It doesn't cover much as I can see most of his thighs. *Damn my eyes.* I urge them to look away, but they disobey me and stare a little too long. He clears his throat, and my embarrassed cheeks heat like they never have before. I quickly close my eyes, in hopes that he didn't see my blatant gawking.

"Um…"

Um? That's all he's got?

Who am I kidding? I don't have much more than that.

"You…um…surprised me," I mutter, looking at the floor and covering my cheeks. "I'll just get the broom and clean up the mess." I don't even bother looking into the closet when I reach in and grasp the first pole-like object I feel. "I'll be right back…I mean, not *right* back. I'm going to go and get your nuts—I *mean* the peanuts…that I spilled…in the kitchen…while you were showering. Not that I was thinking about you showering. I just…" I exhale.

Yeah. Smooth.

I open one eye and peek up at him to assess the damage.

"Are you sure you won't be right back?" he says with a smirk. "That's not a broom you have in your hand."

I look down to find I'm holding one of the crutches.

"Oh," I say, then reopen the closet and exchange the crutch for the broom. "I got it now." I smile awkwardly, then turn on my heel, *so* ready to exit this humiliating ordeal.

When he reemerges from the hall, he's dressed in sweats and a t-shirt. His hair is combed back but still slightly damp. I admonish myself silently at the details I take in regarding his appearance. I shake my head, signaling to myself to back off.

"So, you've cleaned up the mess, I see. The broom worked better than the crutch would have, don't you think?" he teases.

I purse my lips at him.

"Ha! Very funny," I say sarcastically. "Who else, but you, keeps a spare set of crutches in a broom closet—emphasis on *broom*." I cross my arms in front of my chest to show my disapproval.

He laughs.

"I suppose you have a point there."

"Why do you have them anyway?" I ask, all kidding aside.

He sighs and rubs the back of his neck.

"Well, it was going to be a surprise, but…" He looks up almost apologetically. "I've been using them."

Using them? How?

"What do you mean?"

"I mean. It's the first step in gaining back my independence. Elora, I got my first set of prosthetic legs."

I feel my face go from strained and curious to shocked.

"What? Why didn't you tell me? How long have you had them?"

"It's only been a couple of days, and I was going to tell you, but I wanted to be a little more coordinated on them before you had to see me use them." He shrugs an apology.

"Oh, my God, Logan. This is huge! I can't believe you did this!" I'm so excited for him that I find myself clapping like some sort of circus animal performer. He smiles shyly. "Please! Show me what you can do!"

His face falls as he shakes his head.

"No. Not yet."

"Why not?"

"Because I'm not ready for you to see me fall on my face just yet."

"Logan—"

"I'm serious."

Bravely, I squat down in front of him, holding onto his chair.

"Please?" I'm hoping my sincere expression will soften his heart enough to let me help him learn to walk again.

He sighs and rubs the back of his neck again. He seems to be contemplating his answer.

"I don't know." He looks at me again, so I use my expression to silently beg him. "Ugh! You're impossible. Fine. I'll show you how well I can fall." I squeal and grin from ear to ear. "Just don't expect much. I've only been on them a few times with Michael helping me."

"I promise. I'll expect the worst. I'm guessing you won't even make it to a standing position." I smirk, and he smirks back.

"Thanks."

After retrieving his prosthetic legs from under his bed, he holds them out for my inspection. They look very mechanical, in that the replacement shin is a metal rod, and the foot looks as though it was once on a mannequin. He then takes out two, sock-like liners. There's a small pin protruding out from the ends, and I'm guessing that's what makes the prosthetic stay in place. He pulls up his pant legs, and rolls the gel liner onto his right, residual limb. It's hard for me to see his scars and not want to touch them, to ease the pain he must have endured. The scars are pink, and I wonder if they still hurt him. When I look at his face, he's already looking at me. He's wary.

"They don't hurt much anymore, the scars I mean. Although, the new legs do irritate me a bit. They're hot and sweaty at times, and it's hard to scratch an itch underneath all this stuff. It's a lot to get used to," he says by way of explanation.

"I wasn't staring," I lie.

"It's okay. I know you've not really had a chance to see what's left of my legs. I'm not exactly the type to brag about them."

I nod, not really knowing how to respond. We've always had humor to dispel an awkward moment, but now is definitely not the time for that. He continues with the second, sock-like sleeve, then reaches for the artificial limb. He dons one, then the other, then shifts them around a bit until he feels as though they're on properly. He then looks up at me with apprehension and sighs.

"Here we go. Hold the crutches, until I'm ready to take them." I nod, letting him know I'm paying very close attention to his every command.

Scooting forward a bit in his wheelchair, he positions his new legs directly underneath him. He nods at the crutches, so I hand them over. Taking in a deep breath and exhaling forcefully, he pushes himself up from the chair. I'm holding my breath in anticipation of what might happen. Shakily, although not as much as I thought, he stands, then balances, on his new limbs. I'm frozen in place, waiting for any sign that he might topple off to one side or the other. He steps onto them a few times; I guess to make sure they're on tight enough and, after hearing a few clicks, he looks satisfied. Then, once he's confident his balance is in check, he peers over at me, smiling.

"What do you think? Am I taller than you thought I was?"

Taking my cues from him, relief washes over me, and I grin back at him.

"Much." My response is breathy, and I realize it's because I'm still nervous for him. "Are you okay?"

"I'm good. Want to see me walk a bit?" I nod rapidly, and he turns his focus to the floor in front of him. Slowly, his right foot moves, then his left. He continues this way until he's reached the kitchen table. Then, turning around, he makes his way back toward his chair. I place both hands over my face splitting grin. "Well?"

"It's amazing," I say quietly, as if a loud noise might knock him over. "You're amazing." His smile is triumphant…and beautiful. "How much have you been practicing this?"

"They told me to use them for one hour, then off for one hour, and keep alternating like that until I get used to them. But, you know what?"

"What?"

"It's not as bad as I'd imagined. It's not the best thing I've ever had to do, but it's definitely not the worst either." His grin broadens. "Elora, I can *do* this. I think I really can do this." His triumphant expression warms my heart.

"Without you, I'd have no motivation to do anything. Without you pushing me—no, *badgering* me, to fit into a world that so clearly wanted me not to survive, I wouldn't be in this position…literally." He turns slightly to come face to face with me and for the first time since we've met, he's taller than me. I look up into his thankful eyes. Then, propping his crutch securely under his arm, he reaches out and touches my cheek. My eyes close automatically as I feel the warmth from his fingers graze my skin, and I lean ever so slightly into his touch. My heart races at the wayward thoughts, which run through my head, and, for a moment, I'm lost in my own imagination. "Thank you," he says and, when I open my eyes, we're almost nose to nose.

Holy shit. I can hardly remember how to drag in a breath. I feel as though the room has suddenly become a vacuum, and all the air has been sucked out. Is he going to kiss me? Oh, God, he might actually be going to kiss me. Should I kiss him back? *Should* I kiss him back? It's then that the proverbial bucket of cold water is thrown into the mix, and the word *client* rattles around us. I suck in a huge gulp of air and step back a bit, trying, successfully I think, to put an emotional and physical distance between us. The momentary wounded expression on his face all but kills me, but he recovers, as I'm sure he realizes what almost happened. He steps backward, stumbling a bit, but steadies himself perfectly.

"I'm...uh..." he stutters, then stops.

His loss for words is mirrored by me, and we stand paralyzed for what seems like an eternity. Finally, the silence is broken.

"Elora...I...I'm sorry...I don't know what came over me." His breaths are labored, making this situation even more dire. "Please..." He bows his head and shakes it marginally. "Forgive me." He looks back at me for...what? A response, no doubt.

Say something.

"Um...no, I mean, yeah. There's nothing to forgive. It's a great accomplishment. You're happy. I'm happy *for* you. It's all good," I lie, knowing full well I want him, but he's the one man on this planet, right now, that I can't have. "We're good," I reiterate, begrudgingly. And now, I know, I'm in trouble. I take another step away from him as he sits back in his chair. For the rest of the day, we're oddly professional, which makes me both satisfied and heartbroken simultaneously.

Another week passes, and Logan and I have gotten into a routine. Every afternoon, after we eat lunch, he and I go for a walk around his neighborhood. The practice and exercise is good for him and, each day, we lengthen the walk by fifteen minutes or so.

Today is a beautiful, spring day. There's a slight breeze, which blows the newly sprouted greenery back and forth, and I can't wait to walk around in this glorious weather.

"Hurry up, slow poke," I call to Logan while waiting on his front porch.

"I'm coming," he says as he steps over the threshold. "Why are you so impatient?"

"It's a gorgeous day today!"

"I see that. No jackets this time."

He walks toward the sidewalk, mindful that the stairs are his first obstacle on our hike.

"Just go slow. You've been doing so much better with them lately, but I still get nervous for you."

"Yeah," he snorts. "I get nervous too."

There are only two steps to go down, but there's no railing. He removes the crutches from under his arms and holds them, only with his hands. Right foot, left foot, he clears the first one. Then, he goes for the second. His right foot lands safely onto the sidewalk but when he picks up the left one, his shoe gets caught on the edge, causing him to lose his balance.

"Ah!" he shouts, as his leg gives out from under him, sending him sailing onto the concrete below.

"Oh, my God! Logan! Are you okay?" I instinctively grab onto his arm, trying to help him up.

"I'm fine," he says. His voice is a bit gruff as he balances on his hands and knees. "I'm good. Just stay near me while I get back up."

"Do you want me to help you?"

"No. Stuff like this is going to happen, and you might not be around. I need to learn to handle things on my own."

Amazingly, with little effort, he stands back up unassisted. I clap politely at his finesse, and he bows slightly.

"Nice recovery, Mr. Turner. How did you learn how to do that?"

"At therapy, but I've also been watching a lot of videos online."

"Doing some extra studying? I'd say that's worth at least ten extra credit points."

"Why thank you, Miss Foster. That's very generous of you," he says, then winks.

We both laugh, then begin our walk.

"So, really, did you get hurt when you fell?" I ask while walking beside him.

"Not really. I think the fear of falling is worse than the actual fall." He looks at his hand. "My hands got scratched up a bit, that's all."

I stop, take his hand in mine, and blow on it. Then, I place a very gentle kiss on the heel.

"There. How's that?"

He smiles appreciatively.

"It feels better all ready. You must have a magic touch," he says.

"I'll never tell," I reply with a wink, and he smiles fondly at me.

"I have a question," he says, as we resume walking.

"Yes?"

"I got a call from a friend the other day."

"Oh?"

"Yeah. Apparently, he's getting married and invited me to go."

"Well, that'll be nice. I think you should go."

"Yeah," he says, then swipes his forehead with his hand. "Um...I was wondering...would you want to come with me? Be my plus one?"

I raise my eyebrows in shock. I wasn't expecting this.

"Oh. Um..."

"You can say no. It's fine. I just thought that maybe, since I don't really have anyone else to go with, that you'd be willing to hang out with me for a few hours that day. But, if not, I understand."

Oh, my. What should I say? I'd be his *plus one*? What exactly does that imply? He's looking anywhere but at me, and I think he was really nervous about asking me. I could just think of it as a way to make sure he's safe.

"Sure," I say, and his head swings over in my direction.

"Really?"

I smile and nod.

"I'd love to go. Thank you for asking me."

His face erupts in a huge grin.

"Great!" he says, keeping his elated expression. "It's about a month from now. I hope that's okay."

"That's fine. How should I dress?"

"Well, I think it's being held at a more formal venue, but whatever you decide to wear will be fine."

It looks as though I might have to go shopping.

8

LOGAN

I'm rooting around in my closet, when I finally spot my suit jacket and pants. I pull them out, from way in the back, and dust off the shoulders. Sheesh. How long has it been since I've had to wear it? It's a simple navy suit, with very small pin stripes. The tie that Bethany suggested is still wrapped around the hanger. I remember now it was her friend's wedding.

As I finish trying it on, Michael knocks on my door, but doesn't wait for me to answer, before barging right in. His eyes fill with horror, when he sees my attire, as realization dawns.

"Damn it. It's formal?" he says with a grimace.

"I'm afraid so," I say, and chuckle a bit.

"Seriously? I'm not even sure where my two occasion suit is."

"Your what?"

"You know, the two occasions in which I'm forced to wear it: weddings and funerals."

"Ah, yes. I have one of those too," I say, tugging at the lapel of my current clothing. I reach out and cross my arms in front of me, testing the tightness of the fabric on my back. "It's been so long since I've worn it; it feels a bit small. I may have to buy another one."

"Wait. So you're telling me that I not only have to wear a stiff, throat strangling suit, I may also have to take you *shopping* to buy another one?" I shrug, and he rolls his eyes. "Just kill me now."

"Oh, come on. It's not that bad. We'll just go to a department store inside the mall. They're sure to have some."

I laugh when Michael's face contorts even more.

"*The mall?* Why do I even have to go to this wedding?" he whines.

"You have to go because Ryan is friends with *both* of us. He invited *both* of us, and it's only polite."

"Can't you just go and tell him I'm sick…or better yet, dead?"

I laugh again.

"If I have to go and wear a monkey suit, so do you. Now, go find yours and see if it fits, so we can go get a new one for you at the same time."

ELORA

"These are all so pretty. How am I supposed to pick just one?" I say, while grabbing yet another dress off the rack.

"I don't know, but what a problem to have!" Melanie says. We erupt into a fit of giggles as she follows me to the dressing room.

"What do you think of this one," I ask, emerging from the small changing area.

She tilts her head to the side, then smoothes out a wrinkle at my waist.

"I'm not sure. I'm not fan of this style."

"I agree. I like the color though. It reminds me of the sea."

"Yeah, go back in, and try on another."

A few moments later, I open the door again.

"How about this one?"

Her eyebrows shoot up.

"Whoa. I'm not sure what statement you're trying to make, but I'm pretty sure that '*take me straight to the bedroom*' is not the right one."

"Yeah…not at all the message I'm trying to send." I laugh uneasily. "I'll try another," I say, then go back into the changing room.

"So, who's wedding is it again?" she asks.

"Oh, some old friend of Logan's."

"Uh huh."

"I guess he and his brother have known him for a while."

"Hmm," she says.

I poke my head out of the door.

"Now, what does *hmm* mean?"

"Nothing," she says, feigning innocence. "I just hope he knows that this is strictly business and not a real date. You did make that clear, didn't you?"

"He knows that," I say, clearly irritated.

She holds her hands up in surrender.

"Okay. I believe you. I'd just hate for this to become a misunderstanding."

"Melanie, Logan and I have a very professional relationship, nothing else, so stop worrying about it, okay?"

"If you say so, I have to believe you." She starts to walk out, but turns back to face me. "I just hope he feels the same way."

I scoff at her and wave her away, then close the door to finish trying the next dress on.

"Okay. I like this one. It shows just enough cleavage but not too much. It hugs me in all the right places without accentuating the bad spots." I laugh at my own words. "And, the fabric is so soft. Are you ready to see it?" She doesn't answer. "Melanie? Are you there?" There's still no answer. "Melanie?" I say, while opening the door. My reflection is the only person I see. She must've gone out. In my bare feet, I tiptoe out of the changing area, looking for my lost friend. "Melanie?" I call out again, but I can't see her, nor hear her reply. I call her name again then, finally, I hear her faint voice.

"Hang on. I found a really pretty one. I'm just trying to find your size."

"Okay," I say, then turn to head back inside.

"Elora?" a familiar voice says.

I turn around to see two men standing in the aisle near me. I swallow hard, and instinctually, I wrap my arms around myself.

"Logan?" I say, shocked to see him at a mall. "Hi." I walk closer to the two men. "How are you?"

"I'm fine. You?"

"I'm good."

What the hell is he doing here?

"I was just here buying a new suit…for the wedding," he says, answering the question I didn't actually ask out loud. His eyes are large and round as they sweep across me, inspecting my attire, no doubt. "Wow. You look…" His voice is hoarse, and he doesn't finish his sentence, before I begin blushing. I cover my heated cheeks in an attempt to hide my embarrassment. "Amazing."

"Thank you," I say, trying desperately to recover my wits and calm my rapid heartbeat. "It's nice to see you out and about." I'm hoping my nervous laugh doesn't give me away.

"Yeah…thanks. Someone once told me, I should get out now and then." I hear the other man clear his throat, then nudge Logan's shoulder. He breaks eye contact with me to shoot his friend a puzzled look. Then, suddenly, he remembers his manners. "Oh. Elora, this is my brother, Michael. Michael, *this* is Elora."

Michael reaches his hand out to me, and I gladly accept and shake it.

"He's so rude," Michael says with an exaggerated eye roll and a toothy grin, then he laughs at his brother's expense. "So, you're the elusive Elora. Logan has been going on and on about you for months. Although, now I can see why." He gets an elbow thrown into his side, and winces slightly. "I mean, it's nice to finally meet you."

"I've heard a lot about you too." I lean into him a bit. "But, don't worry, I don't believe any of it." Logan's gloating smile is triumphant, as Michael laughs and shakes his head.

"I appreciate that," he says.

"Is that the dress you're going to wear to the wedding?" Logan asks.

I look down, having forgotten I'm still wearing it.

"Uh, I'm not sure yet. I still have a few to try on."

"Well, you look beautiful in it, but then, I'm sure any dress in this place would look lovely on you."

"Thank you." I think I'm blushing again.

"Mr. Turner!" Melanie says, as she strolls over with two more dresses in her arms. "It's so nice to see you on your feet."

"Please, it's Logan, and thank you. I'm happy to have the opportunity to be on my feet again."

He introduces her to his brother, and they exchange pleasantries.

"So, I understand that Elora will be going to a wedding with you next month?" she says.

"Yes, she was nice enough to agree to go with me." He looks at me and smiles. "I'll be the most envied man there."

I smile shyly, and he winks.

"Well, I can't argue with that. She's the best."

"Yes, she is," he says without breaking eye contact.

"Logan, we should let them get back to shopping," Michael says, then he turns his head toward us. "It was very nice to meet both of you." He looks at me directly. "And I hope you find the one you're looking for."

"Thank you," I say, as my eyes shift between him and Logan.

"Yeah, we should go. Melanie, it was nice to see you again. Elora… I'll see you on Monday."

I nod, say my goodbyes, then head off the dressing room to change.

As Melanie and I sit drinking our coffee, I'm catapulted back to the department store. It's ironic that we ended up in the same place as Logan and Michael. I recall the shy feeling I got when he saw me in that beautiful dress. He seemed mesmerized by it. I wonder what he was thinking.

"Hello?" Melanie says, trying to get my attention. "Anybody home?"

"Um, yeah. I guess I was daydreaming," I admit.

"I can see that. How are things going with Logan? Are you doing okay?"

"What? Oh, yeah. Everything's fine. I'm fine. He's fine. Everybody's...fine."

"Good. I'm glad it seems to be working out." Then, she shakes her head slightly and snorts. "Those first few days, I was so afraid you were going to tell me some horror story, and ask me to move you."

"He's not that bad." I chuckle.

"Not according to the last few aides."

"I guess I can see why they didn't like him. Hell, I almost walked out after the first day. But, I'm glad I hung in there. He really is very kind and sweet."

Silence hovers.

"Really? He's kind and sweet? Are you sure you're going to the right house?" She chuckles softly. "Although, I have to say, he did seem like a different person today than he did before."

"Yeah, he was rough around the edges at first. You have to understand where he's coming from though. He's only had a short time to adjust to his predicament. I've been researching people who've had a limb amputated, and some of them take years to come to terms with it. Some of them *never* get over it. I'd say Logan is doing very well."

"Hmm," she says.

"What?"

"It sounds like you've really become attached to him."

"Yeah, I guess I have. I'm fascinated by his story. He's been a war vet and a medic, no less. He's a hero in many ways, and I just want to give him the help he's given to others."

"Well, just don't get too personally involved."

"What do you mean?"

"I saw the way he looked at you today. He was enjoying the view of you in that dress."

"What? No. He was just being polite. What did you expect him to say? '*Ugly dress, it looks like shit on you?*'"

She laughs.

"Well, no, but he was definitely having trouble looking anywhere else but at you. He kept staring."

I smile inwardly.

"Oh, please, that was just your imagination."

"Maybe…Look, I want to tell you a true story that happened to a girl from our agency. I'm not saying that you're in the same situation, but I also know how quickly feelings can be formed." She adjusts herself so that she's leaning closer to me. "A few years ago, one of our caregivers started a relationship with her patient. He was a handsome, young man who became paraplegic due to an accident. While she was taking care of him, they apparently fell in *love*." She accentuates the word *love*, as if she doesn't believe it was true. "When it came out, it was all very scandalous. His parents were upset, even though he was an adult, and threatened to sue the company. She kept going to see him, even after they fired her. The company ended up taking her to court, claiming breach of contract."

"Oh, no," I say, stunned.

"Yeah. She lost the case and was ordered to pay thousands of dollars. The whole thing was a disaster. To top it all off, they broke up shortly thereafter. Their relationship was tainted and doomed from the start. I think he may have thought he was in love with her because she was his caregiver. It was so sad."

"Oh, my God. How awful," I say, covering my mouth and noting some similarities.

"Yes. It was. That's why I'm telling you to be careful. I'm not saying that you're in love with Logan Turner, but I know how easy it is to get too attached."

"Yeah," I say, dazed. "Well, don't worry, he's charming, but not *that* charming." I laugh uneasily, because I know that's just not true.

"I hope you're smarter than that. I hope you can keep your relationship professional."

"Yeah, I mean, absolutely. I don't have any feelings for Logan other than the fact that he's my patient. and I'm his caregiver," I lie. "I only look out for his best interests. No worries."

She sits back and breathes a sigh of relief.

"Good. I'm glad to hear that. I worry about you. I know how much money and effort it takes to get through nursing school, and I'd hate to see that ruined because of a lapse in judgement."

"Yeah. Me too."

The subject changes to something lighter, but I'm not really paying attention. Could I really lose my job, my chances of being a nurse, and be sued, all for falling in love with the wrong man? The thought is depressing. Is it worth it? Maybe, I should back off now, before we get any closer. But, how? How can I back away from a man I've grown to care so much about? Does he even care for me the way Melanie seems to think? I can't deny the way he looks at me sometimes. Still, maybe it's just my imagination. Oh, how did I get myself into this situation?

LOGAN

"**G**ood morning," I say with a smile, as Elora walks through the door.

"Morning," she replies quietly.

"You okay?" She nods, but I can tell something's off. "Are you sure? You don't seem like your usual happy self."

"Yeah, I'm fine. I'm just in one of those moods, I guess. What can I make you for breakfast?" She lays her bag on the floor and walks toward the stove.

"How about if we make breakfast together again. Eggs and bacon sound good?"

"I'm sorry, I'm not hungry. I ate at home, but I'll be glad to cook for you."

I wheel myself over, stopping right in front of her. Reaching out, I touch her arm, and she noticeably stiffens.

"Hey. What's going on with you?"

"Nothing. Really." She moves her arm away from my hand, pretending to push a nonexistent lock of stray hair from her face. "I just didn't get a good night's sleep, I guess."

"Elora…" I probe.

"I'm fine!" she shouts, as she spins around to face me. "Just leave it alone, okay?" She rolls her eyes and sighs in exasperation, then turns back to the task as hand. I'm shocked into silence. What the hell is going on? I've never seen her this angry…and at me, no less. I nod my head, even though she can't see me, and back away, wheeling myself to the table. I pick up the newspaper, but comprehend none of what I'm reading. The whole while, I'm trying to figure out what might've happened since I last saw her.

She places my breakfast in front of me then retreats to the living room, presumably to study. I eat the most solitary meal I've eaten in a long while; the silence fills the room. I look over at her occasionally, to see if she's watching me, but she keeps her head down. The only movement I see is the intermittent turn of a page. I want to say something. I want to let her know that I'm here for her, for whatever is bothering her. But, I chicken out. After I place my dishes in the sink, I turn toward the hallway.

"I'll be in my bedroom, working out, if you need me."

She looks up and nods sullenly. I start wheeling myself down the hall when she speaks up.

"Logan?" she says, so I stop and look at her. Her face is so sad, and so apologetic, and I now understand, just a bit, how she must've felt when I first met her—when I was so angry at the world that I was willing to hurt anyone who tried to help me.

"Yes?" I try to keep my voice free from irritation.

"I…I'm…sorry."

"It's okay," I say, then smile sincerely. "We all have those days. I'll see you after my workout."

She hesitates, but eventually gives me a subtle nod. I continue on, into my room, to give her the space I know she needs right now.

After a vigorous workout, I exit my room with my legs on. I walk into the kitchen but don't see Elora. I take a few steps in the direction of the living room, where I last saw her, but she's not there. Perplexed, I walk in a bit farther. Nothing. Did she leave? My heart begins to panic. I walk back toward the kitchen when I notice some movement on the front porch. I hold my breath as I near the window, then exhale when I see her sitting on the step.

"What are you doing?" I ask, after opening the front door. She turns to look behind her and smiles wistfully at me.

"Just sitting here in the warm sun. Are you ready for lunch?"

I shake my head. No. I'm not going to ask her to take care of me today. It's my turn.

"No, but if it's okay with you, I'd like to make lunch for *you* this time."

She snorts.

"That's not your job, it's mine. I'll do it." She insists, then stands.

I hold up my hand.

"Not a chance. You're having a bad day today. Let me do this for you. If you don't want to talk about what's bothering you, I'll respect that but, if I can't help with your problem, at least let me take a bit of your burden off."

She smiles appreciatively, and I can't help but feel I've gained a little bit of my Elora back.

"Logan, taking care of you is anything but a burden to me."

"I know, but still. Let me do this for you." Her expression is apprehensive. "Please?"

Reluctantly, she agrees. I hold the door open for her, and she steps inside. The fragrant smell of her hair wafts past me in her wake. I close my eyes briefly and absorb every molecule.

"So, what'll it be? Soup? Sandwich? Soup *and* a sandwich? What are you in the mood for?"

"Um, I don't know. Grilled cheese?"

She picked something easy. She thinks I can't handle something more complicated. I'm onto her. My mouth twists.

"That's it?" She nods. "You know, I'm capable of cooking something a little more elaborate."

She covers her face splitting grin, which tells me she doesn't believe me, but it's so good to see her coming back to me. My chest warms in response.

"I'm sure," she says, then bites her bottom lip to keep from laughing.

"Do you doubt my abilities as a chef?"

"*A chef?*" she blurts out, as if her words could no longer be contained.

"You're laughing at me," I say, teasing her.

"I'm not. I promise. I'd just never describe you as a chef."

I try to act affronted, and lean against the counter with my arms crossed. She laughs, which is exactly the reaction I was hoping for.

"Well, I was planning on cooking Coq au Vin for dinner, but forget it now." I put my nose in the air and look away from her.

"No, you weren't," she giggles. "You don't even know what that is."

"Okay, you're right. I have no idea, but it sounded French, so I figured it had to be fancy."

"Grilled cheese for lunch will be just fine," she says, smiling and shaking her head at our conversation, and I know I've got her back.

"Yes, ma'am. Coming right up."

ELORA

How on earth am I supposed to keep my distance when he's being so damned charming? I watch, in utter amusement, as Logan butters both the outsides *and* insides of the bread. I want to say something, give him some pointers, but I refrain. This is his show. He wants to do this for me, and I'll give him that. It was such a sweet gesture, and it only solidifies my feelings for him. What the hell am I going to do?

Within minutes, a grilled to perfection, hot, cheese sandwich is set in front of me, complete with a pickle on the side, and a glass of tea. It smells great and since I lied to him earlier about having eaten breakfast at home, I'm positively starving. He sits down adjacent to me, with his own plate of food, and I watch as he unfolds his napkin and places it on his lap. His parents have trained him well.

"Well, dig in...unless you're afraid," he says with a smirk.

"Just one thing missing," I say, then I get up to go to the refrigerator. I take out a large container of salsa, and pour some into two bowls. After putting it back in to the fridge, I carry them over, placing one in front of him, and the other at my place setting. He looks at me, perplexed.

"You want chips with your sandwich?"

"No. I like to dip my grilled cheese in salsa, and I thought you'd like to try it too."

His brow furrows, as he thinks about this new cuisine but ultimately, he gives it a go.

"This is really good," he says, after swallowing a bite of his salsa dipped sandwich. "Why have I never thought of this?"

I shrug.

"I don't know. I made it up one day. My mother used to make grilled cheese with tomatoes inside. One day, I was craving one of her wonderful creations, but I didn't have any tomatoes, so I improvised. And voila! A new dish was born."

"Well, I'd say you're a genius, but I don't want to overstate the obvious," he says.

I roll my eyes and giggle.

"So, are we still going on our usual, after lunch, walk today?"

"Do you want to?" I nod. "Okay then, we'll go."

We finish our lunch and begin our stroll. He's chosen to use only one crutch today, but I'm holding the second one, just in case he needs both. As we walk along our usual path, we talk about nothing in particular, but our conversations always flow like water. There've not been too many times that we've struggled to connect in this way, and I'm finding it very difficult to keep my distance.

"So, tell me about your parents. Do they live nearby?"

"My mom lives just over the Indiana border. She moved there a few years ago after she met her current boyfriend. We don't get to talk much, but she's very eccentric, so I'm okay with that. We talk on the phone mostly now."

"And your dad?"

I sigh.

"I never knew my dad. He left just after I was born. It's been my mom, my brother, and me ever since."

"I'm sorry," he says with regret.

"Don't be sorry. You're not the one who left." An uncomfortable silence hovers, so I change the subject. "So, lunch was delicious. Thank you," I say with a sincere smile.

"You're very welcome. It was my pleasure, and the least I could do for someone who does so much for me every day."

"That's very kind of you to say, but it's my job."

"Something tells me that you'd do it even if it wasn't in your job description."

I chuckle.

"Probably, but you're lucky you're no longer that grumpy man I used to know, or I might put a little *extra something* in your food." I say with a smirk. His mouth falls open.

"So, that's what it means when someone says they put love into their cooking…it's really spit?"

I giggle and nod slowly, as if to suggest I've already done it. He shakes his head with a smile.

"Miss Foster, you're terrible. I'm glad I cooked today, and I think from now on, I'll keep doing it," he says, then his mouth twists. "Then again, knowing how stubborn you are, you won't let me."

My eyebrows lift.

"Stubborn? Me? What about you? It was like pulling teeth to get you to start transferring yourself from chair to chair, let alone how long it took me to convince you to try wearing prosthetics."

He smiles fondly.

"I know. That's why I appreciate you so much. You've never given up on me, no matter how much I protested. For that, I can never re-pay you."

9

ELORA

The next day, as we arrive back at his house after our walk, a thought occurs to me.

"You know, when we're at your friend's wedding, you might be expected to dance."

"And, exactly who is going to be expecting that?" he says, with pure confusion on his face.

"Me," I say, smirking.

"You? Really? Why on earth would you want to see me dance?"

"Well, not *see* you dance, but dance *with* you." I feel my cheeks heat, and I'm a little shocked that it came from my mouth. "I mean, what else is there to do at a wedding if you don't dance a time or two?"

He wraps his fingers around his jaw and seems to contemplate my words.

"I suppose you do have a point. What do you suggest we do about it?"

"Well, the wedding's still weeks away. You should have a better feel for walking on your prosthetics, but until then..."

"You think we should practice." He finishes my sentence. I shrug and nod, still blushing. "Okay. Why not."

With his crutches, he strides over to an old, record player I hadn't noticed, and turns it on. Selecting a black, vinyl disc, he places the needle onto it, and the music begins. Soft, smooth waves of sound come through the speakers. They're sounds from a different era. I look at him and smile.

"Old school. Nice."

"Do you like it?" I nod. "It's something my father gave to me. He told me never to underestimate the power of the classics." His expression then changes to somewhat mischievous, as he makes his way back to me. He leans one crutch, against the counter, then the other, but grabs for my hand and waist rather quickly. "Whoa," he says, as he tries to correct his balance. "I got it now." I giggle as he holds onto me for dear life.

"Don't worry, I'll help you," I say.

"I have no doubt." He smiles playfully and winks.

As we gently sway to the music, I feel his grip tighten now and then. I can tell he'd have a lot more trouble if he wasn't holding on. We're basically stepping side to side until, a moment of bravery sends me backward a bit. Then, a step forward for me. I'd imagine walking, or in this case, dancing backward, is difficult, but he's doing very well.

"You're very light on your feet," I say, grinning. "You've only stepped on me twice."

"Have I?" He takes a step back and looks down. His expression is repentant. Then, I let him off the hook, telling him I'm kidding. "Just for that..." He pushes me away slightly and raises his left hand, unexpectedly twirling me around once. I gasp quietly, but giggle on the return to his arms. "How's that?"

"Not bad," I laugh. "Though I'd prefer you'd play it a little safer for now."

He scoffs. "There's a time and place to play it safe. Having a beautiful woman in your arms isn't that time."

I grin from ear to ear as I feel my cheeks heat. He thinks I'm beautiful?

"You're too kind."

"It's the truth. And, to top it off, you're a great dancer."

"Well, you lead very well. You've done this before."

"Yes. I was never shy about school dances. I'd watch all the other guys holding up the walls, while I was dancing with their girls."

"Impressive."

"Thank you. I do my best."

He pushes off again,] and twirls me. I squeal at this maneuver, knowing he's got his balance this time.

"You're getting really good at this...balancing, I mean. You've hardly wavered."

"It's getting easier." His carefree expression changes to more serious. "I'm so glad the agency chose to send you to take care of me."

"Yeah?"

He nods.

"Yeah. There was something about you. I noticed it from the moment you walked through my door. You were a force to be reckoned with. I knew you'd challenge me; I just didn't realize just how much." He chuckles, as if recalling some memory.

"Well, *you've* definitely been that—a challenge." I giggle. "I wasn't sure I'd even come back the next day, let alone stay as long as I have. God, you were so hard to deal with."

"And, look at us now, dancing and laughing at ourselves," he says.

"Yes, look at us," I say with a grin.

Just then, a wrong step makes him stumble a bit, so he grabs onto me. I gasp and instinctually wrap my arms around him, in an attempt to steady him. He recovers his balance, but something has changed. His eyes seem to look straight into my soul, his breaths are shallow and ragged, and his lips part fractionally as he glances down at mine.

Oh, God. What's happening?

He looks into my eyes again, for permission I think, then slowly the gap between us closes. My eyes close as I feel the warmth of his mouth on mine. It's a soft, warm peck, but when he comes back in, his lips are parted. Tentatively, my tongue touches his and without thinking, I pull it back. In the recesses of my mind, I know it's wrong. So, why does it feel so right? With his hand at the small of my back, he pulls me in tighter, desperately urging me to continue. Our tongues slowly wind around each other's in our own private dance. This kiss is so innocent, so pure, yet it conveys so many emotions that have been building for so long. I feel the vibration from his throaty growl, and it sends my heart into a frantic rhythm. I feel my chest pounding thunderously, but I'm not really sure if it's mine or his. Maybe, it's both. And, in this moment, there are no barriers, no imaginary lines, and no missing limbs. It's just us.

Then, I realize I'm walking backwards. I stop when I feel the crook of the counter against the lower part of my back. He has me boxed in. Feeling almost drunk in the moment, I thrust my hand into his hair, grabbing a fistful in the process, and again, his reaction can be heard and felt.

Finally, after several minutes have passed, he pulls back. Our foreheads rest against each other, and I can feel his sharp, shallow breathes against my lips, as we attempt to reconcile what just happened.

LOGAN

"That was..." I can't even find a word in the English language that would describe that kiss adequately.

"Logan—"

"My God, Elora, you're so—"

"Logan."

I look up to see tears streaking down her face.

"What's wrong?" I asked, concerned. She bows her head, shaking it ever so slightly.

"We shouldn't have—"

"No. Don't say it." I lift her chin and wipe a tear away with my thumb, desperate to make this okay for her. "Please...just don't."

"This was wrong," she whispers, and it almost sounds like a sob.

"*No.* How can you say that?" I push off the counter, effectively releasing her from the corner. "This was not wrong."

"But—"

"No! I felt something—*we* felt something. I know you did. How can that be wrong?" I turn to face the counter next to her when I hear my fist pound onto the top. She startles, so I quickly recover my composure. Reaching for her hand, I try desperately to convince her. "It's going to be fine. This wasn't a mistake. Please don't regret this."

Her head is bowed again, as she takes in a deep breath.

"I work for you. You're technically my boss. How is this right?"

"Who cares if I'm your boss? It doesn't matter!"

"It's unethical," she says, as she peeks up at me.

"Fine then, you're fired. I'll call the company and tell them I don't need you, or anyone else, to come over anymore."

She chuckles slightly at the absurdity, then looks back down at her hands.

"It's not that simple. I signed a contract."

"Stating?"

She goes on to disclose the binding nature of the contract she signed, then she looks up at me. "I can't take the risk."

I push my hands through my hair as I lean with my back to the kitchen counter. There's got to be something we can do about this.

"What if I call the company? I could tell them...I don't know... that this is what I want, and not to hold it against you." I'm desperately grasping at straws now. I take both of her hands in mine, turning her to face me. "Please. You've brought me back to life. Don't make this about anything but us." I'm pleading with her not to leave. I've become one of those poor, desperate saps that no one wants to be around.

"My shift is almost over. I have paperwork to do." She drops my hands, passing me, and heads for her bag near the front door. I watch helplessly as she scribbles something down, gathers her belongings, and reaches for her jacket. She then stands with her head bowed. "I guess I better go," she says, in an eerily quiet voice.

"Will you be back on Monday?"

Please say yes.

"Goodbye, Logan."

Shit! She's dodged the question.

Too stunned to move, I watch in horror as she exits, closing the door softly behind her. I turn my head to follow her figure as it walks past the kitchen windows. I witness her shoulders shudder. Is she crying? I think she's crying. What the hell am I doing?

She's *leaving.*

Walking as fast as I can, in my wobbly state, I chase after her.

"Elora!" I shout as I open the door. I haven't got my crutches, and I'm moving faster than I ever have without them. I almost fall while trying to step over the threshold, but manage to stay on my feet. "Elora, wait!" I get to the edge of the porch, just as she's getting in her car, and look down at the challenge before me. Two innocent looking steps. I haven't tried going down them without holding onto anything or anyone yet, but I need to get to her. Carefully, but as swiftly as I can, I reach down for the first one. I hear her car start, so I look up. "Wait!" As I do, I lose my footing, and I hear the sound of the wind as it comes whooshing past my ears, and I come crashing down, knees first, onto the unforgiving sidewalk. "Agh!" I cry out, as a sharp pain lances through my legs, and I'm forced onto my hands and knees. Her car, which was already backing out of the driveway, halts momentarily, and I pray that she stays. Raising up, I try to stand before she can move again, but my hopes are dashed when I watch her pained expression as she resumes her mission, and she pulls all the way out. My heart drops completely out of my chest, as I watch her taillights get farther and farther from me, until she's completely out of sight.

The world is still. As I lie here in my bed, I can hear nothing but the tick, tick, tick of the wall clock that tells me it's time to get up. I don't want to get up. I've got nothing to get up for. My alarm goes off. Several seconds go by before I smack it. I then resume my focus on the ceiling. Parts of the texture look like familiar shapes. It's sort of like looking for pictures in the clouds. I spot a man's face. It's distorted. He has eyes that are uneven and an odd-shaped head. I've been staring at him for days now. Days and days. Since she left. I can't unsee him now. Every time I look up, there he is. He stares back. I think he's laughing at me. I turn my head away. I can't watch his amused expression anymore.

Michael comes in frequently. He says he's worried about me. I haven't been out of this bed for days. Days and days. Since she left. He's threatened to call our mother, but I don't care. I don't care about anything anymore.

"Well, can you get someone else? He needs help, and if she refuses to come back, then send us someone new."

He listens as the person on the other end of the line talks. I can hear him sigh and mumble under his breath.

She's not coming back.

"Logan, you have to get up and eat. I know it's fast food, but at least it's something. Please. Eat *something*."

I'm not hungry.

"Here," he says, trying to hand me the phone. "It's mom. She wants to know what's going on. Do *you* want to explain it to her?"

I turn my head away and close my eyes. I don't need this right now.

"Dude, she's threatening to come here and see you. Do you really want that? Because I don't. So, please, just talk to her."

I know he's bluffing. He wouldn't say things like that when she could be listening.

Nice try though.

"Can I just talk to her? She should know what she's done to him. He's a wreck. She needs to fix this," he says angrily, then listens again.

"Fine, my number is 216-555-6405. Thank you. I'll be waiting for her call."

I'm alarmed at his words. She's done nothing wrong. He's saying bad things to the people at her work. He's going to get her fired. I feel a fire starting to build, and I sit up.

"Michael!" I shout. He walks in, frustration, then relief, written on his face. He exhales forcefully.

"You're up."

"What the hell do you think you're doing?" I ask, ignoring his observation.

"What are you talking about?"

"Who were you just talking to?" I say, even though I already know.

"Elora's home health agency."

"Are you trying to get her fired?"

He smirks. He actually has the nerve to smirk.

"I'll do whatever it takes. She did this to you. They should know."

I rip the comforter off my legs and pivot to the edge of the bed.

"Are you fucking stupid? Why would you do that to her? She's done nothing wrong. Call them back right now and tell them that!"

"I'm not doing a damn thing. If you want it done, *you* do it." He leans against the doorway and crosses his arms and legs—legs I wish I could take out from under him.

"Fine." I reach for my cell phone, but it's dead. Then, I see *his* phone in his hand. "Give me your phone."

"Fuck off. I'm not your servant."

I'm furious now, so I maneuver myself near my wheelchair. I grab onto it, swing my ass over, and sit. Then, I follow Michael into the kitchen.

"Give it to me," I say, ready for a fight.

"Come and get it, asshole." He's leaning against the counter, dangling the phone just out of my reach. I stretch up and touch it, but he pulls it away before I can grab it. I try again, to no avail.

"What the fuck, Michael? Give me the damn phone!"

"If you were wearing your legs, you could reach it."

"Don't fuck with me. I'm serious. Give it to me, *now!*"

"It's such a shame Elora screwed you up so much. Hey, maybe she'd date me. What do you think? Should I call her?" He wiggles the phone in his hand and smiles.

That's it. I pull my fist back then launch it at him, punching him, as hard as I can, in the gut. Taken by surprise, I'm sure, he doubles over, lowering the phone in the process. I grab his wrist, then take the phone from his hand. He begins laughing.

"So, this is what it takes to get your attention?" He laughs some more. "If I'd known that, I'd have done it days ago."

"Fuck you!" I spit.

As I glance at the phone, wondering what to say to her boss, it rings. The caller ID displays a number I don't recognize.

"Maybe that's her," Michael says, so I throw up my middle finger at him, then wheel myself into another room.

Once in the dining room, I press the *on* button and raise it to my ear.

"Michael, is everything okay? My boss called to tell me you've called several times. Is it Logan? Is he all right?"

The bitter sweet sound of Elora's worried, angelic voice, dances into my ear as a lump forms in my throat. She's breathing harder than usual, and I can't stop my mind from recalling the same sound the last time I saw her...when we kissed.

"Um...hi," I say quietly. She hesitates before responding, but when she does, it's in an equally soft voice.

"Hi."

"How are you?"

"Fine. How are you?"

"I'm okay," I lie. "There's no emergency."

"But, your brother—he's been calling."

"I know. He's an alarmist. Everything's fine."

The truth is, nothing is fine.

"Oh. Okay."

The silence between us is too loud. I need to say things...lots of things.

"How've you been?" I ask, hoping she's feeling the same, shitty way I am.

"Good, I guess."

"And nursing school?"

"Logan, is there something you need from me?"

My heart screams *yes*, but I know that won't get me anywhere.

"I'm…it's just that…" I sigh. Let's just put it all out there. "I wish you'd come back." She sighs heavily. "I know, I know, you don't want to break any rules, but we could just go back to the way it was before the kiss. We could do that, don't you think?"

"Logan…"

"I still need help. You know my track record with scaring people off. I'll go through the whole company, before I find someone to re-place you." I hear her soft giggle.

Good God, I've missed that sound.

"Yeah, your track record really is bad."

"Then, will you come back?"

She sighs again.

"I can't."

"Why not?"

"You know why not and, besides, I've accepted another client."

My mood plummets. I'm running out of ideas.

"Well, what about the wedding? Will you still accompany me?"

"I don't know."

"Please? I won't find anyone else to go, and I'd really like to take you."

I wait, on pins and needles, for her answer.

"I don't know. Let me think about it."

Well, that's not a *no*.

"Take all the time you need."

"Okay. I have to go now. I'll be late for work."

"All right. It was nice talking to you," I say, because it truly was.

"You too," she says, just before our call disconnects.

I sit, stunned for a moment, when Michael enters the room.

"So, what'd she say?"

"Nothing much."

"Is she coming back?" I shake my head, sadly. "Oh," he says, then places his hand on my shoulder. "I'm sorry." I nod, unable to speak at the moment.

"It is what it is," I say, turning my chair in the direction of my bedroom.

"You're not going back in there," he says.

"Just leave me alone."

"I just got you out of bed. If you think I'm letting you wallow in self-pity for one more minute, you're crazy." He then steps in front of me, blocking the way.

"Damn it, just let me go! I don't want to think anymore. All I want to do is sleep."

He places both hands on the arms of my chair and looks me dead in the face.

"I'm not going to let you do this to yourself. If you want that girl, then we'll find a way to make it happen, but I'm not just going to sit idly by and watch you wither away and die. You're my brother. You've had to endure a lot of shit lately, but you're still a good person...in here." He points to my chest. "If Elora's half the woman you say she is, then she already knows that. You just have to remind her."

I look up at him, unsure if it's even possible.

"But, how?"

"Work hard at being the person she's come to know. Work on your therapy. Get stronger. Make her forget all you've lost. Show her you're just like everyone else. No. Show her you're *better* than everyone else. Work on getting rid of the crutches and cane. If you do that, she can't help but notice. And then..." He raises his eyebrows, silently suggesting I finish that sentence.

I've never thought of my brother as being super smart, but he's right. Elora wouldn't want to see me regress. She'd want to see me overcome my obstacles. My best chance at winning her over is to present her with the best version of myself. *Yes.* This could work.

"I'll do it…but, I'm going to need your help."

He grins broadly.

"Anything you need, you know that." He pats me on the back. "I'm glad to have you back. I was beginning to think you were gone for good."

"You sure tried hard enough." I chuckle.

"Yeah, I wish I'd used the girl card sooner. It worked quite well."

"So, you did it on purpose?"

"Kind of. I sort of stumbled onto it, but your reaction was perfect. I wish I could've anticipated the punch to the gut though." He rubs his stomach. "That fuckin' hurt, man."

I give his stomach a playful slap.

"You deserved it, asshole."

He laughs loudly.

"Just wait, until you get back on your feet again…literally. Then, we'll see a fair fight."

"Well, let's start now. Go get my legs."

He nods and heads in the direction of my room.

ELORA

I hang up, then sag into the couch. That was almost painful.

"Is everything okay?" Daniel asks while holding onto his can of beer.

"Yeah. I mean, I guess so."

"What did his brother want?"

I throw my phone onto the coffee table, then stand, and walk into the kitchen.

"I'm not sure."

"Isn't that who you were talking to?"

"Logan answered the phone," I say, opening a bottle of water.

Daniel frowns.

"How'd that go?"

"I don't know." He looks at me expectantly. "What? I really don't know. He asked me to come back to work for him. I told him I couldn't, end of story."

"Is it?"

"Is it what?"

"The end of the story?"

"Daniel stop."

"What? Elora, you've been moping around here for days. Your eyes are puffy, which tells me you've been crying, and you've been baking like crazy. I don't know what you're doing, but I think your heart has declared war on your head."

Well, if that's not the truth…

"Yeah well, my head won, okay?"

"You've gotten yourself into quite a predicament here, and you need to think long and hard about what it is you want. It sounds to me like you can either have your job or a love life, not both. Are you willing to risk one to have the other?"

I sigh. I'm just not sure.

"I don't know," I say, secretly wishing I could have both.

He stands in front of me with his arms crossed at his chest.

"I don't like this. I don't like what this is doing to you. He shouldn't be putting this much pressure on you—"

"He's not!" I shout my interruption. "I've taken myself out of the picture! It's done!" My small tantrum has made me feel a bit better, and I sigh again, feeling the need to apologize. "I'm sorry. I know you're just looking out for me, but I can handle this. Trust me."

"I hope you're right."

He glances at me with a disapproving expression, before he exits the room, and leaves me alone with my thoughts.

Maybe, he's right, but it's not like I'm in my dream job. I can find another one. Wait. What am I thinking? Falling in love with someone I'm taking care of could really reflect badly on me as a future nurse. What if I go through all this schooling just to be denied a job based on what happened the other day? Could that happen? Then, my whole career would be over before it started. And, what if I quit and the company sees my car in his driveway, mistaking my intentions for being over his house? They could take me to court, just like that other girl. No. I think it's best if I just forget about Logan Turner. I've done all I can for him. He's on the road to recovery now. He doesn't need me anymore.

But, even as I think it, tears threaten.

10

ELORA

nother week has passed, since I talked with Logan on the phone, and now, I find myself driving toward his neighborhood. It's late evening, and I've been circling the area for about an hour now, trying to talk myself out of driving all the way to his house. What am I doing? Why am I pulling down his street? What on earth am I planning to say to him? For what reason am I dropping in, unannounced? I stop a few houses away from his, and park my car in the street. The dusky camouflage hides my identity should I decide to abort the mission. Turning off the engine, I sit and contemplate my words. *Hi, Logan. How are you? Do you miss me as much as I miss you?* No, that's no good. *What am I doing here, you ask? I'm...hoping you still want me and...* Ugh! This is so frustrating. I have no good reason for being here. I came here in the hopes that on the way, I would come up with a reason for stopping by and the words to say what I want to convey. But, my brain has failed me, as it's my heart who is leading me.

As my hand touches the door handle, I close my eyes and say a silent prayer for clarity. I don't know what will come from my lips, but I hope whatever it is, will be well received. I tug the handle and the overhead light pops on. Just then, a cute little VW Beetle comes clipping in front of me and pulls into Logan's driveway. I quickly shut the door. Then, I watch in horror as a young, slender female exits the car and flounces up to the house.

Who the hell is she?

I hear the doorbell ring, so she must not be someone who feels comfortable enough to just walk right in.

Please don't answer the door.

My hopes are dashed as the porch floor is illuminated by the opening of the front door. Maybe, it's someone to see Michael.

"Oh, my God, Logan! You're standing!" I hear the woman squeal from a distance, then she throws her arms around his neck.

My heart sinks.

He says something to her, but I'm too far away to hear him. Then, he opens the door farther. She walks in, and he closes the door behind them. Tears trickle down my cheeks, so I dash them away violently. How stupid could I have been? This was a ridiculous plan. I knew I wasn't thinking straight. I put the car into drive and pull away rather abruptly, leaving my hopes and dreams behind me.

LOGAN

"**O**h, my God, Logan! You're standing!" Bethany says, as she hugs me around the neck, knocking me off balance slightly.

"Take it easy. I'm not that steady yet. What do you want?"

"Is that any way to treat your ex? We need to talk. Can I come in?"

I sigh, irritated at her tenacity, but hold the door open wider, to allow her entry. As I'm about to close the door, I see an unfamiliar vehicle race away from in front of the neighbor's house. For a split second, I think the driver looks like Elora. I squint to see the woman's silhouette from behind but can't really see too much. Give it up, Logan. She's probably nowhere near here. I close the door and turn to see Bethany making herself comfortable on the couch.

"So, you look good. It's nice to see you vertical again," she says with a smile.

"Cut the crap, Beth, what do you want?"

"What makes you think I want something? Maybe, I just wanted to see how you're doing."

"Because you always want something. It's just not always immediately apparent."

"Logan Turner, be nice!" she scolds, but I'm just not in the mood for her bullshit tonight.

"Believe me, that *was* being nice." I take a sip of the beer I've been nursing for the better part of an hour and lean against the half wall by the foyer. "Why are you here?"

She scoffs at me, as if I care.

"All right, here it is. As you know, Ryan is getting married in a couple weeks, and I thought it'd be nice if you were my date for the evening." My jaw drops open, and I'm sure my expression resembles that of someone who just walked into a Limburger cheese factory. "I know what you're thinking—"

"I'm pretty sure you don't."

"You're thinking, *why would I want to go with my ex-girlfriend?* Well, let me explain."

"This ought to be good," I mutter, then take another long draw from the bottle in my hand. On further inspection, I notice I've emptied it, so I head to the fridge for another one.

"Logan, are you listening to me?"

"I'm all ears."

"Okay, here's the thing," she says as she stands and walks over to me in the kitchen. She comes to stand right in front of me and picks at an imaginary piece of lint on my chest. "I made a mistake. I shouldn't have left you when you were away with your little, army friends."

I grab her wrist and hold it away from my chest, anger coursing through me.

"*Little army friends?*" I say, menacingly soft. "What exactly do you think me and my *little, army friends* were doing over there? Playing G.I. Joe?"

"Now, Logan, you know that's not what I meant. I just meant that...well, you know. I've missed you, and I realize now, that I made a mistake." She takes the last step between us, looks up into my eyes, and kisses me.

She fucking kisses me.

As soon as her lips touch mine, I grab her shoulders and hold her away from me, halting anymore progress she might've made.

"Are you crazy?" I ask, really wondering. "Why are you doing this?"

"I just thought that…"

"You thought what?" I say, letting go of her and walking to the other side of the kitchen. "You thought that I'd be so desperate for someone—anyone who'll have me that I'd let you come crawling back into my life?"

I'm livid.

"Not exactly, but…" She shrugs as if in agreement with my hunch.

My jaw hits the floor this time. I can't believe the audacity of this woman.

"Well, you're wrong. I don't need you or anything you have to offer. I'd pick being alone for the rest of my life over being with someone who runs when the going gets tough."

"I know, and I'm so sorry. Like I said, I made some mistakes and—"

"And, one of them was coming here tonight," I say as coldly as I can.

We stare at each other. Me: furious and breathing heavily, her: repentant and sad, although I'm not sure how much of her expression is real. She bows her head, and her sharp intake of breath stutters a bit. There was a time when seeing her cry made me want to comfort her. I'll admit to myself that that feeling hasn't entirely gone away, but knowing how she is, and what she's done, brings that feeling to heel. Still, I need to calm down. I don't love her anymore, but I don't want her to get into a wreck from crying on the way home.

My deep sigh causes her to look up at me.

"Look, I didn't mean to come across as that much of an asshole. I just…I just can't go back to where we used to be."

"But, why not? We were good together." She takes a step forward, but I hold up my hand, stopping her in her tracks. "The wedding is weeks away. Won't you at least think about it?

"I won't change my mind," I say adamantly.

"Are you seeing someone else? Is that what this is about?"

My eyes reach for the ceiling.

"This has nothing to do with anyone but you and me. I think it's time for you to go." I walk toward the door, expecting her to follow, and she does. Opening the door for her, I stand awaiting her departure. She takes a few tentative steps toward the threshold before turning around to face me. She reaches up and grazes my cheek with her fingertips. I stiffen but don't move away. She then rises onto her tip toes and kisses my cheek. Again, I'm still.

"Call me if you change your mind. You know the number." And, with that, she's gone. I close the door and lean against it, letting out a long, steadying breath.

That woman still gets to me.

"Cindy called last night," Michael says with a mischievous gleam in his eye. "She said she found the perfect dress to wear to Ryan's wedding and that I'm going to want to see it up close and personal." His eyebrows lift twice.

"That's great, Michael. Are you two going to get busy right in the middle of the dance floor during the cake cutting ceremony?" I roll my eyes, and he laughs.

"No, I'm classier than that. We'll wait until the place clears out a bit and find a quiet corner." I sneer in disgust at his lack of respect for the newlyweds and his date. "What? She puts the *sin* in Cindy." Again, he grins and nods knowingly.

"You do realize her name starts with a C, not an S, right?" He waves me off, and I sigh at his immaturity. "Do whatever you want. I'll find my own ride home."

"Wait, isn't Elora driving you?"

"I'm not sure if she's going or not," I say, my heart instantly contracting.

"Have you talked to her about it?"

"Just that one day that you were trying to get her in trouble at her job." I shoot him a dirty look, and he smirks.

Asshole.

"Well, you have her number now. Why don't you call her?"

"I can't. It'll be…weird, and make me seem desperate."

"You are weird and desperate," he says, then laughs. I grab an apple and chuck at his head, but he catches it, then takes a bite.

"Thanks, man," he says with his mouthful. "So, if you're not going to call her, how will you know if she's coming?"

"I won't."

"Well, that's a great plan," he says sarcastically.

"Shut up."

"No, seriously. Why *would* you want advanced notice of having a date? I mean, that might lead to a healthy anticipation of this event and cause you to lighten, the fuck, up…We wouldn't want that, now would we?"

I sneer at him again. I know what he's doing. He's trying to goad me into calling her. Well, I'm not playing his game today.

"Fuck off," I say and push away from the counter, headed in the direction of my room.

"There you go. Do the one thing you're really good at: running away when faced with a challenge."

I stop, mid stride, and turn around. I've had enough. Walking aggressively toward him, I don't stop, until I'm right in his face. Nose to nose. I can almost feel his breath.

"Don't you *ever* say that to me again. If you've ever had to go through what I've had to go through, you'd never say that to me. I've been through—"

"Hell," he interrupts. "You've been through hell, Logan. I know. You've told me often enough. I can practically recite your monologue by heart." His tone is castigating and condescending, and I want to beat the look of sarcasm off his smug little face. He rolls his eyes. "I get it. Poor Logan. He's had it so rough, and it just keeps getting worse, doesn't it?"

My jaw tightens, and my fists constrict, as I think of every reason I can not to beat the shit out of him.

"*Stop,*" I say through gritted teeth. "Just shut the fuck up, right, now."

"What're you going to do about it? Huh?" he continues. "Clearly you're too weak and wounded to fight for anything anymore. You used to be tough, you know? You used to go after whatever you wanted. What happened to that guy? Did the surgeons hack him off when they cut off your legs?"

That's it! I ball up my fist as tightly as I can and pull back, landing a right hook onto Michael's jaw. I stumble forward a bit but recover my balance, anticipating his retaliation. I don't have to wait long as Michael swings at me, punching me in the left eye. I fall backward against the counter but manage to right myself fairly quickly. I come at him again with a punch to the gut, which makes him double over, then a left to the side of his face. He then rushes me, while wrapping his arms around my waist, and jams his shoulder into my ribs, effectively slamming my back into the refrigerator. I hear the rattle of glass jars behind me, and the air exits my lungs in a rush. I keep swinging at him, but he won't let go. Then, finally, he twists and shoves me hard. I lose my balance and land with a thud onto the kitchen floor.

Breathless and panting, and with his hands on his knees, he stands over me.

"Had enough?" he asks.

I say nothing.

He then does the unexpected. He reaches out and extends his hand, as an offer of help to get me off the floor. I hesitate. I'm still pissed and panting, but satisfied that I can still hold my own in a fight.

"Hey," he huffs out, then smiles and gestures again for me to take it. I roll my eyes at myself as I accept his offer, allowing him to pull me to my feet. We eye each other briefly before he gives me a quick, brotherly hug. I reciprocate.

"Damn," he says, while holding his jaw. "You've still got it."

I smirk, looking at the damage to his face.

"I can see that," I say, pointing out the bruise already starting to form on the right side of his face.

"Don't think you came away unscathed, little brother. Your face is bleeding."

I reach up and touch my eyebrow, feeling something wet. I pull my hand away to inspect the blood on my fingers.

"Thanks for that, asshole. I'll look great at the wedding with a shiner."

"We'll be a set of bookends, won't we."

I chuckle.

"Yeah our dates probably won't find it amusing though."

He nods, and I sigh softly, resigned to the fact that I'm about to admit he's done it again. He's gotten me to agree to do something I was dead set against, and for my own good, no less. I grab the phone and turn to go into my room. I can almost hear his smug, triumphant smile.

The phone rings once, twice, three times. By the fourth ring, I'm about to give up, when suddenly, she answers.

"Hello," she says as more of a statement, because caller ID doesn't lie. She knew it would be me on the other end of the phone.

"Hi," I reply quietly. "How are you?"

"I'm okay."

"How's your new client?"

"Fine," she says, then swallows. "How'd you get my number?"

"You called me first, remember?"

"Oh. Yeah, I guess I did."

The silence that lurks hurts my heart. I need to fill the space.

"So, I'm using a cane now."

"That's...good. That's really good, Logan."

I smile at the sound of my name on her lips.

"Thanks. I've been working hard, you know? Probably too hard. You'd probably yell at me to know how hard, but I've made a lot of progress."

She snorts.

"I'm wagging my finger at you right now."

I grin broadly and chuckle softly. God, I miss our daily banter.

"So, the reason I'm calling is to find out...well, the wedding is a week away now, and I was wondering if you were planning on going." I squeeze my eyes shut, hoping to block out the word no.

"Logan..." she starts, then sighs into the phone. "I'm not sure it's a good idea. I mean, I'd love to but..."

"I know. I understand. I had to ask again, and let you know the offer still stands. I won't hold it against you, should you decide not to come."

I'm disappointed, I'll admit, but I don't want to push her into doing something that could potentially make her uncomfortable. That's the last thing I want. I want her to come because *she* wants to be there.

"Can I think about it a bit longer?"

"Don't worry about it. It's fine. Michael's going too. I'll just hitch a ride with him. Although, I might get a crash course in driving afterward, just to save us all from a DUI."

She giggles. I sigh silently at the sound.

"So, it'll just be you and Michael then?" she asks, and for some reason, this question strikes me as odd.

"Yes. Well, the two of us and his date, Cindy."

"Oh," she simply says, but I can't help but wonder if there's something else.

"Why do you ask?" I say bravely.

"No reason. I just thought that maybe...you found a backup date."

What? Why would she think that?

"If I had, I wouldn't be asking you to come, would I?"

"I guess not," she says, then laughs at herself. "I don't know what I was thinking." She laughs again, but it sounds forced. Another awkward silence paralyzes the conversation. Neither of us says a thing for several seconds. "Well, I guess I'd better go."

"Okay. Um, I guess if you decide to come, I'll see you then. If not, well…"

"Yeah," she says with an eerie finality. "Goodbye, Logan."

"Bye, Elora."

I push the end button and hold the phone to my chest. Closing my eyes, my mind goes blank. I don't want to hope. I don't want to pray. I don't want to think or talk about it anymore. What's done is done, and I've said all I can. It's up to her to decide what to do now, and I'm helpless once again.

11

LOGAN

With a drink in my hand, I stand against the wall of the reception hall. I'm keeping a silent watch over the entryway that's across from me, as if I'm some sort of guard. Is she coming, or did she decide not to? My heart sinks each time someone enters who's *not* her. Maybe, she's not coming after all. I take another sip of my drink and wait.

"Any sign of her?" Michael asks on his approach.

"Not yet," I say.

He places his hand on my shoulder.

"Stay positive. Give her time. She might show up."

"I know. I'm trying."

"Hi, Logan. It's nice to see you again," Cindy says as she saunters over to hang on Michael's arm. He wasn't kidding about her dress. Holy shit. It doesn't leave much to the imagination.

"Hi, Cindy. You look lovely," I say with a small smile.

"Thank you. Is your date here yet?"

I want to roll my eyes. The more they ask, the more frustrated I become. Clearly, she's not, otherwise she'd be standing next to me.

"No. But, I'm sure she'll be along soon." I smile politely again.

They look at each other, and the expression that passes between them is sympathy. God, I wish they'd just leave me alone.

"Let's go find our seats," he says to her. "We'll see you at the table, Logan."

I nod and take another sip.

The frequency of the guests coming into the hall has dwindled greatly now, and my hope for her arrival has all but vanished. The dinner music begins, and the DJ asks everyone to find their seats, as the bride and groom have just arrived.

Shit. She's not coming.

"I'll ask you all to rise, so I can introduce to you, the bridal party!" the announcer says, and the crowd rises and cheers. "First, we have junior bridesmaid, Lacey Masen, and her date, who happens to be one of the groomsmen, Joshua Underwood!" The crowd erupts again with applause and a few *awws* at their cuteness. They enter holding hands and take their place in the reception line. Jeez, even the eight year olds have a date. I clap politely. "Next, we have bridesmaid, Sarah Underwood, with Groomsman, John Everett."

The announcer continues introducing the bridal party, but I tune him out. I'm half paying attention, when Ryan and his new wife, Sydney, enter to wild applause and whistles. Again, I clap politely, but all I really want to do is go home. They walk through the doorway to take their place in the lineup, when someone behind them, in a blue dress, catches my eye. I crane my neck to get a better look, when my grateful eyes land on the wide eyed expression of Elora Foster.

My heart stops.

"Oh, my God. She's here," I whisper to myself, but apparently it's loud enough to catch Michael's attention.

"Where?"

"In the doorway," I say, not wanting to take my eyes off her, for fear she's not really there.

"She looks hot," he says.

"No, she's breathtaking."

Everyone at our table sits down, but I remain standing. I'm mesmerized by her beauty and at the fact that she's here.

She's really here.

She's looking around, no doubt trying to find a familiar face, when at last our eyes meet. A shy smile graces her face, and I can't contain my face splitting grin.

"Excuse me," I say to the group, then start walking toward her.

ELORA

I finally spot Logan, and my nerves are electrified. He's stunningly dashing in his black, well-tailored suit which hugs his muscular physique. His hair is perfectly styled and has just enough wave to make me want to run my fingers through it. He looks wonderful. His chest falls, and his lips part, as if a breath he'd been holding has finally been released, and I watch as a slow, crooked grin creeps into his face. He makes his way over to me.

"Elora, you look...beautiful," he says, as his eyes sweep across my body. He doesn't even try to disguise his awe.

I blush furiously at the compliment and cover my heated cheeks with my hands. He then takes one of them and plants a soft kiss on the back. I almost fall off my high heeled pumps at the contact.

"Thank you. You clean up well yourself." He smiles broadly.

"Thanks. Our table is...well, you already know." He chuckles nervously. "Come on. Let's get a drink and settle into our seats."

Still holding my hand, we begin walking toward the bar, when I suddenly stop.

"Logan, you're walking unassisted," I say in amazement. He looks down at his legs.

"Yes. I was hoping to surprise you."

"That you did," I whisper, hoping my pride is obvious. "It's wonderful. I'm so proud of you." I shake my head and smile, knowing I can claim my part in his recovery, but I'm unwilling to take any credit for it.

"So, what happened to your eye?" I ask, assuming he fell at some point while trying not to use his crutches or cane.

"Oh, this? Let's just say that my brother and I don't always see eye to eye." He smirks ironically.

Hmm. I wonder what they fought about.

We get our drinks and head back to the table. I place my white wine on the table, then he pulls out my chair, and I sit.

"Elora, it's so good to see you again," Michael says as he holds out his hand for me to shake. "Your guy was a nervous wreck before you showed up." Logan shoots his brother a *back off* look and he wisely backs down.

"Was he? I wouldn't know it to look at him. But then, he's always so calm and collected." Logan sputters into his drink from the thick layer of bullshit I just laid out there. I smile at him and wink. I also notice a rather large bruise on the side of his brother's face and giggle inwardly. Secretly, I'm proud that Logan had a bit of success in their fight, and I feel the need to let him know I noticed. "Nice bruise," I whisper, and Michael's mouth twists with humor.

"Thanks," he says and narrows his eyes at Logan, who then beams back at him.

"I'm Cindy, by the way, Michael's date."

I shake her hand, and my eyes widen as I instantly notice her dress. There's not much to it.

"It's nice to meet you, Cindy."

"Did you have any trouble finding the place?" Logan asks.

"Not really. I got a little lost when I had to follow a detour, but I'm here now."

"I'm glad." He smiles at me, and looks as though he wants to say more, but he doesn't.

The wait staff comes around and places salads in front of us, then soon after, the main course. We all make small talk as we dig in.

"You know, this is good," Michael says, "but, I like the way you cook it better."

I'm a bit shocked by his compliment and blush just a bit.

"Well, thank you. I'll make it again for you sometime," I say.

"You can come over and cook for us anytime you want."

I smile and nod then look at Logan, and his eyes are hopeful. It's then I realize I've just promised to see him again, and I'm not sure if that's a good thing or not. I look down, determined to be more careful of what I say from now on. These waters are difficult to navigate, and I certainly don't want to get his hopes up.

Around 7:00, the DJ's music changes tempo, and the modern rhythms of today's top forty comes blasting through the speakers. The bride and groom are the first to step onto the dance floor, followed by the maid of honor and best man. The party is in full swing when Logan leans in.

"Do you want to dance?" he asks.

"Are you serious?"

"Yes, why?" He laughs.

"I don't know. I guess I thought I'd have to pry you out of your seat to dance with me."

He scoffs.

"Elora, you made a real effort to be here for me today. The least I can do is dance with you. Besides, isn't that why we practiced?" His smile is genuine, but my mind can't help but wander to our kiss that day and what it meant for us afterward. I sigh and smile, trying to shake the memory of me leaving his house for the last time out of my head.

"Yes. Let's dance," I say.

He stands, then offers me his hand. I take it and rise from the chair. But, before walking me to the dance floor, he searches my face.

"Thank you for being here," he says softly. "It means more to me than you know."

Oh, Logan. I wish I could wave a magic wand and make all the complications go away.

But I just smile and nod, and we head toward the pounding beat.

"We're going to slow this down a bit now, so all you couples, get ready to sway," the DJ says, just as we reach the floor.

"Slow dance," I say, then laugh nervously.

"Don't worry. I had a great teacher."

I feel his hand at the small of my back while his left hand holds my right. The shock waves that pulsate through my body keep me on edge, no matter how much I tell myself it's just a dance.

"You know, if you step on my foot, I may not feel it, but my whole leg could come off, and then you'll have to hold me up while trying to pick it up," he says. I'm in shock.

"What?"

"Just kidding. You had such a serious look on your face that I thought you could use a little humor."

I giggle.

"You're something else, you know that?"

"That's what they tell me," he says with a cocky smile. I just roll my eyes.

"Well, if I step on your foot, it's your own fault. Your foot shouldn't be on my side of this dance space."

"Really?"

"Really."

His mouth twists, and I smile, awaiting his comeback.

"So, what's been going on in the life of the best dance teacher, slash, caregiver there ever was?"

"I don't really want to talk about that stuff right now. Can we just enjoy the time we have together on this night and worry about everything else some other time?"

"Absolutely," he says. Then, suddenly, he twirls me out and back in. I squeal in surprise. "Now, watch this." He pulls me in tight against him, and we spin quickly in a circle. I can only see his face, as the background blurs from the speed of our spin. When we slow, we're both grinning from ear to ear.

"You've really gotten good at balancing."

"I told you, I've been working hard. I'm hardly ever in my chair anymore."

"That's great, Logan. That's really great. I can't believe how far you've come."

"I know. When I met you, I was this grumpy person who could barely function."

"And now, look at you," I say. "It's been quite a transformation. I wonder what you'll accomplish next."

"The sky is the limit," he says.

The music changes again, to a faster beat, so we decide to mingle a bit.

"I'm going to visit the ladies room."

"Okay. Come find me when you're done."

I nod and begin my trek.

When I arrive at the bathroom, several of the bridesmaids are hovering around one stall. It's then that I realize they're assisting the bride with bustling her train.

"You missed a button, Georgia. Actually, you've missed several," Sydney says.

"Well, if you'd quit moving around so much, I could see them."

"Here, let me help," says a woman who I remember being introduced as Sarah. She must be the groom's sister.

They finally get her all put together, and she emerges from the stall.

"Oh, hi. Elora, right?"

"Yes," I say, confused as to why she would know me.

"Logan mentioned that you might be coming. He speaks very highly of you."

"Oh."

"He's such a great guy. Too bad about his accident, eh?"

I wonder how much she knows about it.

"Yeah, he really is. It really threw him for a loop."

"I feel awful for him, but he seems to be recovering nicely. I hear that's, in part, because of you."

I shrug.

"He gives me more credit than I deserve."

"That's not what I was told. Ryan said you saved his life just as much as he did."

Huh?

"What do you mean?"

"I mean that Ryan saved Logan's life initially, but you saved it somehow as well. Maybe, by helping him recover?"

Ryan saved his life?

"I guess so. If you want to look at it that way."

I want to ask her for more details, but I feel like I might be prying. After all, if Logan wanted me to know, he'd have told me about it already.

"Well, it was nice to finally meet you. The two of you should come over sometime."

"Sure," I say automatically, and she exits the bathroom.

I lean against the sink, trying to imagine how Ryan saved him. Was he a doctor in Logan's platoon? I've got to get to the bottom of this somehow.

As I walk out, someone is grabbing my arm. It's Michael, and we're headed toward the dance floor.

"What are you doing?" I ask.

"Shh. I want to dance with you, but we'll have to be quick before Logan interrupts us."

We arrive at our destination and assume the position. Hm. This might be a great opportunity to pump his brother for information.

His hold is much looser than Logan's, but I'm glad for that.

"I wanted to ask you something," he says.

"Okay."

"What are your feelings toward my brother?"

"Um—"

"I don't mean to come right out and ask like this, but I need to know if there's a chance for the two of you. If there isn't, then I need to stop, um, encouraging him." He points to his injured face, and now I understand what their fight may have been about.

"Well, that's sort of a personal question, Michael. I'm not sure how to answer that."

"I know, and I'm sorry. Just tell me, is there a chance at all?"

I contemplate my answer.

"How about you answer a question for me, then I'll answer yours?"

"Okay. Shoot."

"Sydney said that Ryan saved Logan's life initially. How so?"

"That's all you got?" He scoffs. "That's easy. When Logan had his accident, Ryan happened to be right behind him. He saw the whole thing. Ryan, being a vet, knew what to do. He wrapped make-shift tourniquets just above Logan's knees and called the ambulance. If it weren't for Ryan's quick thinking, Logan wouldn't be alive today."

"Did they know each other before that day?"

"They'd met a few times before, but Ryan was *my* friend from college, so no, they really didn't."

"Who's they, and what didn't they do?" Logan asks, as he reaches us. "And why are you dancing with my date?"

My heart speeds up. Did he hear us?

"We were just talking about—"

"Nothing important," I interrupt. "Are you cutting in?"

He smiles smugly at Michael.

"Yes. I am."

Michael hands me over, but before he leaves us, he directs a statement at me.

"You owe me another dance." Then, he winks.

Ah, yes. I never did get the chance to answer *his* question.

"What was that about?"

I shake my head.

"Nothing to worry about," I say. "Let's dance."

The cake has been cut, the bouquet and garter have been thrown, and all the typical wedding reception traditions are over. Now, as the guests begin to leave, I realize my wonderful night with Logan is almost done. Although I'm glad I came, I'm sad it has to end.

"Are you sure you want to give me a ride home?" he asks.

"Of course. Why wouldn't I?"

He shrugs.

"Thank you," he says appreciatively. "I'm going to find whatever corner Michael and Cindy are making out in, and let them know we're going."

"Okay," I giggle. He touches my arm just before walking away. I sigh and smile wistfully.

He's on his way to the opposite side of the hall when a young woman walks by. She smiles at me, so I smile back.

"So, you're Logan's new girlfriend?" the woman asks.

"Um, no," I snort. "I'm just a friend."

"Mm," she says, looking me up and down. "Does *he* know you're just friends?"

I can't hide my puzzled expression.

"I'm sorry, who are you?"

"My name's Bethany. I didn't catch yours."

"I didn't throw it." I smile sarcastically. There's something I don't like about this woman, though, I'm not sure what it is. "I'm Elora."

"Elora." She repeats my name, but the tone she uses puts my body on high alert.

"Can I help you?" I say, thrusting my brows toward the bridge of my nose.

"I'm so glad you asked. Can I ask you a question?" I nod, subtly. "What are your intentions with Logan?"

What?

This seems to be a popular question today.

"That's really none of your business," I say, peeking over her shoulder to get a glimpse of Logan.

"I know it's not, but I'd like to know the answer. Are you interested in being *more* than just friends?"

"Well, I work for him so…"

"You work for him? Doing what?"

"I am, I mean, I *was* his home health aide."

"Ah, I see. And now you're not?"

I shake my head.

"No, not for a couple weeks. Why?"

"Did he fire you?"

"What? No. I left him. I mean, he didn't need me anymore, so I stopped taking care of him. Why are you asking me all this?"

I'm really beginning to get irritated.

"I'm just curious. I'm a friend of his too. He never mentioned you, and I'm wondering why."

I shrug.

"I don't know, but I'm sure if you were any kind of *close* friend, you'd have heard about me."

Ha!

"Well, the truth is, Logan and I haven't been close for a while now. I knew him in his military days. I'm his ex-girlfriend."

Oh, shit. His ex. This is making sense now. But what the hell does she want?

"He told me all about you—or at least the part about how you left him after his accident."

She laughs.

"You've *almost* got it right. I didn't leave him *after* his accident; I left him *before* it, while he was still in the military. I wrote him a 'Dear John' letter, of sorts. I got a lot of flak for that bad judgement call, but even I'd have the decency *not* to break up with a man after an amputation. Imagine what people would think."

Huh?

"Is there a point to this conversation?"

She sighs, and has the audacity to look sincere.

"I needed to ask if you are interested in Logan because I want him back." I close my eyes and inhale, hoping I didn't just hear that. "If there's a chance he'll have me, I want to know who my competition might be. The two of you looked pretty cozy out there on the dance floor. Are you sure there's nothing between you?"

My mouth goes dry. There's nothing going on between us, but that doesn't mean I don't want it to. The truth is, I was hoping we could find a way to be together. But, now...

"No. Nothing," I say, regretfully.

She smiles broadly, and I suddenly feel sick.

"Good. You won't mind if I drive him home then."

I swallow reflexively.

"Well, that would be up to him. I already promised him a ride."

"How sweet of you, as his *employee*, to offer that. Your job is all encompassing, isn't it?"

"You could say that."

This lady's really starting to piss me off.

"Can I ask a favor?"

I laugh loudly, and I see Logan's head turn. He's headed this way, and he does not look happy.

"Sure," I say.

"I'll need you to back off. If I'm going to get him back, I don't need him making goo-goo eyes at you," she says with a sneer.

I curl my upper lip, suddenly wishing I wasn't wearing high heels.

"What's going on here?" Logan asks me as he observes us. "Beth, what are you doing?"

"Hi, Logan. I've met your ex-employee here. She's lovely."

"Cut the crap. What do you want?"

She looks affronted.

"I was just asking how you're doing. That's all. No need to get so angry."

"It didn't look that way to me." He then turns his attention back to me. "Are you all right?" I nod. "I think we're done here," he says to Bethany as he glares at her. "We're going home." He places his hand at the small of my back to steer me toward the door.

I'm a little shell shocked at what just happened. She's got a lot of nerve, thinking she can just march back into his life after leaving him while he was away. And, where has she been since his accident? Has she come back now only because he has legs again? His reaction to her was quite cold, but a wayward thought enters my mind. I wonder if he loved her…or if he still does. She's very beautiful, and he admitted to me how much she hurt him. I decide to test the waters.

"Um, Bethany offered to drive you home."

He scoffs.

"Are you trying to get out of it?" He smirks.

"No, no. I just wanted to relay the message in case you'd rather…"

He stops me in the doorway and turns me to face him. His hands are on my shoulders, and his intense eyes burn into mine.

"I don't want to look back. I hope to look forward to a day when everything will change." His eyes search my face, then, out of nowhere, he kisses me.

He kisses me.

I feel his fingers push through my hair, and he's holding my head, as his thumbs caress my cheeks. I'm holding onto his arms because this has completely taken me by surprise.

Oh, my God, here we are again.

After a moment, which is too short for my liking, our mouths separate, and he looks over at Bethany. She looks as if she's eaten something that's left a bad taste in her mouth. I look at him, looking at her, and he smirks.

What?

"There. That should send her a message," he says, and looks back at me. "Come on. Drive me home."

12

ELORA

D riving home, a million thoughts race through my mind. He kissed me. It was our second kiss—not as good as the first time, but way up there on my list of second kisses. Then, there was the conversation I had with his ex. She seems like she might be trouble. And, what about the way Logan looked at her after our kiss ended? What was that about? Was that kiss for *her* benefit? Could he have been trying to make her jealous? Does he still have feelings for her? I'm more confused than ever, and I'm not sure what to think.

"I'm sorry about that," he says.

I look over at him briefly.

"Sorry for what?"

"Kissing you. Well, that's a lie. I'm not sorry I kissed you. I'm just sorry it was that abrupt. I'd hoped that the next time we kissed it would be a bit more planned."

"Oh."

"Oh?" I look over and shrug. "You were okay with it, weren't you?" he asks, a concerned tone to his voice.

"I think we should talk about this another time."

"Um, I'm sorry. I thought…" He's at an obvious loss for words. "Sure. Another time." He looks out his window, and we drive the rest of the way to his house in silence.

I pull into his driveway, put the car in park, and we sit, listening only to the sounds of the night. The breeze, which has picked up considerably, rushes through the newly budded trees, and the occasional noise from an adjacent neighbor breaks some of the awkward quietness. I sigh and pick at a pleat on my dress.

"I should probably get going," I say softly, though I can't look at him.

"I don't want you to go," he says, equally as soft.

I look at him with regret in my eyes. I know what he wants, but I'm not sure I'm ready to give it to him.

"Logan—"

"Elora, just come in for a few minutes. We can talk. I'll make some coffee. We can just sit and spend a little more time together." He turns in his seat. "I'm not ready for this night to end just yet." His eyes are sincere as they bore into me. It's as if he's seeing right into my soul.

I break the visual contact and look back down.

"I don't know."

"I'm not asking you to commit to anything but coffee," he says. "Please?"

When I look back at him, he's got the most heartfelt expression. It's as if the fate of the whole world is depending on my answer. It's only coffee, right? It's not like I can't walk out if I don't like where things are going.

"Okay, fine. Coffee."

His face-splitting grin warms my heart, and we exit the vehicle.

LOGAN

O nce inside, I begin to set up the coffee pot, and I notice her looking around, nonchalantly. She's probably wondering if my brother is here.

"I'm fairly certain Michael and Cindy went back to her place. We're alone," I say.

"They looked very...*involved*, at the reception." She raises her eyebrows, no doubt bewildered at the sight of the two drunken lovebirds. I laugh.

"Yeah. He's been looking forward to spending time with Cindy for a while now." I shake my head at my brother's lack of couth. "As much as I disapprove of his method, this night with her will do him some good." I take out two coffee mugs and place them on the counter. "Would you like anything to eat?"

"No, thank you. I've eaten way too much today already." Her hand rests on her stomach, as if she could gain an ounce.

"Okay. Have a seat on the couch. I'll join you in a minute."

She walks over and sits at the far end, while I pour the coffee. After bringing both cups over, I sit at the other end, fold one leg under the other to face her, and rest one arm on the back of the couch.

"The reception was nice. Sydney looked beautiful," she says as she takes a sip.

"Yeah, she sure did. Ryan cleaned up well too." She nods her head in agreement. "But you, you look exquisite in that dress." She blushes and looks down at her hands which are wrapped around her cup. "What, don't believe me?" She shrugs.

"Thank you. I guess I'm just not used to such compliments coming from you." She smirks.

"Well, I'm sorry for that," I say. "I'll make a mental note to do better in that regard."

An awkward silence takes over, and it seems neither of us know what to say next. I want to say so much to her, but I don't want to overwhelm her with everything I'm feeling. I want her to come back to work for me, but I'm not sure she'll agree.

"Can I ask you something?"

"Sure."

"Would you consider coming back here? To work, I mean."

"You don't really need anyone anymore. You're pretty self-sufficient, wouldn't you say?"

"Some days. But, I don't want just anyone; I want *you*."

"Logan—"

"I'm serious. I might not need you to help me get around anymore, but I'd love help with things like cooking. Michael and I really suck at it." I chuckle to relieve some of the tension.

"So, you want me for my chefspertise?"

I laugh loudly.

"You and your made up words. Yes, that and so much more. Consider your care more like companionship."

She smiles.

"You'll see, some day, people will be using my made up words, and I'll be famous like William Shakespeare."

"I have no doubt," I say, "but seriously, won't you consider it?"

She readjusts her position on the couch, so she's mirroring me.

"I wasn't lying when I said I took on another client. He's 87 years old, with Parkinson's. I'm the first aide he's connected with, and I can't just dump him. He needs me."

I know the feeling.

"What about after your shift with him? I could call and request a late shift with you."

She sighs in resignation.

"Logan, I know what you're trying to do, but the problem remains. We can't have any kind of personal relationship if I work for you. I'd be going against company policy. I'm not willing to do that."

"Okay, then, how about if we just hang out as friends. You could come over and have dinner with us occasionally, and maybe go out sometimes. I can help you study. We'll just be friends with our options open for whatever could come out of this. There shouldn't be a problem if I'm not your boss."

If we have to start over as friends, I'll take it.

"Except for that little document I signed. They'll think I'm working for you on the side and sue me. Logan, I just don't see a way around any of it."

I take in a deep breath and wrack my brain for a solution. I open and close my mouth twice, grasping at any idea that floats into my head. There has to be a solution. I can't let this girl slip through my fingers.

"Okay, let me get this straight. You're not opposed to hanging out here. It's the thought of getting caught and having them think you're breaking your contract that scares you?"

"Basically."

"Well, then it's simple. We'll hide your car."

"What? How?"

"Either we'll put it in the garage, or...I don't know..."

"Or, I could drive someone else's car, like my brother's. It's the one I've been driving you around in."

"That's perfect!"

I shift closer to her and take her hand in mine. She stiffens slightly, which tells me I need to curb my enthusiasm a bit.

"This is going to work. I know it will," I say.

"Please understand though, that we're going to move slowly with our new...friendship. This will be foreign to both of us, and I'd hate to see it end badly."

"I understand completely. No pressure," I say, holding my hands up in surrender.

"Okay then...we have a deal." She holds out her hand, and we shake on it.

I'm beyond excited about the prospect of having her as a friend, but in the back of my mind, I'm praying it turns into more.

"So, what do we do now?" she asks.

"Well, we could watch a movie."

"It's kind of late for that."

I nod.

"How about a board game?" I suggest.

She shrugs.

"I'm very competitive. I'd probably wipe the floor with you," she says with a smirk.

"And, you're modest too." I smile and shake my head. "How about we make a fire out in the back yard? Some beer, a little music playing softly in the background, and my new friend sitting in a lawn chair beside me. How's that sound?"

"Oh, I *love* the smell of a campfire," she says with a huge grin.

"Then, it's settled. Let's do it."

I rise and hold out my hand in an offer to help her up. She takes it and stands.

"Thank you," she says with a nod. "What can I do to help?"

"You grab the beer. I'll get the lighter and chairs, and I'll meet you out back."

"Okay." I watch as she practically skips to the fridge, removes the bottles, then heads for the patio. Her child-like glee warms my heart, and I think I've fallen a little more in love with her. As I reach in the drawer for the lighter, I see some movement on the front porch. I squint to try and identify what it might be.

"What the f…" I don't even get my full sentence out before recognizing Cindy with her arms wrapped awkwardly around Michael, who is staggering toward the front door. I walk quickly to the entryway, opening the door as they approach.

"I'm delivering your brother, Logan. He's about to pass out and has thrown up no less than three times—one of which was in his car," she says with a look of utter disgust. "You can tell him to call me in a few days, when his hangover is done."

I take him from her and sling his limp arm around my shoulders. "Thanks, Cindy. I'll take it from here." She nods, then exits.

Nearly his full weight rests on me, making it difficult to balance, as I trundle toward the hallway with Michael in tow. Thank God Elora comes back into the house because I'm ready to just drop him here in the middle of the foyer and let him sleep it off. She gasps when she sees us then rushes over.

"Let me help," she says, as she takes his other arm and drapes it over her shoulders, then she wraps her arm around his waist. A very drunken Michael, looks at me, then turns his head toward Elora and smirks.

"You guyz-zar wonderful. You know that, right?" Michael slurs. He looks back at me and frowns. "I'm sooo sorry 'bout ruinin' your ev-ning with Lora."

"It's fine, Michael. Let's just get you in bed," I say, irritated. His crooked smile tells me he's not done talking.

"I know how much you love 'er, Logan. Jus' finish woo-wing 'er. I'll be jus' fine right here."

My God, Michael, just shut up.

"You should stop talking now. We're putting you to bed."

I mouth the words *I'm sorry,* and she smiles and mouths back *it's okay.* Then, I look at her and roll my eyes, letting her know I'm not happy about this at all. She giggles softly and shakes her head, as if to say she understands. Suddenly, his legs go limp, and Elora and I are forced to carry his dead weight all the way to his room. The hallway leading to the bedrooms is narrow, and we struggle but, ultimately, succeed in dragging his tall frame all the way to his bed.

"I'll get the covers," she says. "Can you hold him for a second?"

"Yeah, I'm fine. Go ahead."

She nods and lets go, yanking his comforter back, then resuming her place beside him.

"Let's sit him on the edge, then tip him into bed." She nods, and we do just that. I grab his upper body, while she takes his legs, and in one smooth motion, he's laid flat on his back.

"Shouldn't we lay him on his side? You know, in case he gets sick again?"

"Yeah. You're probably right," I reply. So, we roll him over. He grumbles a bit, smacks his lips together, then falls asleep, snoring quietly.

"Come on," I whisper. "He's out for the night. Let's continue with our evening." I walk toward the door.

"Wait," she says quietly, then reaches across my sleeping brother and pulls the covers over him, tucking him in neatly. "There. Snug as a bug in a rug." She smiles at me, and I at her, then we leave to let him recover.

"That was kind of you to cover him up. If it were me, I'd have left him right here on the floor," I snort.

"No, you wouldn't have. You care too much about him."

"Maybe, but I'm kind of pissed at him right now for almost ruining our evening. By the way, let's get that fire started," I say.

"Logan, I think I'm just going to go home."

"What? Why? Michael's not going to interrupt us again. He'll be asleep until tomorrow afternoon. We can still salvage this. Come on. Let's go," I say, hoping I can convince her by walking in the direction of the patio door.

"I'm really tired. Can we do this another time?"

My shoulders slump. I don't want her to leave, but I understand that we've all had enough excitement for one day.

"Okay. Another time."

She grabs her purse and heads toward the front door. I follow, but I'm trying hard not to let her see the disappointment in my eyes. She opens the door, then turns to face me.

"I had a really nice time tonight. You did a great job dancing." She smiles.

"Thank you. I was hoping you'd notice," I say, smiling back at her.

"Well, this is it."

I frown inwardly, not liking the negative thoughts that sentence conjures.

"When will I see you again?" I hold my breath, waiting for her answer.

"When do you want to?"

My heart screams *now*, but I know I can't say that.

"Tomorrow?"

"Are you sure that's wise? Your brother might need you."

"No, he'll be fine. We could have that campfire...or just take a walk, like we used to. It's up to you."

She rubs her chin and contemplates her answer.

"I'll call you and let you know."

I'm a little defeated that I didn't get a definite answer, but I'll take whatever time she's willing to give me.

"Okay. That sounds good."

And, then comes that awkward moment, when two people are silent and standing in the doorway, waiting and wondering if now's the appropriate time to kiss. She's not making an attempt to leave. Does that mean I should lean in and—

"Goodnight, Logan," she says, and leans in, kissing me on the cheek. I smile, even though I wish it was more. The truth is, something about that kiss says more about how she feels than if she would've kissed my lips. I'm satisfied with that for now, knowing I have to devise a plan to win her over.

"Goodnight. Be careful driving home," I reply, then I watch as she strides gracefully toward the steps, stopping briefly to turn and wave. I wave back, then wait to close the door, until her taillights disappear around the corner.

ELORA

"Hello there, Cinderella. Back from the ball so soon?" Daniel says with an eye roll. "I thought for sure you'd be out much later than this."

I smile and place my handbag on the table.

"I would've been, but Logan's brother had a bit too much to drink, which cut our evening short."

"No booty-call then?"

"Daniel!" I shout, while throwing my shoe in his direction. He's barely able to duck out of the line of fire, and I smile because I'm just in a good mood. "It was never going to be a booty-call. You're an ass."

"Maybe, *you* didn't think so, but if he's a typical male, you can bet he was hopeful." He snorts, so I throw the other shoe at him. "So, I take it you had a good time?"

"Yes. It was very nice," I say with a cheesy grin. "I'm probably going to go over again tomorrow."

His eyebrows shoot up.

"Really. Is it an official visit, or are you helping him with his middle leg?"

"What has gotten into you? Is sex all you can think about?"

He cocks his head to the side and raises one eye brow as if to remind me that *all* men think this way.

"Hey, it's not often I can tease my sister about her boyfriend—I'm assuming that's the decision you've come to."

"He's not my boyfriend; he's just a friend...who happened to kiss me again." I turn to walk into my room, but Daniel wraps his hand around my arm, halting me mid-step.

"Oh, no you don't. You're not going to drop that bombshell and expect me not to react. What happened?" he says, as he guides me to the couch, insisting I sit. He stands before me with his arms crossed at his chest and sways a bit, making me aware he's been drinking... again. "He kissed you again. Am I going to have to kick his ass?" I smile and bite my bottom lip in an attempt to reign in my excitement.

"No, relax. If you don't want to know anymore, I won't say another word."

He rolls his eyes at my aloofness.

"I don't particularly like hearing about my sister's sexcapades, but it looks as though you'd like to talk about it. So, go ahead. If you say you're just friends, what were the circumstances leading up to it?" He rolls his eyes again, clearly a little uncomfortable with the subject.

I think back to just a few hours ago and frown. Since Logan and I had our talk, I'd temporarily forgotten about how our second kiss happened, and that Bethany might have been the reason behind it.

"Um..." I look down at my dress, smoothing the skirt.

"You look sad. Was it a bad kiss?" His eyes close, and his face twists as though he's only asking for my benefit.

"No, not at all. It's just that it came after the two of us had a run in with his ex—who, incidentally, wants him back."

He sits down.

"Oh. That doesn't sound good. So, you don't think his kiss was genuine? Like, maybe, he was doing it to show her he's not interested in her anymore?"

"Exactly," I say. "Or..."

"Or?"

"Or, maybe, he was trying to prove to himself that he's done with her."

"Huh?"

I realize I'm coming down, quite hard, from my high, and I slump into the back of the couch.

"I'm not sure what to think. He kissed me, then looked right at her and said '*That should send her a message.*' He admitted it wasn't as romantic as he'd have liked, which makes me wonder even more if maybe, he still loves her...or whatever. Maybe, he was testing his feelings for her."

"*What?* Have you talked to him about it?"

I shake my head.

"No. I wasn't in the mood for a conversation like that. Then, his brother came home drunk and sick, so I helped Logan get him into bed. After that, I left." I turn to him. "What could he be thinking? You're a guy. Tell me what it could mean."

I see a few different emotions cross his face, concern being one of them. I think he knows it's possible that I'm right about this.

"Elora, I have no idea what he could've been thinking. Maybe, it was just a spur of the moment kind of kiss that simply meant he wanted to kiss you. I'd say, talk to him about it the first chance you get. I wouldn't let this fester longer than it has to."

"Okay," I agree. "Maybe, you're right. I'm going to sleep on it." I rise from the couch and hug Daniel. "Thanks."

His brotherly arms engulf me.

"Anytime," he says, then pulls back to look at me. "Be careful, okay?" I nod. "This could very easily get ugly." I nod again and he sighs. "Get some rest. It might be clearer in the morning."

"I know. Goodnight."

"Night."

And I stalk off in the direction of my bedroom.

13

ELORA

He walks me backward, until I feel the wall behind me. His lips are on my neck, as he wraps his arms around my waist. Pulling me tightly into him, his pelvis grinds into mine, and I can feel his warm, shallow breaths against my skin. It sends shivers down my spine. My fingers dig at the wall, trying desperately to latch onto something...anything. Then, his teeth graze my earlobe. It takes me by surprise, so I moan and turn my head away, giving him more access.

"Shh," he whispers. "She'll hear you." His hand travels down, reaching for the button of my jeans.

Who will hear?

I open my eyes and look to my left, suddenly spotting Logan and Bethany. He's no longer kissing my neck, but hers. I look in front of me, and he's gone. They both look over and grin devilishly at me.

"Shh," he whispers to her. "She'll hear you."

My eyes fly open, and I sit straight up in bed. I'm covered in sweat and panting. Wiping my brow, I look around, half expecting to find them both in my room, but reality sets in, and I realize it was only a dream. My heart races as I recall the events that just played out before me. The unanswered questions even plague me in my sleep.

"Good morn—," Daniel stops abruptly and raises his eyebrows. "What the hell happened to you? You don't look like you got much sleep last night."

I smooth my hair down and gaze at my reflection in the microwave door. Dark circles have taken up residency on my sleep deprived face.

"I didn't. Is there coffee?" He pours a cup then pushes it at me, as if I'm a wild animal he'd rather not get bit by. "Thanks," I say, taking the cup from him.

"So—"

"Shh," I interrupt him. "Not before I've had a least a couple sips." He nods and waits. I walk over and sit at our kitchen table, warming my hands on the cup and nursing it quietly. "I tossed and turned all night. My mind conjured up one doozie of a dream."

"Want to talk about it?"

"No. I really don't."

"Was it Logan Turner related?"

"Of course."

He sits down adjacent from me. His expression drips with concern.

"I'm guessing that means that you'll be going over there again to talk to him about it." I nod my head and he looks vaguely disappointed. "Well, if nothing else, it might just get you a better night's rest."

"Yeah. I think I might surprise him this morning with donuts from Carlisle's Bakery."

"You know, you're putting a lot of effort into whatever this relationship is. I hope he's doing the same. He really doesn't deserve you."

"Thank you, and I promise you, he is. Now, I have to go," I say as I kiss the top of his head, like I used to do when we were kids.

I sneak in quietly, as I don't know how well Michael is after a night of binge drinking. The scent of the freshly baked doughnuts I bought permeates the air, and I giggle as I wonder if the aroma alone could cause him to wake up. I peek around at the kitchen table, but Logan isn't there. He must've slept in. I set the bag on the counter and walk toward his room. But, before I get halfway there, I hear a horrible sound.

"No!" he shouts. "Stop! Don't leave!"

I sprint over to his door, and this time, I don't hesitate before opening it. He's in bed, in the middle of a nightmare, no doubt, and he's thrashing around, screaming in agony. I rush to his side, and I'm about to wake him when he shouts again.

"Where are you going? Why are you leaving?"

I retract my hand, as self-doubt crashes in all around me—large and loud. Who is he talking about? And, I wonder…is it Bethany? Has the fact that he saw her yesterday triggered his feelings for her and brought them to the surface? Is he dreaming of when she left him, and he's calling out to her, begging her to stay?

I cover my mouth, suddenly feeling like a voyeur. I shouldn't have come here unannounced. This is private, and I'm sure I shouldn't have heard him. I back away, but feel tears welling up in my eyes. My worst fears are being realized. Even in his sleep, the truth comes out. I have to go. I need to get out of here before he wakes up and sees me. I turn and head for the door, when I hear him again. His voice is calmer this time, and his body no longer fights against a sleep induced enemy.

"I love you," he whispers.

I slowly turn back around, a sick feeling in the pit of my stomach. Who is he talking to? My negative side whole heartedly believes he's talking to her, but what if he's not? I take a deep breath, swallow my fears, and step closer to him. Not wanting to, but unable to stop myself, I bravely lean in.

"Who? Who do you love, Logan?" I whisper, then I close my eyes tightly awaiting his answer.

"You," he says quietly. "I love *you*, Elora."

I gulp in a breath and hold it in, afraid to make a sound.

Did I hear him right?

Am I sure he said *my* name?

My mind quickly compares the sound of my name to hers, just to make sure they sound nothing alike.

Elora.

Beth.

Bethany.

Nope. They're not even close.

My heart melts and panics at the same time. He loves me? Is he sure? Can I believe this nocturnal confession? Now, I really need to leave. If he wakes up and finds out I've been listening, I'll—

"Elora?" Logan's groggy voice says. I smile awkwardly because, well, I'm incapable of doing anything else. "What are you doing here?" He rubs his eyes as if he's seeing a mirage. I laugh guiltily.

"Hi," I squeak out.

Well, that didn't sound suspicious at all.

Confusion washes over him but leaves just as quickly. He smiles and begins to sit up, as he realizes I'm not a hallucination.

"Hey. What's going on? Why are you here so early?"

"Um, you said you'd hoped to see me today." I toss my hands into the air. "So, here I am." I smile again, but I'm sure it looks more like I've just stepped on a stray Lego.

"I'm thrilled that you're here. I just thought you'd call first." He swings his body to the edge of the bed and reaches for his prosthetics.

"Well, I did, but you didn't answer, so I figured I'd surprise you. I brought you some doughnuts." I gesture over my shoulder with my thumb.

"Great. As soon as I'm done with this, I'll make some coffee," he says, rolling the first liner onto his leg.

"No need. Take your time. I'll go make a pot."

I exit the room with my head practically spinning. Whew! That was close. I'm so relieved to get out of there. I thought for sure he'd see right through me. I'm better than I thought when I'm under pressure.

Just as I'm done setting up the coffee maker, he comes walking out. His hair, which was the definition of bedhead, has been tamed, and he's wearing only pajama bottoms, which hang from his hips in a way that makes me wish for a little bit stronger gravitational pull.

Damn. He's hot.

I shake my head to ward off any wayward thoughts. I came here for a reason, and I'll need to keep a clear head.

"I wasn't sure what kind of doughnuts you like, so I just got a variety."

He inspects the contents of the bag.

"It's perfect. Thank you," he says with a lazy smile, while brushing his fingers against my arm. "So, you're up early, and I hope you don't mind me saying this but, you look tired. Didn't you sleep well?"

"Not really. I tossed and turned most of the night. You're not the only one who had nightmares last night."

His expression turns to curiosity.

"How'd you know I had a nightmare last night?"

Oh, shit.

"Um...well, I sort of...heard you when I came in." My eyes dart around the room, hoping to land on my next sentence.

"Did I say anything?"

I shrug.

"Not really. You were moving around a bit though," I add. "Do you remember what you were dreaming about?"

He tenses, then relaxes, and walks over to the cabinet to retrieve two coffee mugs.

"No. I rarely remember my dreams." I breathe a sigh of relief. "But, you must've had a bad one too."

"Why would you think that?"

"Because you just told me. You said that I wasn't the only who had a nightmare last night. So, what was yours about?"

"I don't remember either," I lie.

He pours the coffee into our cups and hands me one.

"Well, here's to not having to relive our bad dreams in the daytime." We lift our mugs and clink them together. "So, what do you want to do today?"

I shrug noncommittally.

"I don't know. How about if we do something where we can talk?"

"Like?" I shrug again. "Okay, I think I have an idea. Let's finish our breakfast, then we'll go downtown. There's an arts festival going on, and I think today's the last day for it."

"I heard about that. I haven't been there since I was a kid. That sounds like fun," I say.

"Great. It's a date."

⟡

As I cruise down the busy city street, I'm reminded of several trips I'd taken here as a child with my mom. The culture downtown is so different from that of its suburbs to the south, and I can't help but feel as though I'm in a whole different world. The rolling fields of Medina County have turned to skyscraping, office towers here. The high-end restaurants are mixed in with mom and pop shops, and graffiti is mixed with modern art. I feel a bit out of my element, but I'm fascinated just the same.

I pull into a parking space and turn off the engine. When I look at Logan, he's already staring at me.

"What?" I say, grinning at him.

"Nothing."

"You can't look at me like that and say *nothing*."

"I don't want to freak you out."

My face falls.

"Is there a spider in my hair?" I begin to panic, but I keep still because I have no idea where it could be. He laughs, loudly.

"No. It's nothing like that, although it's cute that you're afraid of something that's a million times smaller than you."

He chuckles.

I frown.

"Then, what?"

"I just think you look pretty today. That's all."

"Oh." I relax, and smile timidly. "Thank you. That's very sweet of you to say, but why would I freak out about that?"

"I just don't want to screw this up."

I lay my hand on top of his.

"Stop worrying so much. Let's just have fun."

He nods, and we exit the car.

Shutting the door, my widened eyes scan the area, and I take in a deep breath as I drink it all in. The air around us comes to life with the sights and sounds of local vendors which line the streets as far as the eye can see. Everywhere I look is a kaleidoscope of colors, and I'm convinced that every artist within a fifty-mile radius has gathered here to show their wares.

Logan takes my hand and smiles at me, and I mirror his expression. He gently squeezes my hand, but says nothing, as he unhurriedly pulls me along. He must realize how spellbound I am right now.

As we walk, tent after tent stands erect beside us while a barrage of customers flock to them. We move through the crowds at a leisurely pace, soaking up the warm rays of the sun and enjoying the cool, spring breezes. Suddenly, I spot a booth filled with colorful sculptures. I look up at him and raise my eyebrows, silently asking if we can stop by. He smiles and nods, and I drag him inside.

"Look at all this beautiful art. The intricate shapes and colors are all so well defined and perfectly used in combination. I love every one of them," I say, in awe of the spectacle laid out before me.

"I didn't realize you were an art connoisseur," he says, a little surprised.

"I'm not—not really," I say, looking at him briefly then back at the artwork. "I just know what I like."

"I know what you mean," he says softly, and I smile, as I understand the meaning behind his words.

"G'day," says the bleach blonde woman with the Australian accent. "The name's Scarlett. How are you goin'?" She reaches out her hand for us to shake.

"Hello. We're great. I'm Elora, and this is Logan. Are you the artist?" I ask, as I wave a hand toward the tables.

"Sure am. Do you like 'em?"

"They're fantastic. Great use of colors, I might add."

"Thanks. You must be a collector."

I shrug.

"Maybe, a little. I just love colorful art, and yours definitely stands out."

"Yeah, I make what I see. Mostly wildlife and things from back home."

"In Australia?" She nods. "You lived in paradise. What on earth made you move *here?*"

She shrugs.

"My boyfriend is an American who was traveling abroad when we met. He's an artist too, so when an opportunity to come back to the states came along, he had to take it. I came along for the ride."

"Wow! That's going to be a great story to tell your kids someday."

She smiles and nods in agreement.

"Well, if you want to give my sculptures a fair-go, I'd be happy to quote you a price. Just let me know if you have questions."

I nod and browse the selections.

"These *are* really nice," Logan says, admiring an abstract piece that resembles a brilliantly painted, seaside sunset.

"Oh, I like that one too. The spiral reminds me of a giant ocean wave that was plucked right out of the water. It's soothing, yet vibrant, and evokes so many emotions all at once. I think it's my favorite."

"Should we buy it?"

I look at him, shocked.

"No. I have no idea where I'd put it. Besides, I'm sure it's expensive."

"Let's ask," he says, then lets go of my hand in pursuit of Scarlett. What is he doing? He comes back a few moments later.

"Do you want it?"

"How much is it?" I ask, afraid to hear the price.

"I didn't ask her, but if you want it, it's yours."

"Logan, no. I'm not going to let you buy it for me."

"Why not?"

"Because, it's just…too much."

He frowns.

"But, you like it."

"I like Hawaii too, but I don't expect you to buy it for me," I say, stunned at the mere thought. He shrugs, seemingly unaffected by my words.

"Suit yourself," he says, then walks back over to her. I watch, mouth agape, as he hands her his credit card. She hands him a piece of paper, which I assume is a receipt, then he walks back over to me and smiles.

"Did you just buy that sculpture?" He nods. "For me?"

"No. I bought it for me." He smirks, and his eyes glint as if he's up to something. I narrow my eyes at him, and he grins.

"Where are you going to put it?" I say, as I cross my arms at my chest.

"I don't know yet. I thought that you might like to help me decide. Besides, it may give you motivation to come by more often to visit me…I mean, *it*."

I smirk.

"We can pick it up on our way out." He grins broadly and shakes his head. "Come on. Let's keep going."

As we stroll leisurely along, taking in all the sights, our hands remain connected. Once in a while, I feel his tighten around mine, and he pulls me into him. I've come to the conclusion that he does this whenever we pass someone he deems an unsavory looking character. I'm not sure if it's a conscious effort or instinctual. Either way, it makes me feel safe and protected.

It's now early afternoon, and the crowds have migrated toward the concession stands. My stomach growls loudly as a friendly reminder that we passed the lunch hour. Embarrassed, I cover it with my hand as if that would quiet it down.

"Are you hungry?" I shrug, then nod. "Why don't we stop for lunch? I saw an interesting little restaurant near where we parked," he says.

"That sounds like a wonderful idea. We can drop off your sculpture on the way there."

After picking up Logan's art, we make our way through the crowd and back to the car. While en route, I notice Logan stops frequently to adjust his right leg.

"Is everything all right?"

"Yeah. It's just that the socket on this side seems to be a little loose."

"Loose? Is that normal?"

"My therapist said that my residual legs will change shape, which will necessitate an adjustment or replacement of the prosthetics. I guess that's what's going on. It's been bothering me for a few days now."

"Why didn't you say something? We could've stayed at your place. You could've taken them off, to give yourself a break, and just used your wheelchair."

He shakes his head adamantly.

"No way. I don't want to be wheelchair bound ever again," he says. "I'm enjoying the lifestyle you encouraged me to live, and I'm not going backward."

"Don't think of it as going backward."

"Let's just talk about something else, okay?" he says, and if I'm not mistaken, he seems a bit irritated.

"Okay," I reply quietly, and the subject is closed.

We enter the Sand-Witch Shop, and wait as the hostess gathers two menus. The décor is nautical, with a definite mermaid theme. She seats us at a booth by the window which faces the main road. From this angle, we can observe the quirky pedestrians as they walk past us.

"This place is cute," I say.

He looks around.

"Yeah, it's not bad. I hope the food is good. I'm starving."

I nod in agreement. Then, the unbidden image of our second kiss and my nightmare come into focus. I need to talk to him about it.

"Logan?"

"Yeah?"

"I need to…ask you about something."

I have his full attention now.

"You can ask me anything."

"Well, you know when you kissed me at Ryan and Sydney's wedding?"

He smiles broadly.

"I remember. What about it?"

"I noticed that…" I stop mid-sentence as he reaches down and winces a bit. "Are you sure you're okay?"

"I'm fine. It's just a little sore from all the walking we did. Please, continue." Nervously, I look at the table next to us. It's quite close to ours. There's a young couple eating their lunch, and I wonder if they'd be able to overhear our conversation. "Earth to Elora," he says, and I look back at him. "Go on. What were you going to ask me about?"

"Um, maybe I should wait until we're alone." I glance back at the couple.

"You're just going to leave me hanging?" I shrug. "Please continue. I'm dying to know what you're thinking."

He reaches across the table and caresses my hand.

I smile awkwardly.

You can do this.

"Well, it just seemed like—"

"Hi. My name is Tammy and I'll be your waitress. Can I start you folks off with something to drink?" she interrupts.

"Uh, yeah," Logan says. "I'll have iced tea and she'll have…" He looks to me for an answer.

"The same, please."

She nods and writes in her notepad.

"I'll bring them right over," she says, then she walks away to fetch them.

Logan looks back at me.

"Now, where were we?"

I sigh, frustration lingering in the air.

"I'll just wait, and we can talk at your house."

His eyebrows lift, and he seems concerned as to what the topic of conversation might be.

"Is everything okay? You're not upset about something, are you?"

"No. It's nothing like that," I say, even though it sort of is like that.

"Are you sure? Because your expression is worrisome."

He gently squeezes my hand, and I try to fake a sincere smile, though I'm not sure I'm pulling it off.

"Please don't be worried. It's nothing. Really. Let's just enjoy our lunch."

He's skeptical, I can tell, but he says nothing more about it.

The drive home takes about thirty minutes. We're making small talk, and I'm trying to avoid the subject of our kiss. Most of the way there, he's fidgeting with his leg.

"When we get you home, I want you to take that off, and let me have a look at it."

He smiles mischievously.

"You want to play doctor with me?" He raises and lowers his eyebrows seductively.

"Yes," I giggle. "Something like that."

I pull into the driveway and put the car in park. As Logan exits the car, he winces.

"Agh!" he exclaims and grasps his leg. I rush to his side.

"Hey. Is it bothering you that much?" He shrugs, which is man speak for, *yes*. "Here," I say, putting his arm over my shoulders. "Let me help you into the house."

We hobble in together, and he sits on a kitchen chair. Slowly, he removes his right prosthetic leg then, the liner.

"Hm. It's gotten bigger," he says while wincing. I look down and spy a huge ulcer that has formed near the bottom.

"Logan! When did this happen?"

"I told you, it's been hurting for a few days. It wasn't this big yesterday."

"And, you still walked around on it like this?" I'm upset with him for not telling me about it. "This needs to be cleaned out. I'm getting the first aid kit." I turn toward the hallway, ignoring his pleas to not make a big deal of it, and fetch the supplies I need. When I come back, he's removed the other leg as well. Upon further inspection, I determine that the wound is isolated to one leg. I place a large bowl underneath the chair and pour a sterile, saline solution on it while trying to dab it gently.

"Ow! That stings," he says, gripping the seat of the chair tightly.

"Well, if you'd told me about this when it started to hurt, it might have been a lot less painful." I shoot him a scolding look to let him know this was a bad decision.

"I know, I'm sorry. I just didn't want to miss the wedding, and then when you showed up this morning…well, I couldn't say no to you."

"Seriously?" He shrugs apologetically. "Ugh! You're impossible." He grins, then winces again, as I dab his blister a little harder.

I finish tending to the wound, using a wet to dry dressing with an ace wrap over the whole thing. He then takes a hold of his prosthetic leg and liner.

"What are you doing?"

"Um, putting my leg back on."

"No, you're not. You won't be able to wear it until that blister heals.

"Like hell!" he says. "I'm not going back in that chair. There's no way!"

"Logan—"

"No. I'm not doing it." He grabs his liner and begins to roll it on. I watch his face harden while it rubs against the wound.

"This is ridiculous. Who cares if you have to stay in your wheelchair for a few days? You did it for several months after your surgery."

"I. Am not. Staying in that wheelchair." He says each word slowly and clearly, and there's a menacing finality to his tone. I cross my arms in front of my chest, my stubbornness erupting with his.

"Fine. Then, I'm not coming back over until your wound is completely healed. The longer you wait to give it a chance to rest, the longer it is before you can see me."

I flash him a cocky smile. His responding expression is clearly irritation, as he's just realized two can play this game. We stare at each other intently. It's a showdown, and may the best man—er—woman, win.

"Really," he says. I nod. "You'd stay away just to win this argument?"

"I hadn't realized we were arguing, but it seems you're willing to let me stay away to prove a point." I purse my lips and raise one brow.

His mouth twists.

"Touché. I guess you win. But, for my concession, I'm throwing in a condition." He too raises one eyebrow.

Why do I find that so sexy?

"What condition?"

"That you sit here and tell me whatever it is that you started to say at the restaurant, and you don't stop until you've said it all."

I bite the inside of my cheek, as I decide if this is the best time to talk about it.

"And, if I don't?"

He snorts.

"Then, I guess it'll be a while before we see each other again."

I sigh, frustrated that the solid lead I had is now nonexistent. How the hell did I lose this battle?

"Fine." I uncross my arms and stomp off toward his room. Coming back into the kitchen, pushing his wheelchair in front of me, I line it up with the chair he's sitting on and lock the wheels. "Get in," I demand, pointing to the seat.

"You're so bossy," he says, then smirks. I roll my eyes at him.

He follows me into the living room, where I sit on the couch. He lines up then transfers himself. After getting comfortable, we face each other, and he begins.

"First, let me just say I'm sorry. I didn't want this day to turn into an argument. I know I should've stopped wearing my legs at the first sign of pain, but you have no idea how much I want to be normal for you." He scoots closer and takes my hand. "I have a lot to learn about how my life works now, and I'm so grateful you've agreed to be a part of it. I want to be whole again…for you. I want you to be proud to walk down the street with me. I don't want people to look at us and wonder why you're with me, in whatever capacity that means. So, I guess that means that if I have to endure a little pain, so be it. I'd go through a lot more than a pressure ulcer for you."

I look down at my lap. Because of me, he's intentionally hurt himself. If I weren't in the picture, he would've taken them off and had them repaired. I close my eyes and sigh.

"I'm sorry too. I shouldn't have pushed you so much. If I've given you any reason to think I'd only want to be seen with you in pubic, while you're wearing your legs, then I'm sorry. The truth is that I don't care if you're in a wheelchair with a purple hat on your head, playing folk songs on a harmonica. As long as you're happy, then I am too."

"Well, that's an interesting image," he says with a smirk.

I snicker.

"I think we need to communicate more…which is why I want to talk about a concern I have."

His brow knits, as his face turns serious.

"Okay. By all means, tell me what's on your mind."

I swallow and push my hair behind my ears.

"Um…I'm nervous about your feelings toward Bethany."

"Why?" he says, perplexed.

"Well, she wants you back. She told me so."

"So what? I don't want her. I've told you that already."

"I know, but there's something that's been bothering me."

"Okay…"

"At the wedding, you dragged me away from her then kissed me. As soon as you ended our kiss, you looked straight at her. The kiss was abrupt, and the look you gave her seemed to come at an odd time. I thought that maybe it was more for her than for me. You know, like, maybe, you were trying to make her jealous or that you were testing your feelings for her." I look down at my lap again. I'm so afraid of what I might hear next.

He shifts closer to me again and brings his hand to my chin, gently lifting it, so I'm looking at him. His eyes shift back and forth, examining my expression.

"I'd never kiss *you* to spite *her,* nor would I do it to see if I'm over her or not. I'm over her—completely. And, if you need proof of that, I'm willing to give it to you." I look back down, and he reaches up and caresses my cheek. "Elora, you have no idea how many ways you've saved my life." I glance up at him. What is he talking about? He looks away as if to gather his thoughts, or maybe he's contemplating whether or not to tell me something. "Do you remember the very first day you came over here?" I nod. "Do you remember I had you move Michael's boxes into his bedroom?"

"Yes," I say quietly. "You got really upset with me the next day, when you couldn't find some wooden box you were looking for."

"Yes. That's right. That box was very important to me, but I never told you why." I look at him, silently wondering where he's going with this.

"Elora, that was a very difficult time for me. I was a different person than I am now. I thought my life was over, that there was no way I could live a normal, let alone *happy,* life ever again." He takes a deep breath, the exhales forcefully. "That day, you took the one thing from me that I wanted most in this world. You took my death. There was a gun in that box. I was planning on killing myself that day." He bows his head, obviously ashamed at his former self.

My hand flies to my mouth.

"Logan, no!" I say in shock. "Why on earth would you even think about doing that? My God. I'm...*sick* at the thought that you could've succeeded."

My heart races at all the what ifs.

"I know, but as I said, I thought my life was over. I had no legs—no hope for a normal life. I was forced to have someone else do things for me that I should've been able to do for myself. It was humiliating, to say the least. I felt like a useless human being, and all I wanted was out. I'd chased away so many aides who couldn't care less about me. But, then, you walked in." He grins and pushes a hand through his hair. "God, you were different. It was as if you were a light, shining on the darkened path of where my new journey would take me. You cared, and you challenged me. You pushed me to want more for myself. You gave me a reason to fight for my life. And, that's when I felt it—hope. I felt it instantly—the minute you walked in, and it scared the shit out of me. Until that point, I'd never dared to hope for anything more than the cards I was dealt. And, I knew I couldn't make you happy in the condition I was in. The truth is, you deserve more than half a man, so I let you be the beacon I reached for in my recovery. *You* are the reason I can stand upright again. You. Are. Everything."

14

LOGAN

Silence takes over the room, as her stunned expression has left her speechless. Her lips are parted slightly, and I ache to hear what thoughts will come from them.

Please. Say something.

I touch her arm—my thumb gliding in circles against her skin.

"What are you thinking?" I whisper, hoping her reply is something I'll want to hear. She blinks several times and takes a deep breath.

"I'm thinking…I've never heard anything so beautiful in all my life," she replies, equally as soft, as her sincere eyes look straight through to my soul.

I exhale with relief. Thank God.

"It's the truth," I say, then shrug. "And, now you know."

"I had no idea how you felt…especially in the beginning." She breaks eye contact with me and starts to giggle. "And, you were such a jerk."

I laugh right along with her.

"You're right, I was, and I'm so sorry for that. I wish I could go back and tell that idiot to lighten up."

"Well, it certainly would've made my life a lot easier."

We laugh as we reminisce about our first few weeks together, but soon, the laughter turns serious.

"What are you thinking now?" I ask.

"I'm thinking about all the times I ogled you behind your back and about all the middle fingers that appeared there too."

I chuckle, understanding completely.

"Well, you had every right. But, I'm not that guy anymore."

"I'm glad," she says, then smiles and chews on the corner of her lip. My mouth dries as my breathing becomes shallow.

"Michael is at his friend's house for the night. So, what do we do now?" My voice is hushed—almost hoarse.

She shrugs.

"I don't know. What do you think?"

Then, without another word, I lean closer to her. Reaching up, I let my thumb brush against her cheek, and she closes her eyes, tilting her head into my hand. I lean in and just as our lips meet, I feel a gentle breath escape from her mouth, and I can't help it, I press into her farther. Her hand snakes through my hair, pulling me in, and my arms engulf her. As our tongues touch, an uncontrollable frenzy begins. One of us lets out a seductive moan or, maybe, it's both of us, then we're wrapped round each other. She leans back, allowing me to lie on top of her, all the while, our mouths devour each other's. My hips grind into her automatically, so I stop, unsure if that's going too far. My internal question is answered when her hips rise up to meet mine, and her hand pulls my body against hers. I break our kiss, but only to find her neck. The soft floral scent of her perfume only ignites the fire building inside me. It would take every ounce of will power I could muster to stop now.

"Bed," she whispers, and I can feel the vibrations of her words on her throat.

"Yes," I hiss in reply. Then, I instantly recognize a problem. I don't have my legs on, and I can't put them on because of the blister. I stop kissing her and drop my forehead onto her shoulder. "I can't." I look into her eyes and watch her face go from puzzled to realization in less than a second.

"It's okay. Just use your wheelchair."

And, at those words, the proverbial bucket of cold water is thrown. I let out a frustrated sigh and sit upright. She props herself up on her elbows, a concerned expression on her face.

"What's the matter?"

"It's not supposed to be this damn difficult!" I shout, angry that my legs, or lack thereof, have ruined a perfect moment.

"What's not?"

I peer up at her. There's a fine line between a look of concern and one of pity, and her expression is bordering between the two. I close my eyes and turn away to avoid the rage I feel rising up.

"Everything, Elora. Everything is difficult without legs." I say with a menacing edge. I gaze back at her and continue. "I should be able to sweep you off your feet, carry you into the bedroom, and make love to you, but I *can't*." I shift in my seat, so I'm no longer facing her.

She says nothing for a moment, then I feel her move closer, and her hands land on my thigh.

"Logan, look at me," she says softly. I hesitate, but eventually do as I'm asked. She gives me a small smile. "I don't care how we get there. I don't need a big, romantic gesture. I just want you." I roll my eyes, and she frowns. "Stop being so critical of yourself." She sighs, probably in frustration at me. "Would you still be attracted to me if I dyed my hair a different color?" My eyes quickly meet hers again.

"Of course."

"What about if I lost an arm?"

"I know where you're going with this, and it's not the same."

"Why not?"

"Because you're a woman."

"So," she snorts.

"So, I'm supposed to be the one who's strong and—"

"You *are* strong," she interrupts.

"Not right now, I'm not." I push my hands through my hair, irritated at the point she's trying to make. "I know what you're trying to say, but there are things I should be doing—things I *want* to do, but in my current state, that's nearly impossible."

Her soft hands cup my face, and turn it toward her, so I'm looking at her.

"I don't need you to sweep me off my feet. You've already done that. And, as for carrying me to your bedroom, well, if you think this is the only opportunity you'll have to do that, I have news for you—it's not." She grins mischievously as her eyebrows lift twice. Her smile is contagious and although it takes me a minute, I smile back at her.

"Where did you come from?" I say, amazed at her capacity to defuse my anger.

She shrugs.

"Originally Cleveland." Her smartass grin is one of my favorite expressions. "So, does this mean our," she clears her throat, "*plans* have been thwarted by your chauvinistic ego?"

I laugh.

"My what?"

"Well, if it wasn't for your temper tantrum, you'd already be halfway to a home run by now."

"Really."

"Mm hm." She nods, and her mouth twists.

"Well then, we'd better get started again." I lean in and kiss her, but it's more playful than romantic. She giggles against my lips, and I grin. "What's so funny?"

"Nothing. I just thought of something. Wait here."

She stands and walks into the hallway. After a moment, she returns with a spare blanket and two floor pillows. Moving the coffee table out of the way, she unfurls the blanket and smooths any wrinkles out. Then, she places the pillows at one end.

"What are you doing?" I ask.

"Come on. Come down here, and join me," she says as she lowers herself to the floor and lies on her side, propping herself up on her elbow.

I smile and shake my head, but join her, as requested.

"Now what?" I say, as I lie on my side, facing her.

"Now, we do whatever we want to. If we just want to talk, then we talk. If we want to make out some more..." She raises one eyebrow seductively, "then, we can do that too. But, if you want to make love to me, then this is the perfect spot because the truth is, the location is less important than the feelings behind it."

Without another thought, I wind my fingers into her hair and kiss her hard on the lips. I hear her gasp, but she reciprocates wholeheartedly. As she rolls onto her back, I roll with her, resuming my position partially on top. Her hands rake through my hair, stopping at the back and fisting tightly, as if she had little control over them. It's just this side of painful, which only reignites the fire that was doused just moments ago. My hand roams south as I reach her belly. I lift her shirt slightly, then allow my fingers to explore underneath it. She writhes at the contact, and I watch as her head tilts back, and her eyes close.

My God, she's beautiful.

My lips find her throat again, and for hours we make love, until we both fall into an exhausted sleep.

ELORA

I stretch, with my arms over my head, arching my back off the floor, and yawn. As I look down, I notice Logan's head is laying on my chest. I smile at his sleeping form and run a playful hand through his hair. He stirs, and his sleepy face glances up at me. His lazy smile is charming.

"Good morning," he says.

"Morning," I reply. "Did you sleep well?"

He nods and stretches, then yawns.

"Yes, but my back is a bit stiff from lying on the floor all night."

All night.

All night?

"Shit," I say, as I bolt upright, accidentally knocking him off me. "What time is it?" I search the room for a clock, then finally find one on the wall. "*It's almost seven?*" I grab the blanket, leaving him the sheet, and wrap it around me. "I'm going to be late!"

As I gather my clothes from the surrounding floor, Logan watches me with ill-disguised humor.

"You could call in sick," he tempts me. I shoot him a don't-be-ridiculous kind of look, then continue gathering.

"I cannot be late. This guy I'm working for is a bit of a tyrant about it."

He cocks his head to the side.

"Your new client is a tyrant?" His brow is furrowed.

"Not exactly. He just likes things the way he likes them, and there's no wiggle room." I pull the blanket a little tighter around me and look around. "Is Michael still out?" He nods. "Good." Without another word, I waddle off to the bathroom.

When I reenter the living room, Logan has made a pot of coffee. He's sitting in his chair in just a pair of tight fitting boxer briefs. I pause a moment to remember to breathe.

"Want some?" he says while holding out a coffee cup. His smirk distracts me even more.

"Huh?" I eye his finely sculpted chest, then realize what he's referring to. "Oh, coffee." I laugh guiltily. "No, thank you. I have to go."

"Are you sure I can't persuade you to stay?" he says, as he rolls closer to me and takes my hand, planting a seductive kiss on the back of it. I almost cave, but remember the wrath of my client.

"No," I say, pulling away from him, but kissing his nose to alleviate the frown that now mars his handsome face. "I'll take a raincheck though."

"Story of my life." He shakes his head. "When will I see you again?"

"I'm not sure. I'm working every day this week, and I have classes almost every night. I also need time to study. So…I don't know."

His mouth twists.

"Okay. How about if you call or text me when you get a free moment?"

I nod.

"I will. I promise."

I lean in and give him a quick peck on the lips, then turn to leave. But, he grabs my wrist and pulls me down to him.

"I don't think so," he says, then he wraps his hand behind my head. He pulls me into him and kisses me passionately. For a few moments, I forget my pressing issue and fall into his tender touch. He breaks off the kiss and looks deeply into my eyes. "Now you can go," he whispers. My breath leaves me as I contemplate his earlier offer to play hooky. "Go. You'll be late," he adds. I snap immediately out of my daze and stand upright.

"You're a bad influence on me."

He grins.

"I'm glad."

I plant one more peck on his lips before taking off out the door.

"I'll call you later," I say, as I close the door behind me.

My day has been one of the longest on record. My eight-hour shift at work felt more like twelve, and school seemed to drag on just as long. As I sag into my couch, I close my eyes. I'm exhausted.

"Late night again? Or should I say early morning?" Daniel asks in a snarky voice.

I open my eyes and see my brother looming over me with his arms crossed in front of his chest. I roll my eyes. I'm too tired for his interrogation.

"As a matter of fact, yes. Why do you care?"

"I don't particularly, but a phone call would've been nice. I was worried. I thought you'd be home last night. What if you were in a ditch somewhere?"

"Oh, stop being so dramatic. I was with Logan all day."

His eyebrows shoot up.

"All day *and* all night? Whatever could you have been doing?" he says sarcastically.

"Daniel, stop it," I say as I rise up from the couch. I walk on my aching feet into the kitchen to make myself a sandwich. Daniel follows me. "I wanted to spend the day with him yesterday. Is that all right with you?"

"You don't have to justify your actions to me. I just hope you were safe." His look is expectant, as he waits for information. I don't give him any.

"I know I don't. That's why I'm not saying another word." I smile smugly then turn to make my dinner. He stands behind me for a few minutes, probably trying to think of something clever to say. He says nothing more and eventually retreats.

I take a bite of my sandwich and announce that I'm going to bed. All I really want to do is call Logan, so I close my bedroom door and dial.

"Hey," he says. His voice is smooth and sexy. "How was your day?"

"Hey, yourself. My day was long and boring. How was yours?"

"Lonely. Michael just got home, and I've been missing you terribly."

I smile.

"Good. You'd better miss me. Otherwise, I might start to think you don't like me."

He laughs.

"There's no chance of that, baby."

Baby.

I swoon at the endearment.

"So, what are you doing now?" he asks.

"I just finished eating my dinner, then I'm going to shower and go to bed."

"Have you figured out when I can see you again?"

I sigh ruefully.

"I haven't had time to breathe, let alone think. Can I let you know tomorrow?"

"Of course." He sounds vaguely disappointed.

"I'll make it up to you. I promise. Maybe, we can have dinner one night this week. I'll cook."

He snorts.

"Well, that's a given. You don't actually think I could make anything edible, do you?"

I giggle.

"I have no delusions," I say, then giggle again. I hear him sigh into the phone. "How's your blister?"

"It's getting better."

"You've left your legs off, haven't you?"

"If I say no, would you come over and scold me?" He sounds hopeful.

"No, but I might the next time we see each other."

I hear his grin.

"Don't worry. I've been a good boy."

"Good." I yawn unexpectedly. I'm fading fast. "Well, I'm going to go. I'll call you tomorrow."

He sighs again. This time, it sounds sad.

"Okay. Please be careful driving tomorrow, and text me when you can."

"I will," I say. "Good night, Logan."

"Goodnight, Elora. Sweet dreams."

I smile.

"You too. Goodnight," I say, then hang up the phone. I cradle it against my chest, as though it's him, and sigh. I'm content, and the thought of seeing him again makes me smile.

I take my shower, then I snuggle into bed.

For the next three days, my only form of communication with Logan is through phone calls and text messages. My school workload is so heavy, and the pressure to know everything is so great that I feel as though I have no time for a personal life. Logan has been so great about my busy life, and I pray he can hang in there with me as I do my best to balance a life with him, along with everything else.

"You sound sad today," I say softly into my phone. "Is everything okay?"

Logan sighs.

"Yeah. I'm just tired," he says, but I'm not sure he's telling me the whole truth.

"Me too." Our conversation pauses, as I don't think either of us knows what to say to the other. "Logan?"

"What?"

"I'm sorry about not being able to see you this week. It's just that school is consuming all of my time, and—"

"Don't apologize for trying to better yourself," he interrupts. "I know this is a temporary thing. We'll find time to see each other."

"I know, but I wish there was a way to be together more often."

"Well, you could come work for me again."

I laugh.

"You don't need me anymore."

"Oh, but that's where you're wrong," he says, and I can almost hear his grin. I smile shyly, even though he can't see me.

"You know what I mean. Besides, why on earth would you want to pay for a home health aide, when you're not working right now? I'm sure I don't come cheap."

"For you, I'd manage."

I shake my head, amazed at the affection this man has for me.

"I'd better go. I haven't eaten dinner yet, and I still have a few chapters left to read for school tomorrow."

"Okay," he simply says.

"Aren't you going to ask me when we can see each other?"

"No."

I frown.

"Why not?"

"Because I don't want to pressure you all the time. I know that when you find the time, you'll let me know."

Sadness washes over me, and I suddenly feel like I've unintentionally put him on hold. He's resigned himself to the fact that he's at my mercy, in a way, and he's given up fighting for precedence in my life. This worries me. If he can concede control of when we see each other, could he decide, one day, that I'm not worth all the hassle it takes to be with me? Could he eventually get tired of waiting for me, give up on us, and just walk away? I'm sure I'm freaking out for no reason but, still, the thought of him feeling like he's not important to me anymore weighs heavily on my mind.

"I don't mind."

"You don't mind what?"

"You asking to see me. In fact, it makes me feel wanted."

He scoffs.

"You're definitely that," he says, unequivocally.

I smile.

"I want you too. I've missed you this week."

"What do you miss about me?"

I smile again, broader this time.

"Well, for starters, I miss your smirk."

"My smirk?"

"Yes. It's one of my favorite expressions that you make."

"What else?"

"Hmm. I miss your gentle berating, when you tell me I'm making up my own words."

He snorts.

"And you do it often."

"Hey, sometimes there are no words to describe a situation, so making up your own is the only alternative."

"If you say so." He chuckles. "What else?"

"I miss the feel of your hand gently gliding through my hair, just before you look deep into my eyes and kiss me."

"Yeah?"

"Yeah," I breathe, picturing him in my mind. "It's better than any aphrodisiac."

"Really."

"Mm hm," I hum while closing my eyes.

"Well, imagine if I were with you right now—in your room, sitting beside you on your bed." I touch a spot next to me on the mattress and pretend he's here. "Imagine me brushing your hair aside, exposing your neck." I groan and tilt my head to the side to give imaginary him, full access.

"Uh huh." My voice sounds breathy.

"My lips graze the skin on your neck, very gently, giving you goosebumps."

I touch my arm and find actual goosebumps. I smile, my eyes remaining shut.

"Mmm."

"My finger traces a line down the front of your throat, from your chin, down to that little dip at the base of your neck, then continues its way south. Down...down...down." I groan at his words. "Now, I'm leaning in closer. My hand slides through your hair, holding your head in place, as I plant a trail of soft kisses from your collarbone, all the way up to just underneath your ear. I can hear your labored breaths getting more and more shallow as I go. My mouth encases your earlobe, giving it a delicate tug, as I suck gently on it."

"Ohh," I moan, as my breaths match his description. "Then what?" I whisper, my voice is raspy and filled with desire.

"Oh, then my hand travels down, cupping your breast, as my thumb draws circles around your..."

He stops, and exhales seductively.

"Around my what, Logan?" I ask, craving his words as if I can't go on without them. He says nothing more. "Logan?" I open my eyes, slamming back into reality. "Are you there?"

I hear his smile again.

"I'm here." His voice is low and husky.

"Aren't you going to continue?" I squeak, desperate to hear him tell me more.

"Oh, I'm definitely going to continue, but not over the phone."

What?

"Why not?" I whine.

"Well, if I tell you the rest right now, what reason will you have to come over here and see me?"

Ugh!

"Logan Turner! That was a cruel joke!" I'm frustrated at his trickery, and aroused to a point that makes me want to drive straight over there and make him continue—for real this time. I hear his slight chuckle.

"It was no joke, baby. I meant every word. I'd just rather do it in person than over a distance. And, don't think for one moment that I wasn't equally affected by my own words."

For a single, solitary second, I wonder if he has an erection.

"Now. how am I supposed to concentrate on studying?"

"You could come over and let off a little steam…maybe make some of our own."

His offer is tempting, but if I'm going to see him anytime soon, I'll need to get ahead of my school work. I sigh, defeated.

"I'm sorry, I can't."

"I know, and it's okay. I had to try. I don't want you to feel unwanted."

I smile at my own words coming back to me.

"Thank you."

"Anytime. You know that."

We conclude our conversation and after disconnecting the call, I lie across my bed. The radiant heat of my body, which he created, continues to burn long after his words are gone. I press my thighs together, in hopes that it'll relieve some of the sexual tension. I'm flushed, I'm sure, and I wish, more than anything else, that he was here.

15

LOGAN

It's finally Saturday, and Elora has agreed to come over and cook dinner for the two of us. I've given Michael instructions to leave and not come back tonight. He argued with me, complaining that he wanted to bring a date home, but since it's my house, I won. I told him he could have next weekend with his flavor of the month.

The doorbell rings, and my heart leaps with excitement. A quick look in the foyer mirror, then I open the door. She's standing, grocery bags in hand, on the porch in the dimly lit, dusky light of the evening and smiling from ear to ear. I exhale my relief, as if I'd been holding in a breath for the last six days. My hungry eyes sweep over her perfect figure and in true male form, I picture exactly how I'd like this evening to go.

"My God, you look beautiful," I say, taking the bags from her, then grabbing her hand and dragging her inside. I drop the bags where I stand, and my arms instinctively wrap around her, hoping upon hope that they never have to let her go again.

"I've missed you too—so much. I couldn't wait to get done with my last textbook. I drove straight here. I think I ran a few red lights en route." Her shy giggle fills my chest with a warmth only she could produce.

With my hand still entwined with hers, I lead her farther into the house. Then, turning her to face me, I release her hand and tenderly glide both hands into her hair. I hold her face in my hands, my thumbs caress her cheeks, as I memorize each freckle and line. It's as if I haven't seen her in a decade. Without another word, I close the gap between us and press my lips against hers. She reciprocates by parting her lips, allowing our tongues to touch. I feel her arms engulf me, as she pulls me into her. I moan against her mouth; desire explodes, and all I can think of is continuing our phone call in real time. But. I don't want her to think that's all she came here for, so I break off our kiss, followed by a quicker, less sensuous, peck on the lips.

"Well, hello to you too," she says with a smirk. Now, I see why she likes it when *I* smirk.

"Mmm. I'm so glad you're here."

She grins.

"I'm glad I'm here too." She glances down at my legs. "Can I assume at the fact that you're wearing your prosthetics means your blister is gone?"

I follow her line of sight, then look back at her.

"Yes. Well, almost. I went to have an adjustment made, and he padded the area until it heals up completely."

"That's wonderful. I know how much you hate being less mobile," she says with a grin. God, I've missed that face. I take one last look at my girl, then retrieve the grocery bags from the floor. "Hey, I like where you put our sculpture," she says as she looks into the living room.

"*Our* sculpture? If I recall, you didn't want to buy it."

"I wouldn't necessarily say that's true, but I'm glad you did. It looks great in here."

"I think so too. It makes me think of you, especially when you're not here."

"Well, I'm glad to see I can so easily be replaced," she says with a smirk, as she walks back into the kitchen.

I lean in and kiss her cheek.

"Never," I whisper, then wink. "So, tell me, what are we cooking tonight?"

She raises an eyebrow.

"We?"

"Yes, *we*. I'm not going to invite you over here to cook and serve me. I want to help. Besides, maybe I'll learn how make something other than breakfast."

She shrugs.

"Okay. Let's get started then."

We unpack the food and assemble the necessary cooking utensils. She opens cabinets and drawers, and I watch, with an amused expression, her grace.

"I wanted to cook you a manly dish today, so I decided on red meat. I'm making…" She clears her throat. "I mean, *we're* making Swiss steak. I hope that's okay."

"That sounds great. Although, I'd eat anything you decided to prepare."

I give her genuine smile because it's true. She's a wonderful cook.

"Okay, but it takes a while to cook. I've already browned the meat, but it'll have to simmer for an hour and a half."

"What will we do to fill that time?" I raise my eyebrows suggestively, and she playfully swats my arm.

"Down, boy," she says, but her indignant expression gives way to a wink. "Here, Romeo, start chopping this onion." She hands me a knife and cutting board, and I get to work.

After adding the rest of the ingredients, Elora covers the would-be meal with a lid, then wipes her hands on a towel.

"There. Now, we wait."

I wrap my arms around her waist and pull her closer. Her arms automatically snake around my neck, while her fingers twist in my hair at the back of my head.

"So, now what do we do?"

"We could watch some TV." I silently shake my head. "How about playing chess?" I wrinkle my nose. I *do not* want to play chess with this woman, unless it's strip chess. I shake my head again then walk her backwards toward the couch. She giggles, knowing exactly what I have in mind.

I lower her body down onto the couch, then follow, with one knee between hers and the other foot on the floor. My arms brace myself above her as to not sink all my weight on top of her. Her hair splays out on the cushion. She looks beautiful. I pause to drink in this site.

"What are you waiting for?" she asks.

"I'm just thinking about how lucky I am." She rolls her eyes. "No, I mean it."

I don't want to gush, but I can't think of a single person I'd rather be with in this way than her. She probably has no idea how much I want her and need her in my life. I can never lose her. I can never lose this.

Bending down slightly, I kiss her. I back off, but repeat this move twice more. each time letting my lips linger against hers a little longer. She claws at my back in an attempt to pull me down onto her, but I shake my head. Not yet. I don't want the oven timer to interrupt what could be a spectacular night. I do it once more and in a vain attempt to foil my plans, she pulls down hard, bumping my arm as she does. But, instead of falling on top of her, my elbow buckles, sending me crashing onto the floor beside the couch. She gasps loudly and looks over the edge to see me lying flat on my back.

"Logan! Are you okay?" Her worried tone gives me an idea.

I lie as still as I can with my eyes closed. She rushes to my side. Her eyes sweep over my body, most likely in a panic about what to do.

"Logan," she says frantically as she shakes me. "Please! Open your eyes!" Strands of her hair tickle my face as she lowers her ear to listen for breaths. It's hard to keep a straight face, when all I want to do is grab her face and kiss her. I decide to let her off the hook, and with my eyes still closed, I mumble. She listens intently.

"What are you going to do, nurse Foster? I'm unconscious and lying on the floor."

She scoffs.

"Are you kidding me? You're joking?"

She's angry.

"I'm helping you study. Now, what do you do?" She says nothing, so I crack open one eyelid to view her kneeling beside me with her arms crossed in front of her chest. I prompt her again. "Well?"

"I let you lie there because no one *dies* from falling off a couch," she says with irritation in her voice.

I open both eyes and smirk at her. She rolls her eyes and looks away.

"Oh, come on. I'm just trying to be playful...*and* help you study at the same time."

She looks at me with ill-concealed annoyance.

"I thought you hit your head or something." I laugh. "It's not funny!"

She looks away again, and I realize I might have taken my idea a little too far. I place my hand on her knee.

"I'm sorry. I didn't mean to scare you. Really." She sticks out her bottom lip and blows a rogue piece of hair upward. I lean up onto my elbow and touch her chin. She turns her head to look at me. "*I'm sorry*", I mouth, then give her my best apologetic look. She rolls her eyes again but this time, it's accompanied by a small smile.

"You're an ass. You know that?"

I nod.

"I *do* know that. And, now, my secret is out."

She shoots me a sideways glance and snorts.

"It's not such a secret. I've known it for some time now," she says dryly.

I shrug.

"And, just think, I'm *your* ass." My exaggerated smile is all it takes for her to forgive me. She pushes me down, off my elbows, straddles me, then pins my arms on either side of my head. Her hair, which is loose, falls down on either side of my face, and we're suddenly in our own tunnel.

"I've got you pinned. What are *you* going to do?"

"I'm going to enjoy it," I say with a smug grin. Her mouth twists as an idea pops into her gorgeous head. She leans down, kissing me once, before pulling back to examine my expression. I've not seen the dominant side of her. I kind of like it. She bows again, kissing me again, but this time she lets go of my hands. She leans on her elbows, on either side of my head, and deepens the kiss. I wrap my arms around her tightly, one hand at the small of her back, and the other winds into her hair. I've successfully anchored her to me, as I match her, move for seductive move. She shifts slightly as the crotch of my pants grows tighter, which only fuels my desire for her. But, I'm reminded of our limited time, so I take back control of the situation.

In one motion, I grab onto her upper arms and flip her over, so that she's lying on the bottom once again. She squeals and giggles at the sudden movement but doesn't fight it. She smiles up at me, and with hooded eyes, I smile back.

"Stay the night with me."

Her eyes widen.

"I can't. I have a lot of studying to do."

"Do it here."

"My books are at home."

I shrug.

"We'll go get them."

She contemplates my suggestion.

"Do you really think much studying will get done?" She raises one eyebrow as if in doubt.

"I'll make sure you get some work done. Please? I don't know when I'll see you next, and I'm dying here."

She grins and rolls her eyes.

"You're not dying. And, even if you were, I'm a nurse, remember? I know CPR."

"And, I'd be more than willing to let you practice your skills on me."

She laughs.

"Therein lies the problem. As I said, not much studying would get done."

"Please?" I'm hoping my sincere expression is enough to seal the deal. It takes her a minute, but she finally agrees. I'm grinning like a loon. "Yes!"

"*But,* I do need to study, understand?" I nod in an exaggerated manner. "I mean it. If you want to see me before I graduate, you'll agree to my demands."

"You *are* that: very demanding," I say in jest. She smiles and rolls her eyes again.

"I could say the same about you."

I lean down, kissing her one more time, then swing my leg over, releasing her. She sits up as I stand, and I offer her my hand. She takes it and stands.

"Do you want to go now, or after dinner?"

"Afterward. I'd hate to burn our meal."

I nod in agreement, then we head to the kitchen to give it a stir.

"You know, Daniel might be home. Are you sure you're ready for the brotherly interrogation?" she asks, as she drives us toward her apartment.

"I'll be fine. I'm a soldier, remember? I've been in worse situations."

"I don't know. He can be relentless sometimes."

"I'm sure you'll protect me," I say with a smile.

She snorts as she gives me a sideways glance.

"You're going to need all the help you can get."

She pulls into the parking lot of her apartment complex. The buildings are set at ninety degree angles from each other, with a swimming pool off in one corner. She puts the car in park, then sits back and sighs.

"What's wrong?" I ask, easily detecting the stress in her posture.

"My brother has been…behaving sort of strange lately." She turns to face me. "Please don't take anything he might say to you the wrong way. He means well, and he's just trying to protect me."

"Elora, seriously, I can handle him. He's not the first difficult personality I've had to deal with in my life." I place a reassuring hand on her knee. "I'll be fine. And, who knows, maybe he'll surprise you."

She stares blankly at me for a moment then shrugs. We exit the car and walk to her apartment hand in hand. As we approach the entrance, she turns to me. She opens her mouth, then closes it, twice. Finally, she gives up on whatever last minute advice she wanted to give me and opens the door.

Her apartment is small. The kitchen is off to the left, and her dining room/living room combination is straight ahead. I can see a hallway leading to bedrooms to my right. The décor is basic and neutral, but feminine. She walks in first, searching the rooms for her brother, no doubt. She hangs her purse on a hook as I shut the door behind me.

"Nice place."

"Thanks. It's kind of sparse, but I've got everything I need. It's basically a place to lay my head," she says. "Would you like something to drink? I know we're not going to be here long, but…" she trails off.

"No, thank you. I'm fine."

"Okay then, I'll just gather a few things, and we'll be off."

"Can I see your bedroom?"

She seems nervous, but reluctantly agrees. I follow her into a room at the end of the hallway.

"Well, here it is. It's not much but—"

"Hey," I interrupt. "Stop making excuses for the way your place looks. I'm not judging you. It's a great place. You should be proud."

"I know. It's just…not as nice as your house. It's small and cramped and some days, it looks as if a tornado hit." She shrugs. "But, it's home."

I tenderly touch her cheek.

"It's a great place. Stop worrying what I think. Okay?" She gives me a small smile then nods. "Now, let's get your stuff and get back to what we started." She pins me with her best scolding look. "I meant to study. Get your mind out of the gutter, Miss Foster."

She laughs, gathers her things, shoves them in a nearby backpack, then we exit the room. We're just about out of the hall, when she bumps, almost literally, into a tall man, who I assume is her brother, Daniel. I hear her surprised gasp, as she stops just short of him.

"Hi. We were just leaving." She tries to skirt past him, but he stands his ground at the mouth of the hall.

"Aren't you going to introduce me to your friend?" He crosses his arms in front of his chest as a slight frown forms on his face.

"Of course. Daniel, this is Logan. Logan, this is my brother, Daniel."

I extend my hand toward him.

"Hi, Daniel. It's nice to finally meet you. I've heard a lot about you."

Daniel looks down at my hand then back up at me. His arms stay crossed at his chest.

"I've heard a lot about you too." He icy gaze turns to Elora, and she glares at him.

"We're leaving now." She grabs a hold of my wrist and pulls me toward the door.

Daniel's body turns to watch us.

"So soon? Why are you in such a hurry, and why do you have a backpack? Planning a night hike?"

Elora walks toward him, stopping inches from his tall frame. She fists her hands on her hips and looks directly up at him.

"Back off, now," she insists. "I don't know where this attitude came from, but get rid of it. I don't need, nor do I want, your opinions on where I go, or who I date. If I recall, I've never chastised you for any of your *fine choices*." She draws quotes in the air with her fingers.

His eyes narrow.

"My *choices* have never put my job in jeopardy. I've never dated my boss for that matter either."

"He's not my boss, Daniel. I've told you that. He hasn't been my boss for—"

"For at least a few weeks now, huh?" he snarls.

It's clear he's been drinking. I need to get her out of here. I place my hand on her shoulder.

"Come on. Let's go." Daniel looks at me, and I see the fury in his eyes as he spies my hand on his sister.

"No. He has no right to act this way," she says, still staring at him. "We're a couple, and I have no intention of that changing anytime soon, so get used to it," she tells him.

Then, his stance changes slightly, becoming more erect, and he pulls his shoulders back. My instincts kick in, and I assess this as a threat. With one arm, I hook Elora and push her behind me, stepping forward between her and her brother. If he's going to do something, let it be to me.

"That's enough. We're leaving, before you do something you might regret," I say, looking him straight in the eyes. His nostrils flare, as do his eyes, and I can smell beer on his breath.

"What do you think you're going to do? You've got no legs." He snickers.

"Daniel!" Elora shouts. He looks at her for a second, then his bloodshot eyes fall back on me.

"Don't you worry about me. I can handle whatever I have to." I, too, stand up straighter and puff my chest out a bit.

"This is ridiculous," she says, as she tries to reposition herself in front of me. But, my arm remains stock still, holding her back, protecting her.

Daniel takes a step back and scoffs.

"Whatever. Have your little affair, Elora. And, when you lose your job *and* your nursing license, *and* you get sued, don't say I didn't warn you." He takes one last look at the both of us then retreats into the kitchen. My arm stays put, until he disappears behind the wall. When I know he's not going to do anything stupid, I lower my arm and glance back at her.

"Are you okay?"

"Yes. No. I don't know," she hisses. "Let's just get out of here."

She heads for the door, without looking back.

The ride back to my place is mostly silent. My hand rests on her knee as a reminder to stay calm, even though I can tell she's still enraged.

"Do you want to talk about it?" She blows out a sharp breath through her nose, then shakes her head. "Okay. I'll give you all the time you need." I watch as her shoulders relax, and I hope it's a sign that she's trying to calm down. It only takes her a few more minutes before she opens up.

"I'm sorry about that. He was out of line."

I shrug.

"It's okay. No harm done."

She glances over at me.

"You're kidding, right? Did you hear him? Did you hear what he said to you? It's appalling to say the least. He shouldn't have said that. If you weren't standing in between us, I would've punched him."

"He probably won't even remember meeting me. He'd been drinking."

She looks over at me again, then back at the road.

"Yeah, he drinks a bit more lately than he used to."

I want to press her and tell her he might have a problem but ultimately, I stay silent and let her deal with him in her own way.

We get back to my house, and I gesture toward the couch.

"Why don't you make yourself comfortable. I'll make us some tea and grab a snack. We'll study first, then do whatever else later." My small, sincere smile let's her know I have no intention of seducing her tonight. Daniel made sure to put a damper on those plans. I'm okay with that though. I want to be there for her, no matter what the situation. She nods sadly and sits on the floor in front of the couch. She leans her back against it, then unpacks her books, spreading them along the floor in front of her, and begins.

"Thank you," she says softly, "for helping me study…and for being so understanding with Daniel. He gets out of hand sometimes," she says, as she puts her books back into her bag.

I brush my knuckles against her cheek, and she leans into my touch.

"It's fine. Really. You can't control the actions of someone else."

"I know, but it hurt me to hear him talk about you like that. To say you don't have legs was a cruel thing to say, and…"

I put my arm around her, pulling her into my side.

"He spoke the truth," I say, and she lifts her head from my shoulder, a little shocked by my statement. "What? It's true. I have no legs. I'm not ashamed. *You* taught me that." I smile and touch the end of her perfectly shaped nose. "People are going to say whatever they say, and there's not a damn thing anyone can do about it." A look of deep thought crosses her face. "Can I ask you something?"

She nods.

"Of course."

"When he gets like that, does he hurt you?"

Her eyes widen significantly.

"No, not at all. He'd never hurt me, not intentionally anyway." She looks up through her lashes. "Is that why you shielded me? Because you thought he might hurt me?" I nod gravely, and she looks down.

Then, her arms wrap tightly around me. "Thank you. It felt good, even if there was no real danger."

"I'd do again and again for you, Elora." I pause to collect my scattered thoughts. "I..." I take a deep breath. "I love you." She looks at me abruptly, and I scan her face, trying to gauge her reaction.

"You do?" I nod; a small smile appears on my face where, just an hour ago, rage was brewing. "I love you too," she says, barely above a whisper. "I think I have for a while now. I was just too afraid to admit it."

Her innocent expression begs me to kiss her, so I take her chin in my hand, lower my mouth, and gently press my lips to hers. It's not a desperate kiss, nor is it the kind of kiss that turns into something else. It's the kind of kiss that communicates all the emotions that two people, who have fallen in love, need to convey to one another. I cup her face in my hand and stare into her guileless eyes.

"I will protect you at all costs. Nothing bad will happen as long as I'm with you. You are my light, my love, my Elora, and I love you." I kiss her again, then we meld together as we sit in silence, cocooned around each other.

꒰

As I pull back the covers on my queen size bed, she emerges from the bathroom dressed in her pajamas. They suit her perfectly, with black and white penguins scattered all over her full length pants. I smile at how adorable she looks in them. She sees my reaction, looks down at herself, and giggles softly. She shrugs at her child-like clothing, while I shake my head in awe of the woman I confessed to love.

"Which side would you like to lie on?" I ask.

"I don't care. Whichever one you don't want to."

"Okay then, I'll take the outside. That way, if zombies attack, I'll get bitten first."

She laughs loudly.

"Great. I'll be forced to watch, then you'll be turned into one, and I'll really be screwed."

I laugh loudly.

"Come on. Climb in," I say, and she does.

After removing my prosthetic legs, I crawl in bed next to her. I gesture for her to roll onto her side, then spoon her—my front to her back. With my arm draped over her, I pull her into me. Within minutes, we're both fast asleep.

16

ELORA

My eyes flutter open. Streaks of the morning sun shine in, filtered by the semi-sheer curtains. I feel the weight of Logan's arm around me as I attempt to stretch. I smile and lace my fingers through his relaxed hand. Clearly, he's still asleep. Content, I yawn, but do my best not to wake him up. We were both up late. I sigh and recall the events of last night. We admitted we love each other. That's huge. I'm not sure what comes next for us, but I know we're on the right path.

Then, I remember Daniel's rant and the terrible things he said. I'm still so angry. I don't know what I'll say to him, but he's going to apologize to Logan, whether he wants to or not. What the hell is his problem anyway? He's been binge drinking more and more these days.

Logan stirs, so I freeze, hoping he stays asleep. He tightens his grip on me, pulling me closer to his body, and mumbles something. I have to cover my mouth to keep from giggling.

"Don't go," he says, as he buries his face into the back of my neck. His stubble scratches me a bit, but then he stills. I can feel his face contort as he continues to talk. "Help," he says. I think he's having a bad dream. "*No.*" His voice is louder this time. Releasing me, he reaches down. I think he's grabbing at the air where his legs used to be. Gingerly, I turn around to face him. His face is scrunched up as if he's in agony, and I know what it's about. My heart breaks for him, and I feel the need to rescue him from his nightmare.

"Logan," I say as I shake him gently. "Logan, wake up. It's just a dream." He winces and begins to thrash about. His cries are garbled, as he fights a battle he's already won in real life. My expression goes from concern to panic, as I try to wake him, before his dream goes too far. "Logan!" I shout, and he stills. With sweat dripping from his brow, he opens his eyes. He gazes at the ceiling, in an obvious attempt to regain consciousness. He then looks at me, and his expression softens. I smile timidly, unsure of his mood after this bout. He rubs his eyes, and a small smile appears on his face.

"Hey," he says.

"Hey," I reply.

"Did you sleep well?"

"Yes, I did. I might ask the same of you."

"I slept like a rock." He yawns and stretches, pulling at the covers to adjust them.

"Are you okay?"

His brow furrows.

"Why wouldn't I be?"

"You were having a dream—a nightmare. I'm guessing it was about your accident."

He frowns.

"I don't remember."

"Really? I woke you up from it just a second ago. It seemed pretty violent. You were thrashing around quite a bit."

He shakes his head adamantly.

"Nope. No recollection."

I eye him suspiciously.

"Hm."

"What?"

"It just seems odd, that's all."

"Do you remember all of your dreams?"

"No."

"Then, why is it odd that I don't either?"

I shrug, wondering if he knows, but doesn't want to talk about it. I decide to let it go for now.

"So, what do you want to do today?" he asks, effectively changing the subject.

"I'm not sure, but whatever it is, it'll have to be early in the day. I need to be home before dinner."

"Do you have to go so soon?"

"Yes," I say, as I sit up and dangle my legs off the side of the bed. My back is to him, but I feel his weight shift behind me. I no sooner notice, when two arms engulf me around the waist, pulling backward onto the bed. I screech and giggle, and before I know it, he's on top of me.

"You're not going anywhere," he declares, then he starts to tickle me.

I'm laughing, and wiggling, and trying to drag in precious breaths. And, although I have a definite two limb advantage, he's got me pinned down by my arms and is looking at me, triumphant.

"You can't leave now." He gives me his best evil laugh, then bends down to bury his face in my neck. I'm thinking he's going to kiss me there but, instead, he blows a raspberry so loud that I clamp my chin to my shoulder, holding him there until he stops.

"You win!" I exclaim, and after a few more seconds of torture, he relents.

Still holding himself up off me, he greets me with a smile.

"You look beautiful in the morning. I only wish I could see you this way every day."

"Well, I don't know about every day, but it's a distinct possibility on the weekends."

"I'll take whatever I can get." He kisses my forehead, then climbs back off. "Come on. Let's make breakfast."

After brushing our teeth and starting the coffee pot, we begin making breakfast. Pancakes are on the menu, alongside bacon and eggs. He pours two glasses of juice, then we sit down to devour our mini feast.

"So, now that we've established that we love each other, and that neither of us is going anywhere, I need to ask you a question that's been rolling around my head for some time."

"Ask away. I'm an open book to you," he says.

I take a deep breath, then exhale, to shake any nerves I have out of my body.

"Okay. Answer as much as you're comfortable with."

His fork freezes in midair, and he looks apprehensive.

"Okay…"

"I want you to tell me about your accident."

I jump, as the fork he was holding drops and hits the plate. His flustered appearance makes it very apparent that he doesn't like this question.

"Why do you want to know about that?" He's guarded.

I shrug.

"I don't know. You've never really said much about it, and I've always wondered."

He takes a long sip of his orange juice, then puts the glass down, but says nothing.

I've upset him.

"You don't have to answer. I'm sor—"

"No, it's fine. You have a right to know. I'm just not comfortable talking about it, you know? It sort of brings it all back to me. It makes me relive it all over again." He fidgets in his chair, clearly contemplating his words, but continues, despite feeling uneasy. "It was a motorcycle accident. I was on my bike but only remember parts of it. I remember waking up screaming in pain as two make-shift tourniquets were being placed around both my thighs, in an attempt to stop me from bleeding out."

"Ryan," I mutter, more to myself than to him.

"Yes, it was Ryan. Thank God he was behind me. I found out later that one of my legs was ripped off on impact. The other was so badly broken that they had no choice but to amputate it."

I wince and cover my mouth, horrified and unable to imagine the amount of pain he must've been in.

"Oh, my God. That's awful."

"Yeah. That was the most painful thing I've ever had to endure. It's an agony you can only imagine." His face contorts, and I feel guilty for wanting him to continue. "I can still smell certain things. The odor of gasoline and the smell of burning rubber really stand out clearly. I also remember a revved engine. I think it might've been Ryan's. Anyway, I had several, life threatening injuries, which landed me in the hospital for months. I was in a coma for most of it, but after finding out what I'd lost, I'd wished that Ryan had never found me that day." He bows his head, most likely ashamed of the way he thought at that time. I place my hand over his, reassuring him that I understand. He turns his hand over, letting our fingers intertwine, and squeezes my hand gently. "It was a long time ago. It's over now, and I'm glad I didn't die that day—or I never would've met you." He raises our joined hands to his lips and kisses the back of mine.

"Thank you for telling me. I know it was hard to talk about."

"I don't want to hide anything from you. From now on, if you want to know something, all you need to do is ask." He winks at me, then releases my hand, and resumes eating his breakfast.

I'm reeling from his version of the events, and I'm finding it hard to eat. But because I don't want him to think he can't talk freely about it, I manage to finish most of my food.

Suddenly, the phone rings.

"Who is calling me on a Sunday morning?" he says, a little irritated having been interrupted. I shrug as he answers. "Hello?"

I listen intently to his end of the call.

"Yes, good morning to you too, mother," he says in an exasperated tone.

He waits as she speaks.

"I'm not sure we'll have time today. Elora and I are just finishing breakfast, and she has things to do later. Can we make it another time?"

He listens again, rolling his eyes no less than two or three times in such a short period of time.

"Okay, fine, mother. We'll come, but just for a little while. Like I said, her time is limited today… Okay, fine. Bye."

He hangs up the phone, then pushes his hand roughly through his hair. Finally, he looks at me.

"My mother has requested the honor of our presence at her house for lunch today. I tried to get out of it, but she insisted. And, believe me when I say, you don't say *no* to my mother."

I giggle as he struggles to hide his frustration regarding his mom. I find it adorable that he still listens to her.

"I'd love to go," I say. "Is what I'm wearing acceptable?"

"Baby, you could be wearing a burlap sack, and I'd still drool over you."

I laugh.

"I mean to meet your mother. I want to make a good first impression."

The almost pained expression that washes over his face concerns me instantly.

"Don't take this the wrong way, but my mother has never been a fan of anyone I've dated. It takes a while for her to get used to the idea that her baby boy isn't going to be carried off by some barracuda in a pair of high heels—especially since my accident. So, don't expect her to be welcoming. Hell, I'd be shocked if she even acknowledges you're in the same room."

My face falls. He sees my dismay and reaches out, covering my hand with his to comfort me.

"Sounds like a great time," I say sarcastically, lifting the upper corner of my lip.

"Don't worry. I won't leave your side. And, if she gets the least bit out of line, I'll speak up, and we'll leave. I'm not going to let her scare you off," he says then kisses my temple.

As we pull into the large, circular driveway of the mansion-like home belonging to Mr. and Mrs. Ross, I find that my palms have suddenly become sweaty, and my mouth is dry as a bone. How ironic. Too bad it wasn't the other way around. I'm not sure where to park my car, until I see a man, dressed in a tuxedo type suit, staring at me as he walks toward us.

"That's Malcolm. He's one of the wait staff. He also parks the guest's cars," Logan says, by way of explanation.

"You didn't tell me your parents are rich," I reprimand him for leaving that bit of information out. I glance down at my attire. Is this good enough to greet the wealthy parents of my new boyfriend, who used to be my boss, not so long ago? I suddenly feel *way* out of my league.

"Stop worrying about how you look. You're as gorgeous as ever. If nothing else, you'll get my stepdad's approval. Now, let's get this over with." Malcolm opens my door, and I step out.

"Hello," I say.

"Good afternoon, ma'am," he says dryly.

"Hi, Malcolm," Logan says casually, as if he gets his car parked everyday by a man in a three-piece suit.

"Welcome, Sir," Malcolm replies, then gets into the driver's seat and takes off around the side of the house.

"Are you ready?" Logan asks, taking my hand in his. I must look like a deer caught in the headlights because he chuckles quietly and kisses my forehead. "You'll be fine. You'll see." And, we walk up the massive steps up to the front door.

The doorbell sounds like something you'd hear at church on Sunday morning, and the huge, ornately carved double doors are at least nine feet tall. I'm awestruck, staring at the anomaly, when another man, dressed the same as the first, opens the large doors.

"Hey, Jeffery," Logan says. "How're they hangin'?"

"Very well, Sir. Thank you for asking."

His dry reply makes me wish I'd gone home instead of coming here. Sensing my unease, Logan leans over and whispers in my ear.

"Jeffery is paid to be boring. That's why I try to greet him in a fun way. Pay no attention to him. He's actually a very nice guy."

"Heh," I whimper nervously, which makes Logan laugh.

"Come on. It's time to meet the family."

My vision of what this palace would look like from the inside is pretty much spot on. There's a winding, formal staircase, marble flooring, and carefully hung masterpieces, which line the hallway leading from the two-story foyer into the back of the house. As I take in my surroundings, I'm getting more apprehensive by the second. I feel Logan's hand squeeze mine, and I turn my head to see his broad grin.

"Impressive, eh?" My wide-eyed nod makes him laugh. "You'll get used to it."

"Did you grow up here?" I'm thoroughly in awe. I had no idea he came from money.

"No. My mom remarried a few years back, when I was seventeen. All this," He waves a hand around the room, "is a result of that." I blink a few times, and he chuckles. "Come on. Let's find my parents."

He drags me down the hallway and into the kitchen, where someone, who I'm guessing is also staff, is stirring a pot. She turns toward us as we walk into the room.

"Mr. Turner!" the gray haired woman says affectionately, as she wipes her hands on her apron. "It's so nice to see you again. And, who is this lovely, young lady?"

"Eleanor, please, just call me Logan. This is my girlfriend, Elora. Elora, meet the finest chef on the planet, aside from you, of course. Her name's Eleanor, and she can cook anything you want."

"Oh, you're always going on like that," she says, then turns to me. "He's just being polite, dear. It's so very nice to meet you," she says with a smile.

I giggle.

"Likewise," I say.

"Eleanor, where are my mother and Charles?"

"Your stepfather is sitting in the garden, and your mother should be coming down the stairs any minute now."

"Thank you," he says, then he leads me toward the backyard.

Logan opens the French doors to a burst of sunshine. There, on the patio, sits a man dressed casually and leafing through the Sunday paper. He looks up as we approach.

"Logan. It's wonderful to see you, son." The man rises to greet Logan with a polite hug and pat on the back. His eyes then land on me, and I smile shyly. "And, who do we have here?" He breaks his hold on Logan and takes a step in my direction.

"Charles, this is Elora—my girlfriend."

Charles looks back at Logan, a little shocked, I think.

Didn't he mention me?

"What a beautiful name for a beautiful girl," he says while shaking my hand, I think I'm blushing

"Thank you, Sir. It's lovely to meet you."

"What manners she has, Logan." He brings his attention back to me. "I'm so happy to meet you, young lady." He lets go of my hand, and Logan resumes holding it.

"Where's mom?"

"She'll be along. You know her, she loves to make an entrance."

"What's this you're saying about me, Charles?" a voice from behind us says.

I turn to see a middle aged woman, dressed to the nines, posing in the doorway of the entrance to the house. Logan releases me again to kiss his mother on both cheeks.

"Hello, Mother. You look beautiful today," he says to her. She smiles politely and waves him off, and I can't help but feel like this greeting has been ingrained in him for decades.

"You're too kind, sweetheart." Then, she glances in my direction. "And, who is this lovely creature?" She steps down onto the stone patio and walks toward me, but looks to Logan for an explanation. Logan steps forward, snaking his arm around my waist.

"Mother, I'd like you to meet my girlfriend, Elora. This is my mom, Evelyn."

Her expression is polite although, as I examine it closer, I'd say it's more forced than natural. I extend my hand, and she takes it, shaking it gently.

"It's very nice to finally meet you. Logan has told me a lot about you," I say, hoping to make a good impression.

"Has he now? I hope it was all good." She glances briefly at her son, and his exasperated look tells me a lot about their relationship.

Just then, Eleanor peeks her head outside from the kitchen.

"Lunch is ready," she says, then retreats back inside to serve it.

Evelyn turns to walk in first, followed by me, then Logan and his stepfather. We gather around the lavishly decorated, dining table. Charles sits at the head with his wife on his right. Logan and I sit opposite her, with me closest to Charles.

I look down at the place setting before me. There are more forks than I know what to do with. I can feel my heart picking up speed as I try to reason out which one to use first. I don't want to screw this up. Sensing my dismay, Logan leans in.

"You use them from the outside, in," Logan whispers in my ear, then he kisses me tenderly on the cheek. I nod, thankful for his advice.

"Thanks," I whisper back.

"What are you two whispering about?" Evelyn asks.

Logan clears his throat.

"I was just telling Elora how the color of her dress complements the subtle hues of her exquisite blue eyes."

Huh?

I chuckle nervously at his sentiment.

"Well, she *is* lovely. Isn't she?" his mother says, but I can't help but notice her expression doesn't match her words.

"Yes, she sure is." Logan grins at me and places his hand on my knee. And I know he, whole heartedly, believes that.

The wait staff comes in and places plates in front of us. The appetizer is a salad with mixed greens covered in a light, Italian dressing. Under the advisement of Logan, I pick up the fork to the far left of the plate. He nods his approval, and we dig in.

"So, Elora, what do you do for a living?" Charles asks.

I look at Logan nervously.

"Um, I'm a home health aide." My voice is quiet.

"She's also studying to be a nurse," Logan chimes in. I look at him, and he's smiling proudly.

Charles's eyebrows shoot up.

"Wow! Very good. You have high aspirations. I like that," he says with a genuine smile, which makes me relax a little. He seems nice.

"Thank you," I say softly.

"She's the one who took care of me," Logan speaks up again. "She encouraged me to get my prosthetic legs too." He gazes at me lovingly.

My eyes grow wide, and I smack him under the table. Should he have said that? What do they think of me, now that they know I'm basically dating my boss? I swallow and suddenly, I feel sick.

"Did she now? Isn't that considered unethical?" his mother says in a snarky voice. Logan gives his mom a back-off stare.

"No, in fact, it isn't, *Mother*. It just so happens that she quit working for me long before we started this relationship, if you must know." He's getting angry, so I cover his hand with mine.

"I see," she replies, then lifts her glass and sips her wine.

"Evelyn," her husband says in warning.

A scolding look passes between them and suddenly, the room feels too warm.

"I would never have started dating him as long as he was my patient," I say to try to explain my actions.

"Mm," she simply says.

The next course is served, and the conversation changes to local news, but I remain silent for the rest of the meal. Every so often, I smile and nod, just to make it seem as though I'm a part of it. The truth is, I can't wait to leave.

After the dessert, which is a very fancy, chocolate mousse, Logan leads me out by the garden and toward the lake. The sun reflects against the tiny ripples of the water as a duck skims across the surface, breaking the pattern. Leading me toward a bench, he gestures for me to sit.

"So, that went well," he says, then looks at me. My expression disagrees, and he laughs. "Don't be so worried. They like you."

"What planet were you just on? Your mother hates me. She watched me the entire time with daggers shooting out of her eyes." He grins broadly. "What's so funny?"

"You're so cute when you're upset."

"*What?*"

He reaches up, brushing a strand of hair from my face.

"Look, it could've gone worse. Believe me, I know. You were fine. My stepdad is really impressed."

I roll my eyes.

"This has been a nightmare," I say, covering my face. I feel Logan's arms wrap around me, and he kisses the side of my head.

"Do you want to go?"

I look up at his face. Do I? I want to, but only if he wants to. I shrug and sigh.

"I'll manage. Just stop telling them about how we met. It looked bad, and it embarrassed me."

"Okay. I won't say another word."

I nod then, after a few more minutes of peace, we stand and walk back toward the house. Upon returning, Logan's mother approaches us.

"Excuse me, dear, but I'd like to have a word with my son," she says.

"Of course." I smile and nod, but I can't shake the feeling that her conversation with him might just be about me. Logan turns to me and rolls his eyes.

"I'll be right back."

I stand in the kitchen feeling all kinds of awkward, until Eleanor walks up beside me.

"Would you like some tea, dear?" she says with a warm smile.

"I'd love some. Thank you." She nods and turns toward the stove. "Can I help?"

She scoffs.

"No, ma'am. It's my job to serve you. Just sit right here while I get it ready," she insists, while pointing to a stool at the breakfast bar. I nod and sit, and I do as I'm told, while watching helplessly, as she starts the water.

"How long have you worked for the Ross family?" I ask.

"Since he and Mrs. Ross got married, about a decade or so ago, I suppose. I try not to keep track," she says with a smile.

"They seem like nice enough people." My expression must be one of apprehension because she comes to stand at the counter in front of me, then she looks around before speaking.

"Now, don't you go worrying about Mrs. Ross. She can seem a little hard to get to know but after a while, she'll warm up to you." She winks. I nod, letting her know I heard her, though I'm not sure I'm convinced. Our heads swing over to where Logan and his mother are speaking, at the sound of Logan's raised voice. I then hear his mother's hushed voice, although I can't make out what she's saying. I sigh, ruefully, and Eleanor shrugs.

When the two reappear, Logan's face is slightly flushed. His mood seems a bit agitated, and his mother doesn't look at either of us before going back out to the garden. A look passes between Logan and me, but his expression tells me it's nothing, and he stands by the stool next to mine.

"We should go," he says, and I nod. He then summons his step father to let him know we're leaving.

Finally.

"It was so nice to meet you. Please come back again soon. I'm thrilled to see Logan so happy." Charles pulls back and smiles at me, and I know he approves.

"Thank you. I really care deeply for him. And, thanks for having me. It was a pleasure meeting you."

Logan offers Charles his hand, and his returning hug warms my heart. I can tell he has nothing but love and respect for his stepdad. His mother approaches next.

"You should come around more often, dear. I miss seeing you," she says while giving Logan a formal embrace. She peeks over at me. "And, feel free to bring your date too." He releases her.

"My *girlfriend*, Mother. She's my girlfriend," Logan reminds her.

"Uh, yes. That's what I meant." She chuckles awkwardly at her faux pas.

"Well, goodbye everyone. Thank you for lunch. It was delicious," Logan says, as he nods his head toward Eleanor. Her answering grin makes him smile.

We wave goodbye as Logan opens my door, then closes it, and gets in on the passenger side. I glance over at him.

"Is everything all right?"

"Yes, it's fine. Nothing to be concerned about," he says then looks as though he's trying to change the subject. "I really need to investigate my driving options. I should be driving your beautiful self around town, not the other way around," he says as he kisses the back of the hand he's holding.

"I don't mind driving you. Besides, I'll always know where you are if you aren't able to drive around on your own." I wink at him, and he smiles and shakes his head.

"The only place I'd want to be is wherever you are."

I put the car in park, and we exit, heading into the house. No sooner does he open the door, when a familiar face peeks around the corner at us.

"Hey, guys," Michael says. "What's up?"

Logan lets out a frustrated groan and purposefully bangs his head against the foyer wall.

"Hi, Michael. It's nice to see you again," I say because it's true.

"Elora! Are you still with this butthead? I thought you'd have figured out by now what an asshole he is."

"Hey, now. You're talking about *my* butthead. And, yes, I have him pretty much figured out." I grin at Logan and wink. He rolls his eyes.

"Don't you have somewhere to be?" Logan whines at his brother.

"Nope. You only told me to leave for the night. You said nothing about today. So, where did you two lovebirds go anyway?"

"We went to see your mom and stepdad."

Michael's face is a picture, and I laugh.

"You don't even have to tell me how it went. Our mother can be brutal."

I nod in agreement, but I don't want to be disrespectful when talking about her.

"It went as well as can be expected, I guess."

"Is there any way I can convince you to stay in your room for a little while? Elora has to leave soon, and I'd like a little alone time with her," Logan interrupts our conversation.

"Oh, come on, Dude. I don't want to hear you two getting it on in the living room, while I'm stuck inside my bedroom. If you want to do that, then go in your own room."

"My God. Shut up, Michael."

I touch Logan on the shoulder to tell him take it easy.

"Hey," I say to get his attention. "It's okay. I should probably get home anyway."

"What? No. Come on. Stay here for a little longer. I probably won't see you for another week, and even still, you can't guarantee that."

I rise up and kiss the tip of his nose as consolation for the next thing that'll come from my lips.

"I'm sorry. I had the best time with you these past couple days. I'll miss you terribly, but I'm going to go." His frown makes me sad, but I really do need to go home, not only to study, but to confront my traitorous brother too. "We'll call each other during the week, and text every day. I promise." Grabbing the collar of his shirt, I rise up again and kiss him. It's just a simple peck on the lips, but I don't feel comfortable doing anything more in front of his brother.

He drops his head, so it's resting against mine, and sighs ruefully. "I hate this."

My brows knit together.

"What do you mean?"

"The fact that I don't see you every day. It's killing me."

I cup his chin and raise his face to look at me. His expression is raw.

"I'm sorry. I'm trying to balance everything. I'm doing the best I can. Please, understand."

"I know, and I'm not blaming you at all. I'm just being selfish," he says then kisses my forehead. "You go. Do what you need to do, then call me, before you lay that beautiful head of yours, down on your pillow. I'll wait for your call."

My heart aches for him, as he holds me tightly in his arms. I know how tough it is to want to be together. I know because I feel the same way. Sometimes, I wish I was still working for him.

He pulls back and traces a line on my cheek.

"I love you," I say, and he smiles.

"I love you too, baby. More than I thought possible."

He walks me toward the door and opens it for me. He then follows me out onto the porch.

"I'll call you when I get home."

"You'd better," he says. But, before I'm even a foot away from him, he suddenly grasps me by the arm, pushes me up against the wall, and pins me there with his body. I'm breathless as he stares intensely into my hopeful eyes. "One more thing," he whispers, then he kisses me hard. Our mouths collide, and I push both hands into his hair, grabbing fistfuls at the back of his head. His hands, which were on the wall on either side of my head, are now wrapped around me like a vine. My immensely aroused body is now pleading with me to stay. I feel his hips grind into me, and my knees want to buckle.

My God, do I really have to go home?

He finally breaks off the kiss, but he doesn't move. I'm trapped by the weight of his body which still presses me into the wall. Our foreheads touch, as we try, in vain, to slow our erratic breaths.

"Be careful driving home," he pants. I nod, unable to speak. *This* is how much his passion affects me.

He then pushes away, effectively releasing me, and I stand on my own two, wobbly legs. I turn to walk away and for good measure, he swats my behind. My head swivels, and I yelp in response, but I smirk.

And, with that, I drive home.

17

LOGAN

I watch her taillights, until I can't see them anymore, then I slink wistfully back inside. Not only am I sad, I'm also horny, which is a problem, when I won't get to see her again for another six days or so. I plop down onto the couch.

"Sorry she had to go, man. I know how much you like her," Michael says, holding onto his freshly made sandwich. He sits next to me on the couch.

"I more than like her, asswipe—I love her," I say, as I rid him of his meal.

"Hey! Go make your own," he whines as he reaches across me in an attempt to get it back.

"Fuck off. Because of you, she went home early. I think your penance is this sandwich." I take a bite.

"Fine," he says, "but next time, you should just go to *her* house."

"I wish I could. I don't drive, remember?"

"Well, let's fix that."

"What do you mean?"

"All it takes is a modified car, and you've got yourself a booty-call."

He's so crude…but curiously enough, he could be onto something.

"What do you mean?"

"I saw it on the internet. I found it when you first came home. You can have a car modified to drive with your hands, if you can't drive with your feet. Just look it up."

I rub my chin, contemplating all the possibilities.

"You know, maybe, you're not such a douchebag." I punch him in the arm.

"No, but you are." He retaliates, and a wrestling match ensues.

ELORA

As soon as I get home, I text Logan. I let him know I got home safe, that I love him, and I'll talk to him tomorrow. I know it's little consolation, but it's all I can offer him right now. I relax on the couch with my feet propped up on the coffee table, daydreaming about what would have happened if I *had* stayed.

Just then, a noise makes me jump. It's Daniel. He's knocking into walls, as he emerges from his room. My faces instantly hardens. Just wait until I get a hold of him. As he rounds the corner, I'm ready.

"I could just strangle you, you know that?" I say with a fury I haven't felt before. "What did you think you were doing, talking to Logan like that? That was rude and disgusting, and you're lucky he didn't punch your face in!" I'm panting.

"Shh! Stop yelling. My head is killing me," he says, while holding both sides of his face.

"Good! I'm glad you're in pain. It serves you right for being such an *ass* yesterday!"

He puts his index finger on his lips in another attempt to quiet me.

"I know. I'm sorry. I don't know what came over me. Blame the alcohol." He passes me and goes straight for the kitchen, where he downs some over the counter pain reliever and a tall glass of water. When he turns around, he almost bumps into me.

"I'm not blaming the alcohol, I'm blaming *you*. What the hell were you thinking?"

"Ugh. Go away. Can't you see I'm hungover?"

I bite my lip as an idea forms. Opening a nearby cabinet, I grab a pan with a lid. As hard as I can, I begin banging them together. Daniel winces and covers his ears.

"How's this?" I shout over the noise. "Do I have your attention now?"

He quickly lets go of his head and snares both my wrists, halting my impromptu concert. I struggle to get free, but he holds on tight.

"What do you want me to say, Elora? I'm sorry. Let this horrific hangover be my punishment."

With an evil grin, I open both hands, letting the cookware fall clumsily, not to mention loudly, to the floor. Daniel winces again, so I fake pushing out with my hands then pull in and down, slipping through his grasp.

"I don't want your apology, Daniel. Logan needs it. And, that's exactly what he'll get from you the very next time you see him. Do you understand me?" I glare at him, willing him to answer me.

"Sure," he says angrily. "I'll apologize to him...when he understands the jeopardy he's putting your future in." He brushes past me and sits on the couch. I follow.

"God! Why is everyone making such a big deal about this? Nobody should care if we're dating. Our relationship didn't start until I was no longer working for him. What part of that don't you understand"

"Can you prove that?"

"What? No."

"Well, there's your problem. People assume things, my naïve, little sister. The court of public opinion has more convictions than any court in this country. All your employer has to do is catch wind of this, and you can be sued, which opens up questions about what type of relationship the two of you have. Who's going to hire a nurse who's a liability, assuming you don't get kicked out of the nursing program first?"

I know what he's saying, but I don't want to hear it.

"God, Daniel. Just stop talking."

"You know I'm right. If you have any kind of smudge on your record, your school can you deny you your diploma. You'll have gone through all of that hard work for nothing." I take a deep breath and look at the floor. He rubs his face, out of frustration, then slings his arm around on my shoulders. "I'm just trying to look out for you. I don't want to see you fail just because you fell in love with the wrong man."

I look up at him, as my guard is let down.

"But, I love him. How can I help that?" My head falls against his shoulder again, and a tear drop forms. "I don't think anyone knows. Maybe, it'll be okay."

"I hope, for your sake, you're right. Even still, you have to be careful."

I nod.

I'm getting ready for bed, when a text comes in.

R U up?

I smile and respond.

Yes.

It's only a matter of seconds, before my phone rings.

"Hello?"

"Hey there, sexy," Logan says. "How's my girl?"

"Hi. I'm…good," I say, trying not to sound as if something's wrong.

"Did you get everything done that you wanted to?"

"I guess so. Although, I'm not sure I'll ever feel like I've done enough studying."

"Did you resolve anything with your brother?"

"Sort of."

"Sort of? What does that mean?"

I shrug.

"He apologized for being rude. He says he's just worried about me losing my job."

"Don't worry about that. We've done nothing wrong. We waited, just like we should have."

"I know. I guess whatever happens, happens."

There's a pause in the conversation before he continues.

"Are you okay?" he asks.

"Yes. Why?"

"I don't know, you just sound…defeated. It's nothing I said, is it?"

I sigh.

"No."

"But, it *is* something."

"Yes…No…I don't know. I'm just not in a very good mood right now."

"I know the feeling. I wish I was there to make you feel better."

"Me too. But, I *do* feel better just talking on the phone with you."

"I'm glad. You do the same for me."

Another pause comes, as I listen to him breathing.

"Well, I guess I'd better go now."

"Why is it that you're always the one to end our conversations?" he teases.

"Probably because if I left it up to you, we'd still be on the phone from *last* weekend."

He laughs.

"Yes, I'd say that's accurate."

"Goodnight, Logan. I'll see you in my dreams."

"Goodnight, baby. I love you."

I close my eyes and soak up those last three words.

"I love you too," I whisper, just before we both hang up.

It's Saturday again, and so far this week, Logan and I have talked, texted, and in some cases, sexted, every available moment we could.

We just can't seem to get enough of each other. I've invited him over for dinner tonight and asked Michael to bring him, promising him I'd take him home when we're done. Daniel is staying, but only long enough to apologize for his behavior last weekend, then he's leaving. I'm just putting the finishing touches on dinner when the doorbell rings. Excited, I check myself in the mirror before opening the door.

"Hey, baby," Logan says as he stands in my doorway. I smile broadly, elated that he's here.

"Hi," I squeak and throw my arms around his neck. When I release my hold on him, he brings out a bouquet of flowers from behind his back. It's a plethora of locally grown blossoms and smells like the fragrance of spring.

"That's very sweet of you. Thank you. I love them," I say and kiss him. "Come in, and make yourself comfortable."

He enters the apartment and sets down a bottle of wine he brought with him.

"Something smells delicious. What delectable concoction did you make this time?"

"Chicken Parmesan. I hope you like it."

He wraps his arms around me from behind and nuzzles my neck.

"I have no doubt that I will."

Daniel walks out of his room, and catches our intimate moment. Logan stiffens immediately as the two men size each other up. I hope Daniel sticks to his word.

"Logan," he says curtly.

Logan nods.

"Daniel. It's good to see you again."

Daniel nods back, then inhales deeply through his nose.

"I'd...like to apologize for my behavior the other night. I was out of line, and...I'm sorry," Daniel says with an icy edge to his voice. I'm not convinced he's sincere.

"Thank you. I appreciate you saying that." Daniel nods again. "I want you know that I intend to treat your sister with the utmost respect. I only have her best interest at heart, and I'll do everything in my power to make her happy. Whatever that may mean."

Daniel contemplates Logan's words for a moment.

"I hope so. I won't see her hurt. She deserves someone who will make her happy, even if that means letting her go."

My brow takes a nosedive.

"Daniel," I scold. "Stop it."

"He has to know," he's says as he looks from me to Logan. "Your *relationship*," he draws quotes in the air, "has the potential to ruin my sister's life. She might not *only* lose her job, but this could get her kicked out of nursing school. Or, at the very least, she could go all through school and still not be allowed to graduate, because of being fired from her job, over this *relationship*." He exaggerates the word again. "And, she risks getting sued on top of that. So, I hope you're willing to risk all that to be with her because if she gets hurt over all this, it's on you, man. It's all on you."

I walk straight up to him and look him dead in the eye.

"This is my decision too, Daniel. I would be just as much at fault as he would be. Don't you dare put this all on him. That's not fair."

I feel Logan's hand on my shoulder, as he gently eases me backward, taking my place in front of my brother.

"I'm aware of what this looks like to the unknowing eyes of her employer, and I can assure you, she'll be safe from all that you've just described."

"You can't know that," he says.

"I can."

Daniel shakes his head, then looks over at me.

"I hope you know what you're doing, Elora. It's a big penalty to pay if you're wrong."

"It'll be fine. You'll see."

Daniel looks back and forth between the two of us, before excusing himself, then walking out the apartment door. I exhale at the relief I feel when he's gone. Logan turns me in his arms. Gazing into my eyes, he studies my face.

"Are you okay with your choice to be involved with me?"

My brows shoot up is surprise.

"*Yes.* Yes, of course I am. Why on earth wouldn't I be? My God, Logan, please don't let him get inside your head."

"It's not *my* head I'm worried about. I just want to make sure I've given you the chance to back out of this…not that I want you to."

I step forward, wrapping my arms around his waist, and lay my cheek against his chest.

"I'm in this one hundred percent. I don't care what anyone says. I love you. I want to be with you. And, I hope you feel the same about me."

He reaches down to lift my chin and takes a moment to look into my eyes, before bending and kissing me, very softly, on the lips. He then pulls me to a tight embrace, and kisses my hair, inhaling, then humming his exhale.

"Okay. No more talking about this then. We're good?" he asks. I nod and smile.

"We're good."

"Good, I'm starving. Let's eat."

Another week passes, until it's finally Friday. I'm stoked at the thought of seeing Logan again after a long week, and I'm pulling in the parking lot at the office to turn in my paperwork, when my phone rings.

"Hello, handsome." I smile.

"Hey, baby. Do you know what day it is?"

"Yes, and TGIF has never seemed so appropriate." I giggle.

"Are you on your way home?"

"Almost. Just one quick stop, then I'll be on my way. What do you feel like doing tonight?"

"I have a few ideas, but we'll talk about it when you get here."

"Hmm. It sounds like you might have the same idea I have. I'll see you in a bit. I've got to go. Love you."

"I love you too, baby. Bye."

I disconnect the call then smile broadly, as I anticipate being with Logan for another weekend.

LOGAN

She's late. Where could she be? I've texted her no less than half a dozen times, but I've heard nothing back from her. I dial her number again.

"Hey, I'm really starting to worry over here. Please call me when you get this message...I love you." I hang up and continue to pace. This isn't like her. She always calls or texts me when she's been held up.

Thoughts and memories come flooding back about the day I almost lost my life. I can hear the screeching of tires. I can smell the gasoline. I can see the twisted metal and the blood pooling on the ground beneath me. Suddenly, pain sweeps across the air where my legs used to be, and I'm forced to sit down to try to relieve the ghostly spasms.

"Stop!" I wince and cry out, eventually removing my prosthesis, and giving my residual limb a gentle massage. The ache subsides, and I'm left breathless. Will this phantom torment ever stop?

I check the time again. It's been almost two hours since she should've been here. I have to do something. Grabbing the keys, I make my way into the garage. My car, which hasn't been used for the better part of a year, sits quietly in its spot. The layers of dust are so thick that I could easily write my name on the surface. I hesitate. Should I do this? I haven't driven since before the accident. I can feel my heartrate increase. Could I even make it out onto the main road? Should I wait a bit longer? What if she's on her way, and we miss each other en route? I close my eyes, as my fist closes tightly around my keys. *What if she's not okay.* I open my eyes, and push forward, trying hard not to think about the consequences of what I'm about to do, and I climb inside. The interior smells the same as I remember, and I run my hand over the dashboard. God, I miss driving. With the key in the ignition, I start the car. It purrs to life with a twist of my wrist. I say a prayer, then I open the garage door. Here goes nothing.

Backing out is my first challenge. Operating a vehicle, with what feels like stilts extending from your knees, takes a lot of getting used to. I test the gas and brake petals. The last thing I want is to cause an accident. It takes all my concentration to figure out how hard to press down, let alone steering the damned thing and watching my surroundings. I sigh in frustration. If I'm going to get there in one piece, I'm going to have to go slow. This aggravates me even more, especially while I'm thinking the worst.

As I drive through town, I'm both in a hurry and trying to be careful. The two concepts, being polar opposites, are making my heart leap from my chest.

"Come on, Logan. She's okay. Everything's fine." I repeat this over and over again in my head, hoping to convince myself that it's true.

While I'm not entirely sure which direction she might have taken, I choose a route that allows me to drive past her work, on the off chance that she's there. The parking lot is small, so I assess quickly that she's not. It's both a relief and a distress. Eliminating one of her possible whereabouts, I continue on my journey. At a stop light, I check my phone and send a quick text.

On my way to your apartment. Please stay where you are.

The light turns green, and my overly zealous emotions cause my car to lurch forward, almost hitting the van in front of me. I gasp, then stomp on the brake. My heart is in my throat, as my reality check rings loud and clear inside my head.

"Calm down, Logan, or you may never get to her," I say under my breath.

Finally, I reach her apartment complex. I slowly drive toward her section, as my eyes scan the dozens of cars in the lot. I see her brother's car, which she's been driving, and hope that that's what she drove today. I park, happy as hell to have made it in one piece.

Wasting no more time, I leap from the car, and dash through the outside door, moving straight to her apartment. With unsteady breaths, I knock.

"Elora? Are you home? It's me, Logan." I wait on pins and needles for any sign that she's in there. Then, I ring the doorbell, wanting to make sure I'm heard. "Are you in there?" I ask again, knocking louder this time.

"Are you looking for the young lady who lives in that apartment?" a feeble voice asks.

I glance over at the door, across the hall, and spy a gray haired, older woman. She's standing in her doorway with a coffee cup in her hand.

"Yes. Do you know if she's home?"

She purses her lips and nods.

"I saw her go in a while ago," she says.

Oh, thank God.

"But," she continues, "she didn't look too good. You might want to check in on her."

"I can't get in. I don't have a key," I say, hoping that Elora gave her one for safe keeping.

"It's under the mat," she says. "I told her that wasn't the best place to keep it, but she insisted. Said her brother is always locking himself out."

I look beneath my feet at the mat that says 'welcome'. Reaching down, I uncover the key and blow out a steadying breath, knowing it's the last barrier that stands between us. Grasping it like a lifeline, I look back at the old woman.

"Thank you," I say.

"You're welcome. I hope everything's okay."

"Me too."

I hurriedly unlock the door and peer inside.

"Elora?" I call out but hear nothing in return. I call to her again, as I walk in farther, but still, I hear nothing. Then, as I walk toward her closed bedroom door, I hear the faint sound of someone crying.

Shit.

I grab the handle.

"Elora?"

"Logan?"

Relief washes over me at the sweet sound of my name on her lips.

She's okay.

"Yes. Can I come in?"

"Yes," her muffled voice says, and at her cue, I open the door.

18

LOGAN

Regret lances through me as I find her lying atop her bed. She's curled up in a ball, and her eyes are swollen and red from crying. I rush to her side, throwing myself, knees first, onto the floor beside her.

"Elora. What's wrong? Are you all right?"

She sniffles and wipes her tear-stained cheeks.

"I don't know," she says with a shaky voice.

I do a visual sweep across her body, looking for any signs of trauma.

"What's going on? Are you hurt?" I touch her face, partly to check for fever, partly just to touch her.

"I'm not hurt."

"Are you sure?" I check again but find nothing out of the ordinary. "It's very late. Why didn't you come over? I've been worried sick."

"I'm sorry. I didn't think. I came straight home after leaving the office. My phone is in silent mode, and I guess I didn't pay much attention to the time."

I close my eyes, as my heart settles into a slower rhythm. Standing up, I motion for her to move over, then I sit on the edge of her bed, bidding her to sit beside me. My arm finds its home around her shuddering shoulders, as she rests her head against my chest.

"Talk to me," I whisper, kissing her hair. "What's going on?"

She inhales shakily, before she looks up at me.

"I got fired."

My eyebrows shoot up.

"What?" I say, almost too quietly.

"They fired me, Logan. They saw me over your house. They took pictures of us together. They're saying I've been working for you under the table, and he said to expect a lawsuit." She sniffles again, as her tears flow freely.

"Who said this?"

"Dave Smythe—the owner of the company." Anger starts to burn inside my chest, replacing the worry that was there only minutes ago. "When I tried to explain that I wasn't working for you, that we were a couple, he laughed and said he knew that too. He then showed me a picture of us. He said his next call would be to my nursing school."

"What kind of picture?"

"It was the two of us. I was on your porch, backed up against the wall, with my hands in your hair, and we were kissing. Oh, Logan, what am I going to do?"

I close my eyes and inhale deeply. When I exhale in a rush, I take hold of her face, looking her straight in the eyes.

"I'm going to fix this. This is all my fault. I was warned several times. I'll take care of this," I say with an air of finality.

Her expression changes to panic.

"What are you going to do?" she says, as I begin to stand. She wraps her small hand around my wrist, anchoring me in place.

"I'm going to see your boss. I'll tell him it was all me, and that you're innocent."

"He won't believe you."

I look back at her.

"Then, I'll make him."

I break free from her grasp, and make my way into the living room. I hear Elora's hurried footsteps behind me.

"Logan, wait," she says, desperation in her voice. "How will you get there?"

"I'm going to drive." When I see the concern on her face, my heart softens, and I realize I need to console her and get ahold of myself, before I go. "Come here," I say, reaching for her. She walks into my open arms, and I envelope her in a comforting embrace. She shudders again, her sorrow returning, as she weeps into my chest.

"Please don't go. There's nothing you can do." She looks up at me. "He's determined to make me pay for the time and money he thinks I've stolen from his company. He won't listen to you."

Cupping her face in my hands, I lower my head and plant a loving kiss on her lips. I can taste the salt from her tears, which fuels my fire. I can practically hear my mind screaming at me to fix this.

"I have to go. I have to try to fix this for you." I release her and walk toward the door.

"Logan, stop!" she shouts, just as Daniel walks through the door. He takes one look at the menacing expression on my face, then at his sister, and clearly makes assumptions. Before I have time to react, or say a word, his fist makes contact with my jaw. He hits me hard enough to knock me off balance, sending me careening into the nearby entry table. Luckily, I'm able to right myself instead of hitting the floor. I square up and stare angrily into his enraged eyes.

"I deserved that, but that's the one and only chance you'll get. The next time, I'll defend myself, and I don't think either of us wants that." My nostrils flare in fury, as I turn my head toward Elora. I give her a silent goodbye, then exit.

ELORA

"What the hell do you think you're doing?" I scream at Daniel while pounding on his chest. He quickly grabs my wrists, halting my assault.

"What am *I* doing? What did *he* do?"

"He did nothing! And, you hit him!"

"Hell yeah, I hit him. What the fuck is going on? I come home and see you've been crying, and he looked like he could kill someone. What am I supposed to think?"

"How about finding out what's going on before throwing your fists around?" I yank my wrists out of his grasp and run to the door, hoping to catch Logan before he leaves. But, it's too late. I watch as a car goes speeding from the parking lot, and I have to assume it's his. I close the door and lean against it, defeated.

"If he didn't hurt you, then tell me what happened," Daniel says a bit calmer.

I roughly wipe my tear-stained cheeks before coming to rest on the couch.

"Well?" he insists.

I shake my head, not wanting to reveal that he was right. I don't want the '*I told you so*' right now.

"I was right, wasn't I? Did you get fired?" he asks. I nod my head, and my tears start again. I hear his sigh, but surprisingly, he doesn't lecture me. Instead, he comes and sits next to me. He puts his arm around me as I bury my face in my hands. "I was afraid of this. What can I do?"

I sniffle and wipe my face again.

"There's nothing anyone can do. I've as good as lost my job and my career."

"I'm so sorry," he says, and I look at him.

"Aren't you going to gloat?"

He smirks.

"Do you want me to?"

I shake my head.

"No. Not at all," I say.

"Then, I say we just sit here and come up with plan B."

A few moments of silence are broken when a thought comes to my mind.

"You hit him pretty hard."

"Yeah. I did. But, in my defense, I didn't know what I was walking into. You were distraught and yelling *stop*, and he was angry. I thought the worst. I'm sorry. I'll apologize to him too if you want."

"Apologize if you feel sorry for doing it. I understand your motives."

He gives me a brotherly squeeze.

"I love you, sis, and I'm sorry this happened to you."

I nod.

"I'm going to my room." I then stand, grabbing my phone, and close my bedroom door behind me.

It's late in the evening when my phone rings. I pick it up, acutely aware of who it must be. The caller ID confirms my suspicions.

"Logan? Is everything all right?" I say, with my heart racing.

"Hey, baby. Yes, everything's fine. How are you? Are you feeling better?" he says softly.

I feel relaxed just at the sound of his smooth, calming voice.

"I'm better now that I'm talking to you," I say, honestly.

"Good. Can I come over? I'd really love to see you."

"Yes!" I let him know I'll meet him at the door, and we hang up.

Within twenty minutes, I see a car pull into a parking space near the entrance to my building. It's dark, but I race to the outside door to greet him. I watch as he exits the car with a weary smile, meant only for me, and he catches me mid-stride as I wrap my arms around his neck.

Heaven.

I hear him inhale with his nose buried in my hair.

"God, you smell good," he says. I pull back and look into his eyes. But, before I say a word, I reach up and kiss him. His arms pull me tighter up against his body. After a moment, we break apart, and he sighs. "I'm so happy to see you. Do you have any idea how much?"

"Yeah. I have a pretty good inkling."

He snakes his arm behind my back as we walk toward the building. We stop just short of the door.

"Is your brother inside?" he asks.

"Yes, but I don't think you have anything to worry about."

"Does he know about..."

"Yes."

He nods.

"I want to apologize to him." I'm shocked.

"For what?"

"I should've been more cautious. This was my fault."

"It was both of us," I say in a reassuring tone while laying my hand on his chest.

When we enter my apartment, Daniel's in his room, but upon hearing our voices, he comes out. The tension is thick.

Without warning, Logan thrusts a hand out in Daniel's direction.

"I'm sorry for my part in this whole thing. You were right to hit me. In fact, I'm happy to see you so defensive when it comes to your sister. Please accept my apology for all the trouble I've caused."

Daniel stares at Logan's hand. He looks as though he's contemplating whether or not to shake it. When it's obvious that Daniel's not ready to accept it, Logan drops his hand back down to his side.

"I just wanted you both to know that you don't need to worry about this situation. It's been taken care of," Logan says.

"What? What do you mean? What did you do?" I ask.

Daniel says nothing, but eyes Logan skeptically.

"I had a long talk with your boss. He won't bother pursuing a lawsuit or mention any of this to your school."

My eyebrows shoot up.

"But...how?"

"I handled it," he says, but doesn't elaborate. I wind my arms around his waist. "You didn't threaten him, did you?"

He scoffs.

"No. Let's just say, money talks."

"You paid him off?" Daniel finally chimes in. His tone is accusatory. They stare at each other.

"Yes. I did."

Daniel huffs and rolls his eyes at the notion.

"You know, I don't get you," Logan says to him. "I love your sister. I'd do anything in my power to prevent her from getting hurt, and yet, no matter what I do, you still have a problem with me. Why is that?"

"I don't like the fact that *you* are the cause of all my sister's trouble. You might've bailed her out, but if it wasn't for *you*, she wouldn't need it in the first place," Daniel says with his usual snarky tone.

Logan's mouth twists, and he shakes his head.

"Well, since I can't seem to please you, not that I care to, I guess we'll have to agree to disagree then."

Daniel pulls his shoulders back and puffs out his chest, while Logan remains the same in his posture, clearly unintimidated. I feel the need to step in between the two men in my life before it escalates again.

"Okay. That's enough. Daniel, it's late. If you need me, I'll be in my room. Logan, come with me." I take his hand, leading him into a more private place so we can talk.

He closes the door behind us, then joins me in sitting on my bed. His hands run through his hair out of frustration.

"I'm sorry about Daniel. He's not usually so confrontational." Logan shrugs.

"He doesn't bother me." He turns and softly caresses my cheek. "I'm just happy to see your beautiful face free from worry and tears."

I give him a small smile, then cover his hand with mine.

"So, do you want to tell me about your impromptu meeting with Dave?"

"If you want to hear it." I nod, and he sighs. "I went to your job unsure of what I might have to do to get you out of this situation. I explained to him that you weren't contracted privately, but that I was no longer in need of services. I pulled up my pant leg to show him the evidence. I told him that you were the one who convinced me to work at getting my mobility back, and in turn, get my life back. He laughed and said he didn't care about any of that. He saw an opportunity to win in court, and he was going to take it."

"So, he was willing to ruin my life for a few extra dollars?" He nods his head. "Unbelievable," I whisper.

"Yep. I offered him the cost of what he would win in court, in exchange for him to drop the case. He refused, then pressed me for more money. He said he knew our relationship had the potential to wreck any medical career you would try to pursue, and *that* had to mean more to me than a few thousand dollars. So, after much negotiation, we settled on a price. He tore up the pictures in front of me and gave them to me. I walked out with a bitter taste in my mouth, but I felt relief for you at the same time."

"But, how did he find out? Where did the pictures come from?"

He sighs and looks repentant.

"Bethany was the informant."

My hand flies to my mouth.

"Oh, God. Why would she..." Then, the reason comes into focus: she's jealous.

"I'm so sorry. I didn't think she'd—"

"Shh. It's not your fault." Then, a bigger question come to mind. "How much did you give him?" My voice is small. I've asked the question, but I'm not sure I want to hear the answer.

He shakes his head.

"It's not important."

"It is to me. How much?" His silence reveals that it's most likely a lot of money. "Logan," I press him. "Please tell me."

He bows his head and sighs.

"Ten thousand."

"*What?* Are you *joking?*" He shakes his head and looks at me.

"No," he says quietly.

I stand and begin to pace. I have no idea what to say about this gesture—this *huge* gesture. Why on earth would he do this? Ten. Thousand. Dollars? Is he kidding?

"Why would you do this for me?" I ask as I turn to face him.

"How can you ask me that?" He stands, walks closer, and cups my face in his hands. "I love you. I hated to see the hurt in your eyes that I caused. I had to make it right. No matter what, I had to make it right."

"But, that's a lot of money. You're not working. How did you—"

"That's not your concern," he interrupts.

"Like hell it's not. You bailed me out, which I'll pay back by the way. I can't take your money. You need it."

He looks down.

"You'll do nothing of the sort. I got you in this mess, and I got you out of it. End of story." He takes my hand and kisses the back of it. "Can't we just forget this ever happened and go on with our lives. We can be happy now. There's nothing to stop us."

I sigh ruefully. He does have a point. I should just thank him and start living the life I'd been hoping to, since we started dating.

"You're right. Thank you," I say as I wrap my arms around him. He reciprocates while kissing the top of my head.

"You're most welcome."

"Will you please let me pay you back though? I feel terrible with you being without an income and all." He scoffs, which makes me look up at him. "What aren't you telling me?" I eye him suspiciously.

"I didn't want to tell you this but...I might have a little money in the bank."

"Oh?"

"Yeah. When my dad died, my biological dad, Michael and I inherited some money."

"Okay. But, that doesn't mean you should spend it all on me." He chuckles.

"I didn't." He pulls back, placing his hands on my shoulders. "Elora, Michael and I both inherited one million dollars." I gasp, throwing my hand over my mouth. "I took that initial amount and with a few wise investments, it grew...into a ridiculous number."

"Why didn't you tell me?"

He shrugs, then walks a few feet from me.

"I don't know. It's not like I was hiding it. The subject just never came up."

I let all he's just disclosed sink in, then I turn and walk toward him.

"Is that why your mother dislikes me? She thinks I'm after your money?" He nods, sadly.

"Pretty much. That's what she pulled me out of the room to discuss when we went over there." He shrugs. "I tried to tell her that you're not like that but..."

"I get it. I can see why she would be worried. But, I hope she knows that I'm not here for that reason," I say laying my hand on his chest. "I'm in it for this." Then, I reach up and kiss him. His hands weave through my hair, his thumbs coming to rest on my cheeks. Our tongues touch as we solidify our connection to each other.

Then, I tug on the front of his shirt, begging him to follow me. He does, as we continue to kiss. I feel the bed at the back of my knees, but instead of sitting, Logan reaches down, holding my thighs, and lifts me up, placing me gently on my back. He then follows me down. With his weight on top of me, his lips find my neck. I tilt my head to the side to give him better access.

"God, I love you," I say, which sounds more like a moan.

"Mmm," he hums back. "I love you more."

Before I have a chance to argue that fact, his mouth is on mine again, and I'm lost to the world in a way I haven't been able to be, until this moment.

We're free to love each other as we please.

19

LOGAN

"Elora," I say softly, trying to coax her from sleep. "Wake up. We have things to do today."

She stirs. Her brow furrows, and she pouts her lips at my gentle rousting.

"No. I'm tired," she says, then rolls over. I can't help but laugh.

"I mean it, sleepyhead. Get up. We're going on an adventure."

She yawns and stretches, then manages to open one eye part way. "What adventure?"

"You'll see. Just get dressed, and wear something comfortable."

I reach down and pull at the hem of my shirt, shrugging it off over my head. I see her mouth pop open as she watches me.

"Can't we just stay here?" She's eyeing my bare chest with one eyebrow cocked upward. I throw my shirt at her, and she giggles.

"Although I'm sure that would prove to be a worthy adventure, no, we can't. I have plans...and reservations," I say as I put on a clean shirt.

"But, it's so early."

"That's the best time to go."

"Go where?"

"It's a surprise. Now, get up, or I'll be forced to drag you out by your feet." I narrow my eyes at her.

"You wouldn't dare."

"Try me."

Then, in one swift move, I grab her left ankle and begin to pull. She screeches and flips over on her stomach, grasping at the sheets for any sort of traction. I stop just short of her falling completely off the bed, and let her leg go so that only her torso remains on the mattress. Then, for good measure, I playfully swat her behind. She yelps in response.

"That's not fair," she says, as she turns her head to look at me.

"Hey, I warned you." I laugh.

Her mouth twists, and she laughs too.

"Where are we?" she asks as we drive down the dirt road toward the wooded area about an hour away from our homes.

"We're almost to our destination." I smirk.

"You're still not going to tell me?" Her pouty expression is absolutely adorable.

"We're going zip lining," I say, hoping for a positive reaction.

"Zip lining? You mean, hanging from a wire at really high heights?"

"Something like that."

Her expression is unsure. Is she not up to this?

"I'm sort of afraid of heights."

"Well, are you willing to give it a try? They have a practice run before we begin. If you don't think you're going to like it, we can just find something else to do."

She bites her bottom lip as she contemplates my words. It's several seconds before she responds. I'm waiting with anticipation.

"I'll try it," she says. A ridiculously large grin spreads across my face, and I reach over and squeeze her hand.

"It'll be fun. You'll see. And, afterward, we'll have another, less adventurous, adventure."

She grins and nods her head.

"Then, what are we waiting for?"

I put the car in park but hesitate before getting out. I turn slightly in my seat.

"I want you to know how much I appreciate you trying new things with me. I've always been fascinated with the thought of flying, and I've had this idea in my back pocket for a while now. I was hoping you'd want to go on this adventure with me, so thank you...for being so open minded."

She smiles.

"Logan, I don't care what we're doing, as long as we're doing it together. And, I'm thankful that I get to share this with you."

I lean over and press my lips against hers. She places her hand on my cheek, and my heart melts. When we pull back, my mind suddenly races to our future. In every scenario throughout my flash forward, she is the one constant. Her face is in every picture that my mind has shown me. I smile broadly.

"What?" she asks.

I shake my head.

"Nothing. Let our first adventure begin."

"The first of many?"

"Without a doubt."

After walking around to open her door, we stroll hand in hand up to the front of the building. The rustic look of the log cabin is exactly what I'd expected to find here, in the middle of a forest. I open the door then allow her to walk in first.

"Good morning, folks. What can I do for you today?" says an older man behind the counter.

"Good morning. We'd like to try out your course. We have a reservation." I turn my phone toward the man, and she looks at me, puzzled. "I made them last night after you fell asleep," I tell her, and she smirks.

"Very good, sir." He processes my information, then types into his computer. "I'll need you both to sign this waiver and step on this scale. Then, we'll get started." She looks at me with a curious expression, then shrugs. We both step onto the scale in turn as the man writes the results down on our paperwork. I look over the document briefly, then sign my name. Elora follows. "Have you been on a zip line before?"

"No, neither of us have," I confess.

"Well, you're in for a treat then. If you'll step outside with my sons, they'll get you geared up, then take you up by four-wheeler. When you get to the top, you'll go through flight school. It's only up about ten feet or so, but you'll learn the proper technique, how to self-brake, and self-rescue."

Elora's eyes widen, and my guess is that the word *rescue* has her a bit nervous.

"I'm pretty sure that refers to if you stop moving in the middle of the cable. It has nothing to do with falling." I laugh when I see her relax.

I shake his hand, and we walk outside.

"Ready to go?" the taller son asks as we walk out onto the concrete patio.

"Yes. Very," she says. I look down to see Elora beaming with excitement, and it makes me that much more pleased with my decision to do this.

"I'm Jake. I'll be taking you up. Have you been here before?" We both shake our heads. "Well, I guarantee you'll be back. It's highly addictive. This is my brother Cody, by the way. He'll be coming too." I extend my hand and shake both of theirs and instantly notice the fact that they look like direct opposites of each other. Jake, with his well established beard, has a masculine vibe, whereas Cody is more of a typical, twenty something, although he could pass for a teenager. I wonder if they're blood related. "First, let's get you harnessed up," he says, as he points to a plethora of straps seemingly laid out in front of us. "Just step into the loops, and grab the front and back pieces." Again, he points them out, and we do as we're told. The black tether wraps around my upper thighs, over my shoulders, and hooks to a lanyard at my chest. As Cody adjusts mine to fit me, I carefully observe Jake and Elora. She's smiling and laughing as he cinches her harness tightly. They're talking to one another, but I can't hear what they're saying. Then, I see her touch his shoulder for balance. I close my eyes, trying to get my wayward thoughts under control. "There. You're all set," Cody says, as he pulls my focus away from them and hands me a helmet. I smile courteously, then walk toward my girl.

"Hang on," Jake says, as I hold on tightly to the roll bars. I smile at Elora as she does the same. The engine of the six person ATV roars to life, and we take off up the dirt track.

The road to the top is bumpy and narrow. Jake and Elora are in the front seat, and Cody and I sit in the back. Suddenly, there's a large dip in the dirt road, which bounces us off the seat a bit. Elora lets out a small screech, and Jake chuckles a bit. Then I watch, begrudgingly, as his hand pats her shoulder in a comforting manner and lingers there a little too long. I narrow my eyes as his head turns to look behind him, and he smirks at me. A pang of jealously flares, but I push it down.

You've got to be fucking kidding me.

When we finally get to the top and dismount, I walk over and immediately take hold of her hand.

"You really do look great in anything," I say.

She laughs.

"Sure I do," she says then squeezes my hand. I feel my body relax, and I sigh. "Ready?"

I nod.

Flight school consists of a short platform and a plastic coated wire strung between two trees. It's only a short distance off the ground. Cody begins his speech about safety and technique, and I can't help but think he must recite this in his sleep.

"You'll always be hooked up by your lanyards, two of them in fact, even if you're just walking across a sky bridge. Each one of these has a thousand-pound test, and you'll each have two so don't worry about them breaking. And we'll never unhook both at the same time either. When you're on the zip line, there'll always be one of us in front of you, helping you onto the platform, and one of us behind you hooking you up. We'll make sure you get on and off each platform safely," Cody says. "Now, after hearing all the instructions, who wants to go first?"

"I will," Elora says, bravely.

She steps onto the practice platform, and Cody hooks her to the line. She glances over at me with a smile and a wink, then she's off. Cody tells her to practice her breaking skill, then she self-rescues, moving hand over hand, until she's safely back on the wooden riser.

"Nicely done," Jake says as he pats her back. I sneer at the gesture.

"Okay," Cody says as he unhooks her. "That makes it your turn." He summons me, and I step up repeating Elora's actions.

"I think you're ready for the real thing. We're one sky bridge away from a great time," Jake says. "Let's go."

ELORA

I follow Jake to the mouth of a very narrow bridge—if that's what you want to call it. It really only consists of 2x8s, lined up end to end, and held up by rope. It shakes a lot as we begin our trek. Even though I know I'm held up by my double tethers, I'm still anxious. As we step onto the first real platform, I'm taken aback at the height of our location. The circular, wooden structure sticks out about five feet in every direction and encircles the tree it's attached to. There are no railings to hold onto, and it feels dangerous to get too close to the edge.

"Who's going first?" Jake asks with a smile.

"I will," I say as I raise my hand bravely, but I know I'm anything but brave. "If that's okay with you, Logan." I peer over and see him glaring at Jake as if he was some sort of threat.

What's that about?

"Yes," he finally says. "That's fine." His preoccupied expression causes me to frown.

"Okay then, I'll go ahead of you," Jake says, then he hooks up to the line. "This first one is the shortest at 145 feet. They progressively get longer and faster, with the last one measuring at 1100 feet long. Don't forget to watch for my hand signals when it's time to brake. See you on the other side!" He picks up his feet, and away he goes. In a matter of seconds, I can hear the disembodied voice of Jake coming from Cody's walkie-talkie. "Line clear, Cody."

"Roger that, Jake," Cody says back, then he turns to me. "Are you ready?" I nod nervously. "All right then, stand up on this stump, and I'll hook your lines." I do as I'm told, while holding onto the line above me, then I look back at Logan. I make a quick face of mock horror, which makes Logan grin, but then I smile back to let him know I'll be fine.

"Just pick up your feet when you're ready, and watch Jake for signals." I nod, close my eyes, and go.

I feel my stomach drop, and I squeal with delight as the wind whips past my ears. I'm whizzing across the line, and the next platform is coming fast. In my search for Jake's signal, I don't get much chance to enjoy the view, but my mind is having enough trouble just trying to process the fact that I'm flying. It doesn't take long, before I see Jake. His hands are at his sides but soon, I see the telltale sign that he wants me to apply my hand brake. Placing my palm flat against the line, I apply gentle pressure, and slowly coast to Jake's waiting hands.

"Very good, Elora. You've really got the hang of it already, no pun intended," Jake says with a chuckle as he reels me in.

"Thanks. That was fun!" I declare and stand on the wood floor, as he transfers my tethers to the hooks on the tree. "I can't wait to see Logan's face as he zips over." Jake speaks to Cody through the walkie-talkie again, letting him know I'm here and soon, I hear the zing of another person coming across. I watch as his face is alight with excitement, and a seemingly permanent grin graces his handsome face.

"How was that?" I ask Logan, as he plants his feet alongside mine.

"Awesome!" he says and kisses my cheek. "Did you like it?"

I nod enthusiastically.

"I can't wait to do again, and over a higher height!"

He smiles.

"Me too."

We continue from tree to tree and like before, Jake hooks up and goes, followed by me, then Logan, and finally Cody. When Logan reaches us, I notice his expression is tinged with irritation.

"What's so funny?" he asks, after his feet hit the floor.

"Oh, nothing. Jake was telling me some funny stories about people he's taken up here. Some of their reactions must have been priceless," I say.

"I'll bet." His lip curls up a bit, but I pretend not to see it.

§

After the fourth zip, we get some unexpected news.

"What?" I say, my voice laced with a bit of fear.

"I said we have to rappel to the ground," Cody says, as if it were as easy as walking.

Logan grabs my hand and gently kisses the back of it.

"You can do this. I know you can," he says.

The two men show us how to hold the rope and give us instructions on how to descend.

"You'll have to raise your right foot, keeping your left on the edge, then swing out in a counter-clockwise manner. Like this," Jake says as he demonstrates. "Then, you just loosen your grip on the rope and drop safely to the ground." He disappears below the platform as if he does this every day—which I suppose he does.

Logan chivalrously volunteers to go first, stating that if I lose control, he wants to be able to catch me. It's scary to watch, knowing I'm next, but he nails it.

"I made it," he calls up to me. "Come on. It's not bad at all."

Not willing to look like too much of a girl, I reluctantly do as I've been instructed, and once I'm hanging in midair, I too drop gracefully to the ground below.

"Well done, you," Logan says, as I'm unhooked. I wrap my arms around him and squeeze. He leans down and kisses me.

"That was the single, most scary, thing I've done in my entire life! That first step is so hard to take."

"I know what you mean, but we did it." He smiles down at me; pride is evident on his face.

LOGAN

The next, and final, three zips are the longest ones, and we have plenty of air time to take in our surroundings. The springtime canopy is in its full luster, with every color green you can imagine around us. After dealing with Jake's flirtations for long enough, I decide, after he's already zipped to the next platform, that I'm going next. If he wants to tell funny stories and flirt with someone, he'll have to do it with me from now on. I don't think Elora is even aware of what's been going on, but I'm going to put a stop to it. Sure enough, as soon as Jake realizes it's me coming across, his expression is somber.

The last and longest line measures out at 1100 feet and after we all get across, we get another surprise.

"This is called a quick jump. You'll be attached to this box, which is sort of a spring loaded cable. You'll free fall for about ten feet, then feel the line catch, and then you'll be lowered 60 feet to the ground. Any questions?"

"W-we have to *jump?*" Elora stutters.

"Yes," he says.

She looks at the ground, then at me, with concern written all over her face.

"Do you want me to go first?"

She looks down again.

"And there's no other way down?" she asks Jake. He shakes his head. I watch her throat move as she swallows reflexively. "No. I want to get this over with. I'll go first." She swallows again. She's really nervous. Cody, who's on the ground already, calls up to her trying to ease her mind. She turns to Jake. "Can you push me? There's no way I can voluntarily step off this platform."

"I'd be delighted to," he says with a smirk, and I grimace at the thought that he has to touch her. "It's better to go backwards though. You can't see where you're going." She reluctantly agrees, and he moves her to the edge, facing him. "Ready?" She nods. "On three. One...Two." And he pushes her off before getting to three, by way of laying his hands against her chest and pushing abruptly. She screams as she freefalls, but I hear her giggle as the line catches.

"Thanks for nothing, Jake!" she calls up to him. "What happened to three?"

He looks down and chuckles.

"Sorry about that, but I didn't want you to chicken out." He laughs, and my jaw clamps down tightly, as I wonder if he told her to go backwards on purpose.

"You can stop flirting with her," I say, because I just can't take one more minute of it. His eyes shift to mine.

"Was I flirting? I didn't realize," he says, but his eyes dance wickedly at his words.

"You know you were. She won't give you the time of day though. She's in love with me."

He shrugs.

"I didn't say I wanted to marry her, but it's fun to flirt with pretty girls in dangerous situations. You get to *touch* them...out of safety, of course." His grin makes me want to punch him in the face, but I grab on to every bit of self-control I can muster.

"You're done touching her."

He grins even broader.

"Oh, well, it was fun while it lasted."

My fingernails dig into my palms as I ball my fists. I have visions of knocking him off this platform, but I seem to *need* him to get me down from up here. With a smirk I'd like to wipe from his face, he connects my harness. I elect to jump forward, so I line myself up at the edge. Just as I'm about to go, he adds one more thought.

"Nothing like challenging the man who hooks your straps on. Good luck on the way down. You may need it."

I shoot him a *fuck you* stare, just before jumping. I don't even remember the fall through the malice I have for him. Elora claps politely as I make it down to her. When she sees my face, hers falls.

"What's wrong?"

I shake my head.

"Nothing," I say in an attempt to cover my emotions. "It was just really hard to jump off." I chuckle uneasily.

She smiles lovingly and wraps both arms around my waist.

"Aww. You're safe now, and it's all over," she says to console me. I place my arm around her, kiss the top of her head, then look up at Jake.

"Yep. The danger is gone."

Just then, Jake shows off by falling backwards from the platform in an inverted dive. Elora claps appreciatively, and he bows when he gets to his feet. I roll my eyes.

Asshole.

After walking back to the building, we remove the equipment, and thank everyone kindly. I usher her into my car and take off toward our next destination.

"Where to now?" she asks.

"You're not in a hurry to get home, are you?"

"No. Not at all. What do you have in mind?"

"How about a secluded cabin in the woods?"

Her eyes dance delightfully at my words.

"Really?"

I nod.

"Well, it's more like a treehouse in the sky."

Her hands fly to her mouth, then clap gleefully in front of her while she bounces in her seat.

"Are you kidding me?"

"Nope." I reach over and squeeze her leg. "I already have reservations. We'll just need to stop and get some food for the night."

ELORA

We stand at the foot of wooden bridge, which leads to a log house above the ground. With foliage all around the small building, it looks as though a cluster of trees simply lifted it from the ground as they grew. There are notches cut out, allowing the tall timbers to live in harmony with the man made structure, not just beside it.

"Can we go in?" I ask.

"Of course. I'll get the rest of the gear later."

Rest of the gear? He really has thought of everything.

I walk upward to our home for the night and the closer I get to the top, the more like a bird I feel. Logan takes out a key and turns the lock. The cabin smells of nature, but not in a bad way. As I walk in farther, I can see a kitchenette to my left, with only a sink, microwave, and small refrigerator. To my right is a closet and a bathroom. Straight ahead is a roomy queen sized bed with a plaid comforter, to give it a little more rustic feel. I spin 360 degrees.

"So, what do you think?" Logan asks.

"I think it's wonderfully perfect. It's wonderfect."

He laughs loudly.

"By the time we're old and gray, you'll have made up an entire language of your own."

I beam proudly.

"What should we do first?" I ask.

"After I get the rest of our things from the trunk, why don't we go on a hike? We can gather sticks and twigs for making a fire this evening."

I grasp his shirt and pull him down to me.

"I love you, Logan Turner." Then, I kiss him. His arms find their way around me, and he deepens our kiss, but he breaks it off as quickly as he started it.

"We can't start this now. We've got work to do." I frown, so he kisses the tip of my nose. "Later," he says, then raises and lowers his eyebrows seductively.

After emptying the trunk of the rest of its contents, we head toward a foot trail which leads through the woods. Hand in hand, we walk along the dirt path, admiring the natural beauty of this place. I stoop down every now and then, on our journey, to pick up suitable kindling for our campfire later tonight. He does the same. We're reminiscing about our earlier adventure, as we stroll leisurely along.

"You did a great job today, considering you're afraid of heights. I'm proud of you," Logan says as he smiles affectionately down at me.

I return his grin.

"Thanks. It was a little intimidating at first, but once I realized that I wasn't in any real danger, I was able to relax and let go. How was it for you? Did you get the sensation of flying that you were looking for?"

He closes his eyes briefly and breathes in through his nose.

"Yeah," he says, which sounds more like a sigh. "It was so good to hear the wind rushing past my ears, and to feel it pushing against my body. I closed my eyes at one point, and I could imagine what it must be like to be a bird. There's no freer feeling, I'll bet."

The expression on his face is pure bliss. It warms my heart to know just how much he loved it, and the fact that I got to witness this, is priceless.

"I'm glad you enjoyed yourself. Thank you for letting me be a part of it."

He looks at me, confounded.

"Thanks for being open minded. I was hoping you'd at least be okay with it, but upon hearing you squeal all the way across, my heart was filled with pride. It was wonderful watching you having fun. I couldn't have asked for a more perfect day."

I smile and nod, knowing that we're on the same page.

While looking around at this serene setting, I have to ask.

"Do you think your mother will ever come around? I mean, I'd like to think she'll like me someday…or at least find a way to tolerate me."

His expression is one of dismay as he peers down at me.

"Don't worry about her. I'm sure she'll see who you really are. But even if she doesn't, I don't care. I love you, and that's all that matters. Her opinion, in that aspect of my life, makes no difference to me."

"It sure would be easier if we got along though…for your sake."

"Maybe. But, what about Daniel? Would you change anything based on his opinion of me?"

"No," I say adamantly. "I don't care what he says, you weren't the cause of everything that happened. We both had a hand in it. If anything, he should be grateful to you for fixing the problem."

"I don't think he sees it that way. I don't think he's impressed at my ability to pay off a bully."

I stop walking.

"You didn't have to do that. He'll see what you've done for me as a good thing…eventually. Honestly, I'm not sure what's gotten into him lately. He's not usually like that." We begin walking again.

"He's very protective of you. I'm glad, in a way."

"Yeah, more so lately than normal though."

"I can handle him."

I look up at his confident face.

"But you shouldn't have to. I'll talk to him. Maybe I can get him to see that you're not a bad guy."

He scoffs.

"Hey, now. Don't ruin my reputation."

I giggle and roll my eyes, as we continue our stick gathering mission.

"Do you think we have enough kindling to start our fire?" I say, looking at our haul.

"Probably. Want to head back?"

I nod, and we turn in the direction of our campsite.

Night has fallen, and we've made the last of the s'mores. The meal Logan cooked before that, was perfect. There's nothing like hotdogs toasted over an open fire.

Now, as we snuggle under a blanket together while relaxing on a lounge chair, I have time to reflect on the past months. I'm leaning with my back against his chest, as I gaze up at the countless stars. The serene feeling is heavenly.

"This is so peaceful, you know?" I say.

"Mm," he replies.

"It's hard to believe that our troubles are behind us."

"Shh. Don't say it out loud...you might jinx us." I hear his slight chuckle. Then, his arms give me a gentle squeeze. "I'm glad you feel at ease."

"I do. This is the only place I want to be." I pat his hand which is draped across my torso.

A gentle silence settles across our campsite, as we sit in the calm, just listening to the crackle of the fire and each other's breaths.

"So, where do we go from here?" I ask, breaking the serenity.

"What do you mean?"

"Well, we no longer have to worry about hiding our relationship, and it seems as though there are no more challenges to overcome. Now what do we do?"

I hear his smile, as if the answer is as easy as one plus one.

"How about if we just enjoy each other's company, and savor the journey we're on. I think we both deserve a little happiness, don't you?"

I smile and nod.

Yeah. Neither of us needs anymore drama.

I yawn, then settle further into him.

"Are you tired? Do you want to go to bed?"

"A little, but I don't want to leave this spot. It's comfy and warm."

"The bed is even more comfortable. Why don't we call it a night?"

He attempts to sit up, but I get up and turn to face him. Each of my legs straddles one of his, as I sit in his lap, effectively holding him in place. I then casually lace my fingers behind his neck.

"This is one of the most romantic places we've been since we've met. I'm not going to end this night early just to satisfy my need for sleep," I say. "We can sleep when we're dead, now let's make the most of the time we have here."

I lean into him, pressing my mouth against his, and then feel his arms envelope me, pulling me farther up against him. His readiness is apparent. I wriggle a bit and welcome the friction. He moans softly and pushes his hips upward. We continue to kiss, as our desire for each other explodes. In the back of my mind, I wonder if anyone is close enough to witness this display, but eventually I adopt an *I don't care* attitude.

His hands inch their way up my shirt at the back, and in a split second, my bra is unclasped. They then glide around to the front, as he finds my breasts. I throw my head back, and his mouth finds my throat. I moan, not knowing how much longer I can take his seductive touch.

"Let's go to bed," I whisper, after reuniting with his lips.

"No...Here."

I pull back slightly, as I don't think I heard him correctly.

"Here?" I whisper.

He nods, and his face reveals his intentions.

"Right here," he says. "We've got some cover." He lifts up part of the blanket. "And, the darkness will mask anything else. What do you think? Are you up for another adventure?"

I giggle, then cover my mouth to hush myself.

"Seriously? We can't."

"Why not? No one else is near us. It'll be perfect. Just you and me, making love under the stars." He lifts his eyebrows as a silent plea.

He's serious. Can I really do this? It feels so naughty. I giggle again.

"Okay, but just for a little while, then I want to go inside."

He lets out a frisky growl and bites at my neck. I giggle at his playfulness.

"Shh," he chides, so I bite my bottom lip to stifle my glee.

20

ELORA

Daylight breaks through the windows of our little house in the trees, as if to gently nudge me awake. I stretch and yawn, feeling very well rested. The sheets, which pool around me, cover my bare body, and I can't help but notice that I've managed to steal most of the covers from Logan, who remains asleep. His back is too me, and I sigh as I admire his finely sculpted, naked form. I reach out and gently stroke his back and watch as his muscles ripple beneath my fingers. He stirs and turns onto his back, giving me the full view of his—

"Enjoying the view?" he asks, interrupting my thoughts.

"Hi," I squeak. I've been caught staring. He smiles as if he's just found me with my hand in the cookie jar. Rolling the rest of the way over, he faces me.

"Did you sleep well?"

"Very," I say with a sly smile.

"Mm. Me too. I slept especially well, after last night's exertions." He winks.

"Yes. It was…exceptionally good."

His eyebrows shoot up in surprise.

"My little exhibitionist. Who would've thought?"

I giggle.

"I didn't know I had it in me," I say, grinning from ear to ear. "So, what's on the agenda for today?"

"Check out is at eleven. After that, I thought we'd go to my place. We can talk on the ride home about how to spend the rest of the day." He looks down at the sheet which has inadvertently been pulled away from my body, then he looks hungrily back into my eyes. "But, before we do anything else..." He launches himself on top of me, and nuzzles his stubbly chin into my neck. I laugh and protest, but eventually surrender to his insatiable intentions.

The drive home is bitter sweet. Logan and I had such a good time, I just don't want it to end. He holds my hand, as we make the one-hour trip back to reality.

"You're getting really good at this," I say.

"Good at what?"

"Driving. It must feel great to get even more of your freedom back."

"Yes, it does. I feel almost back to normal." He glances briefly over at me. "Yet another feat I have you to thank for."

"Me? How did I help get you back on the road?"

"Well, I was worried about you, so I was forced to get into my car and drive. Honestly, I wasn't sure I'd even make it to the end of my street." He chuckles and shakes his head.

"And look at you now," I say with pride.

"Yes, look at me now." He smiles broadly and squeezes my hand.

"Hey, why don't you drop me off at my apartment. I'll pick up my car and meet you at your house. That way, I can grab a quick shower and a change of clothes."

"Okay. That'll give me time to chase Michael out," he says with a grin.

Poor Michael.

LOGAN

I watch out the window as an unfamiliar vehicle pulls into my driveway. Upon further inspection, I see Elora behind the wheel, and it dawns on me that I've never seen her vehicle before. She's always driven Daniel's car for the convenience of being more handicap accessible. It's an older model, SUV, but it looks to be in decent shape, although I hear it backfire just before she turns off the engine. I decide to meet her outside.

"Is this what you drive?"

She nods and seems embarrassed.

"Yes, unfortunately." She rolls her eyes. "After I'm done with school, and hopefully get a full time job, I hope to be able to afford to buy something a bit newer—one that's not so vocal," she says, then laughs uneasily.

"Do you want me to take a look at it? It might be something simple."

"Have at it. I'm clueless," she says, as she directs me to the hood.

I ask her to pop the latch, and after fiddling around under the dashboard, she finally finds the lever. She then comes to stand beside me as I take a look.

"Everything looks fine. I don't see any obvious reason behind the backfires. I've checked almost every hose I could reach, and aside from adjusting the timing, I'd say you'll need to take it to a shop." She slumps against the driver's side door.

"It's gotten to the point that it might be more expensive to fix it rather than to just buy a new one."

I wipe my hands on a rag that was stuffed just inside the hood, then sling a sympathetic arm around her.

"We'll figure something out. Come on, let's go inside."

I lead her toward the door, but she stops abruptly.

"Oh, I forgot I brought some extra clothes with me…in case I was coerced into staying the night." She lifts one eyebrow at me as if to dare me to deny that I might be thinking about it. I smile guiltily.

"I'll get your bag," I say. After all, it's the least I can do. She follows me to the back of the car and opens the hatch.

"Is this it?" She nods. "How long do you plan on staying?" I say in jest, pretending it's heavy. Secretly, I'm hoping she has several days' worth in here.

"Ha ha, very funny. I could just as easily go home tonight, you know." She gives me her best look of warning, and I laugh.

"Not a chance."

I lift the bag out and close the hatch, turning to walk toward the house, when a flash of color catches my eye. I glance down at her bumper to spy a small sticker. It's turquoise in color with a picture of a porpoise on it. It simply says, *I love dolphins*, and I can't help but get the feeling that I've seen it somewhere before. Wracking my brain, I begin to walk toward my house. Suddenly, immeasurable pain lances through me, and I drop her bag to grab my head. I cry out from the torment, as a memory comes through from a day I'll never forget. I feel Elora rush to my side as I slump to the ground, hitting my knees against the concrete in the process.

"Logan! What's wrong? What can I do?" Her frantic voice begs me for information, just as flashes of memories come charging through my brain.

A highway.

Taillights.

Screeching tires.

The smell of burnt rubber and gasoline.

I'm watching in slow motion as the vehicle to the side of me begins to change lanes. They're not stopping. I've run out of road. I swerve to avoid the collision, but as my tires meets the gravel on the berm, I can feel my front tire begin to wobble uncontrollably. I stiffen and grab tightly onto the handlebars, trying desperately to regain control, just as I did all those months ago—just before being forced off the road by the SUV…with a dolphin bumper sticker.

I gasp for air as, slowly, my physical agony relents, and I'm left with a horrible reality.

Was it her? It couldn't be. She would've told me…wouldn't she? I try to make sense of what I've just seen, but I'm crushed by the gravity of it all.

Was she the one who caused the accident that took my legs?

I glance up at her concerned eyes, but I don't know what to say. I'm terrified of the answers I seek.

"Logan, talk to me. What's going on? Are you okay?" She gently caresses my face in an attempt to wake me from whatever nightmare she thinks I'm in. She has no idea what I've just uncovered. Hesitantly, I open my mouth to speak.

"Was it…*you?*" My voice is raw and resembles that of a frightened child. "Tell me it wasn't you. *Please*," I beg her.

She's puzzled, as she tries to decipher my words.

"I don't know what you mean. What are you talking about?"

She's shaking her head, completely clueless, and for a split second, I'm jealous. She doesn't know what I'm asking. Her world is as it was, before she arrived at my house today. She has no idea how her world—*our world,* is about to come crashing down.

"The accident. Was it you? Were you driving on the road the day I lost my legs?" I manage to ask, though I'm not even sure it's audible. I'm praying she says *no.* I'm hoping to see innocence wash over her face at my questions, but when her face falls and turns pale…I know.

I cry out again, this time from the anguish of knowing that the one person in this world who I love the most, was the one who took everything from me. Rising to my feet, I pass her in pursuit of the safety of my house. I hear her footsteps as she follows me inside.

"Logan, wait!" she says, trying desperately to divulge some ridiculous excuse, no doubt, but I don't want to hear it. I swing the door to close it, but she catches it and enters. *"Please."*

I turn abruptly, startling her in the process.

"Please what? What could you possibly say to explain what you did? How could you look me in the face, month after month, and *lie* to me?" My breaths come out as if I've just run a marathon, as I wait for her reply.

"I—I don't know what to say." She shakes her head as tears roll down her cheeks. "I'm...sorry." The word *sorry* comes out as barely a whisper, as she bows her head. My instinct is to hold her—to comfort her, but I can't do it this time. It hurts to want to ease her pain, and make her feel the pain I felt, at the same time.

I stride toward the kitchen table and lean over, gripping its edges. My knuckles grow paler as the seconds tick by.

"Tell me about it. What do you remember about that day?" My voice is menacingly soft. I'm sure I must be scaring her, but I don't care. I want answers. I turn my head slightly, and she comes into my peripheral view. She's standing where I left her; her head is still bowed. Her silence causes even more fury to rise up, until I can't take it anymore. I walk back over to her and roughly lift her chin. Looking into her sorrowful eyes only fuels the fire that shows no signs of stopping. "Tell me what you remember," I say with my teeth gritted. "You owe me that much." We stare at each other until finally, her mouth opens.

"It was a warm day in October. The sun was setting behind me. I was coming home from...somewhere, and I remember thinking about how unusual it was that the road was so empty at that time of day. I needed to exit the highway, so I looked back, saw it was clear, and changed lanes. Suddenly, there was a terrible sound. I looked back but the sun was in my eyes. I didn't see what had made the noise. Still, I pulled off to the side of the road just to make sure. That's when I saw the smoke. It was coming from the berm. I was about to go investigate, when I saw a car pull over and park. The driver got out and ran to the scene. I knew there was nothing I could do, so, in a panic, I put the car back in drive, and I left." She gazes into my eyes again, regret washing over her beautiful face. "I'm so sorry," she sobs. "I had no idea it was you. It never even crossed my mind that *your* accident took place outside of a military zone. You never wanted to talk about it, and I never pushed the issue. I just assumed you were injured while deployed."

Her hands cover her face as she weeps into them. I close my eyes briefly and step back, afraid of what I might say or do, if I don't reign in my rampant temper. My heart tries desperately to tell me it was just a freak accident, but my head screams out for justice. How could she, knowing that she caused a horrific accident, just drive away? It doesn't make sense, knowing her the way I do. I can't seem to wrap my mind around it.

I absentmindedly plop down onto a kitchen chair, trying to understand. She slowly comes to stand in front of me. I'm staring at her feet. What does she want from me? Forgiveness? She says nothing, and I wonder what's going on in her mind. Does she regret it?

Good God, Logan, of course she does; she's not an animal.

As we stand at a stalemate, I continue to watch her feet. Her toes wiggle as her natural balance is kept in check. That's something I'll never again get to do. I lean forward, resting my forehead in my hands, while grasping handfuls of my hair.

"I need you to leave," I say, as calmly as I can muster. I hear her quietly gasp.

"Logan, I—"

"You need to go!" I'm losing the grip on my temper again.

"But—"

"*Get out!*" I say, forcefully, as my head swings up to glare at her. I watch her horrified expression as she moves back a step, then two, then I watch as she quietly turns and moves toward the front door. The sound of it latching behind her both satisfies me, and tears my heart out, in equal shares.

Her car's engine roars to life, but I can't watch her leave. Both my life, and my hell, began with her, and I don't know if I can ever forgive her.

ELORA

I race into my apartment and throw myself onto my bed. I'm a blubbering mess, before my head hits the mattress. I wail tears so hot that I'm sure my face will never recover. I've lost him. I've lost him for good this time. There's nothing I could ever say or do to make up for the fact that his legs are gone. My guilt from that day resurfaces, and I can hardly stand to be in my own skin. What am I going to do?

I cry and cry, for hours it seems, until my head is ready to explode. Finally, I sit up, wiping the last few stray tears from my cheeks, and I lean against the headboard in a daze. I've never felt so lonely in all my life. I just want these memories to be gone. The look on his face was one I hope to never see on anyone I love ever again. He was desolate and angry, and it's my fault. My thoughts turn against me, and I come to the bleak realization that we're done. I can never hold him again, never kiss his lips, never feel his arms surround me again. He'll never forgive me. Why would he? Tears threaten, but I need to hold myself together. Daniel will be home soon, and I don't want him to see me like this.

I no sooner think it, when I hear Daniel's arrival. I quickly jump to my feet and dash into the bathroom. When splashing cold water on my reddened face fails to hide my sorrow, I decide to take a shower in hopes that time will remedy my appearance. I hear him near the bathroom door as I step in under the water.

"Kind of early for you to take a shower. I thought for sure you'd be over Logan's house." he says, teasing me. "Uh...he's not...in there with you...is he?"

"No. He had somewhere to be, so I just came home," I lie.

"Well, don't take forever in there. There's only one bathroom, you know."

I snort at the uninvited image of my brother crossing his legs and hopping up and down while waiting for me to finish.

After Daniel walks away, I let the warm water rain down on my face as I think of what story to tell him. He'll start to wonder why I'm no longer going over to Logan's house. I'll need something plausible to keep Daniel from wanting to storm over there and save the day. When I'm fairly certain my face is relatively back to normal, I exit the bathroom to get dressed, then walk into the living room and find my brother sitting on the couch.

"How was work?" I ask on my way through to the kitchen. He eyes me suspiciously.

"Fine," he says cautiously. "Have you been crying?"

Damn it.

"No. Why do you ask?"

"Because you look like you've been crying. What's wrong?" He stands and walks over to me. I keep my head down, but he's hard to fool. "You *have* been crying. What did he do *now?*" His irritation is apparent.

"Oh, just calm down. I'm fine," I say. "Yes, I've been crying, but it's PMS. You know how women get. We had a small fight, and we're taking a break. It's fine. I'm fine. It's no big deal...really." I do my best to convince him that I'm telling truth, and for the most part, I think he believes me.

"Are you sure?"

"*Yes!* For God's sake. *I'm sure!*"

"Okay, okay," he says while holding his hands up. "You're right about the PMS. I'm beginning to feel sorry for the guy," he mumbles under his breath as he walks back into the living room.

LOGAN

"What the hell happened in here?" Michael says as he walks in and sees the aftermath of my violent tantrum. I lean over with my hands on my knees as I catch the breaths that keeps heaving from my chest. When I look up at him, he's waiting expectantly for an explanation.

"Nothing," I pant.

"Really," he cocks his head to the side. "So this room," he looks back at the kitchen, "no, this *house,* has been spontaneously ransacked by unknown forces?" I nod, and he shakes his head. "What the hell happened, Logan?"

I shake my head. I don't want to say it out loud, but I know he'll keep going until I do.

"It was her," I say; my voice is hoarse.

"Elora?" I nod. "What about her?"

I wince as I try to fight back my conflicting feelings for her.

"She was in the SUV. She was driving it." He looks confused, so I elaborate. "*She* is the reason I lost my legs, Michael. She cut me off that damned day. Do you understand what I'm saying?"

Suddenly, his eyebrows shoot up as realization dawns.

"Oh," is all he says. I almost chuckle to think I've nearly rendered him speechless.

"Yeah. How about that? The girl who changed my life was the reason I wanted to end it in the first place. Talk about irony, eh?" I cross the room and open the liquor cabinet. I've never needed a drink so badly in my life. I pour the amber liquid into a nearby glass and drink it in a few gulps. I then repeat the action twice more.

"Are you sure it was her? I mean, did she *say* it was?"

I look at him out of the corner of my eye.

"Yes, she did." I down another swig and pray that the alcohol starts taking effect soon. I just want to forget I ever met her.

"What exactly did she say?"

I slam down my empty glass in anger, and turn to him.

"What does it matter, Michael? Is this twenty questions? I had a memory surface, which included her vehicle. I remembered the stupid, *fucking* dolphin sticker on the back bumper, and it all came back to me. *It was her! She* caused the accident that took my legs and nearly took my life. And ironically," I chuckle sadly. "I wish now that she'd finished the job."

I pour myself another glass, when he swipes it out of my hand. It hits the floor, spilling the contents onto the carpet.

"Knock off this pity party, Logan. You have every right to be angry as hell, but you need to put a few things into perspective. She may have been the cause of your pain, but she's also the cure. Whatever happened that day was an accident, I'm sure. No decent human being would purposely run another person off the road, leaving them for dead, unless there were extenuating circumstances. The proof is in the details. Did you get any? Did you ever once think about how this has affected *her?*"

I scoff at his logic.

"How this has affected *her?* Are you fucking kidding me? She has all her limbs. She wasn't forced to endure months in the hospital and have surgery after *fucking* surgery to put her body back together. She doesn't have to deal with people staring at her as if she's some kind of *freak!*" I laugh, but it's sarcastic. "Don't ask me to consider how she feels when her working here has made her look like a saint." I grab another bottle and drink it without a glass.

My mind begins to run through all the good times we've had together, but I quickly take another swig, hoping to keep those thoughts at bay. It works for the moment. I don't want to think about how much it hurts to both love her and hate her.

21

ELORA

My bed is warm. I don't want to leave it. My heart is broken at what I've done. Logan hates me, and with good reason. Even though I know I need to get up for school, I can't seem to motivate my body to move.

I miss him.

Why did I have to come into his life? Why can't I go back in time?

I pull the covers over my face as tears threaten again. I cannot start this again. If I want to look like a human being today, I need to get rid of my puffy, red face and get on with life...without him. Suddenly, there's a knock at the door.

"Elora?" Daniel says softly, "You'll need to leave soon, if you want to get to class on time."

I sniffle quietly before answering him. I don't want him to know I've been crying.

"Okay. I'm getting up."

"Are you okay? Is there anything I can do?"

Is there anything? I ponder that question for a moment, then push it out of my mind.

"No."

My day drudges on, as I go through the motions of living a life devoid of Logan. I'm doing my best not to think about him, but everything I see and touch, seems to bring my thoughts back to all I've lost. I don't see a light at the end of the tunnel, only darkness and uncertainty, as I fall deeper into despair.

I wonder how he is. Pff! I can guess. He's mad as hell and probably eradicating every errant thought of me from his life. I'm the cause; it's only fitting that I'm suffering now.

School is going on all around me, but I'm not listening. I can't seem to hear anything over the sound of my own heartbeat, which thrums in my ears.

"Elora, what's wrong? What happened?" Daniel asks, trying to make this better for me.

"I don't want to talk about it," I mutter sullenly, as I sit on the couch in my pajamas. Daniel sits next to me and puts his hand on my shoulder. I glance at it, wishing it was Logan's hand instead.

"Did he hurt you? I should go over there."

"No! You can't!" I shout, and perk up immediately. "He didn't do anything wrong. We just…can't be together anymore," I say, hoping he'll just leave it alone.

"Tell me…what happened between the two of you?"

"I told you, I don't want to talk about it. Maybe, someday I will, but not now." I look into his concerned eyes, silently pleading with him to drop it.

"Okay, fine. I'll leave it alone, but please promise me you'll try to feel better…and maybe eat something too." I nod in agreement, knowing full well I'll never be the same again.

LOGAN

"You're not going to mope in bed for days on end like you did before, are you?" Michael says through my closed bedroom door.

I open it abruptly and startle him.

"No. I'm too angry for that. I'm going to the rec to work off some steam." I push past him, headed for the door, but despite my speed he follows me out.

"Mind if I tag along?"

"Do I have a choice?"

"No."

I let out a frustrated sigh. "Come on then. You can drive." I toss the keys at him.

"I planned on it. I want to get there in one piece," he says, then snorts. I give him a sideways glance.

❧

The gym is filled with steroid injected rejects from the area. I roll my eyes, just wanting some time to myself, so I can think. I choose a piece of equipment near the back and set up to do an ab workout.

Breathing in through my nose and out through my mouth, I crank out 100 sit ups with ease. When I see some jock eyeing me, I assume he wants the equipment, so I get off and nod to him. His eyes narrow, but he says nothing. Next, I walk over to the barbells. I'm not even sure how much weight I put on the ends, but I keep lifting, until I'm sure my arms might fall off.

"Hey, take it easy on your muscles. I don't need you whining about hurting yourself," Michael says.

"Fuck off, Michael. I don't need a babysitter."

"I'm just looking out for you, man." I curl my lip up on one side and almost audibly growl at him. He holds his hands up and backs off.

As I sit on the rowing machine, I see that jock again. Is he staring at me?

What the fuck?

"You got a problem?" I say boldly.

He shakes his head.

"No, but it looks like you do."

I inhale deeply and stand up from the rower. With my chest puffed out, I walk toward him.

"My only problem is you staring at me. What, you wanna hug or something?" I laugh sarcastically.

"Fuck off," he says, and turns to walk away.

"Oh, hell no. If you've got something to say, say it."

The muscle head turns back around and steps close, until we're standing nose to nose.

"You better just back off, stumpy, before I teach you how to be-have at the gym."

I snarl as I draw my clenched fist back, and I'm about to launch it at him when it's caught behind me.

"Logan! That's enough!" Michael shouts, as he restrains my arm.

"You'd better take him home before I finish what *he* started," the guy says. He shoots me one last look, before he turns and walks out of sight. Michael's grip lessens, so I pull out of his hold.

"What the fuck do you think you're doing? I had that!" I say, furious.

"Like hell you did! That guy would've pummeled you. Calm the fuck down, dude!"

"Screw you. I'm fine." I step away from him, but he counters and steps in front of me.

"You're *anything* but fine. We're going home, and you're going to call her. Let's go." He grabs my upper arm, but I yank it out of his grasp.

"I'll go, when I'm ready."

Michael looks around the room, when his eyes catch sight of something.

"Come here. I have something you can hit." Reluctantly, I follow him to a bag, which hangs from the ceiling from a chain. "You want to start a fight? Hit this. It doesn't hit back," he says, then positions himself on the side opposite me.

This is ridiculous.

Tentatively, I swing at the bag.

"Is that all you got? Hit it harder."

I grit my teeth and put more effort into my swing.

"Our grandmother can hit harder than that. Let's see something that could do some damage," he says, antagonizing me. I hit it twice more in combination, and he scoffs. Finally, he leans in and whispers, "Hit it like it's Elora's next lover."

At his horrific words, I ball up my fist as tightly as I can and, with a mental image I hope to never see in real life, I unleash my fury on the bag. Punch after anger induced punch, I take all the rage I've dealt with over the past few days and let it out. My heart pounds to the beat of my violent assault, until my knuckles finally become numb.

"Okay, that's enough," Michael says, but I continue. "Logan, stop. You're bleeding," he says, but I keep going. Finally, he lets go of the bag and snakes his arms around both my elbows at my back. I struggle to break free from his hold. "Hey, stop. You're done," he says, quietly.

I feel drops of water fall onto my thighs. It's then I realize it's not water, but tears. *I'm crying angry fucking tears.* I jerk out of his hold and head for the exit, before anyone can witness my pathetic display.

A few minutes later, while sitting in the car, Michael pats my shoulder.

"You okay?"

"I'll never be okay."

He exhales.

"I'm sorry. I thought that comment would help. I was wrong."

I nod my forgiveness, but I can't seem to wipe away that image.

As the days turn into weeks, my heart aches more and more for the girl I thought I knew. My anger has subsided, and sorrow has begun to seep in. I'm trying desperately to wrap my mind around what happened and how much she knew about the so called noise she heard behind her car that day, but understanding eludes me. I'm finding it harder and harder to believe that it was anything more than an accident. Still, I can't condone her behavior in leaving the scene—or mine, the day I confronted her about it. I'm ashamed at the way I reacted, and I feel I need to apologize. Just then, Michael walks into the house with fast food bags in his hands.

"You know, you just need to make up with her already. I'm sick of eating this shit." He plops the bags onto the table and takes out what he ordered.

"I'm not sure what I'd say to her," I say, absentmindedly glancing out the window.

He takes an enormous bite of his burger, then pockets part of it in his cheek to enable himself to speak.

"Start with hello," he says in a muffled voice. He chews a bit, then swallows. "If you miss her, I'm sure she misses you too. Just call her. See what happens." He shrugs.

"It's not that simple. The last time we saw each other…it was… difficult. Where the hell do I start? What do I say? I don't even know if I *want* to talk to her at all. What if my anger surfaces again, and I say something terrible?" I look to him for wisdom, but he just shrugs. "Some help you are." He snorts.

"Dude, just call her. I can't answer these questions for you. You'll just have to see how it feels when you finally talk again. *If* you talk again."

I slump against the back of the chair. I was hoping for some inspiration, but I sink further into my depression.

It takes a whole day to convince myself to dial her number. And, as I hold the phone in my hand, I rehearse my opening line.

"Hello," I say, sort of monotone, then scoff at myself. "Hi," I say with a little more gusto. No, too much enthusiasm. "Hi, Elora," I say quietly, but nothing I say is cutting it. I sigh in exasperation at my idiocrasy. "Good grief, just do it," I tell myself, then I hit '*call*'.

ELORA

My phone rings as I leave for school. I glance down, assuming it's Daniel, but gasp and nearly drop it, when the caller ID says *Logan*.

What should I do?

Should I answer it?

What does he want?

Am I ready to speak to him?

The phone rings for the third time, and I know it'll go to voice mail after the fourth. It's such a difficult decision to make in a fraction of a second. My nerves begin to make me shake, as I press the little green button.

"H—hello?" I say meekly.

"Hi," he says in an eerily quiet voice. There's a long pause before he speaks again. "I'm sorry to bother you. I know this is usually the time you leave for school."

"It's okay. I'm just leaving now." I'm trying to gauge his mood, but he hasn't given my much to go on yet.

"How are you?" he asks softly.

Really depressed and missing you terribly.

"I'm okay. You?"

"I'm fine." His voice is still devoid of emotion. "So…"

"So," I repeat. It's obvious he has no idea why he's called me.

"I'd like to...apologize...for my behavior that day—"

"Oh, God, please don't apologize," I interrupt. "You have nothing to be sorry for. I deserved the reaction you gave me."

He snorts.

"No. I was very angry, and I didn't mean to yell at you like that. I know that what you did was an accident. I know that because I know you, and you'd never do anything like that to someone on purpose. I guess I just need to know...why. Why did you drive away? What happened? Did you know I was there? Did you know I needed help? Did you at least think about helping? *Why?* What made you drive off?"

He needs answers—answers that I can't give him. I sigh, and as I try to buy time to think, the silence overtakes us.

"I know you want answers, but...I can't give you any. I'm sorry that's not what you want to hear right now, but please know that I had no idea it was you on the side of that road. I didn't know until that day in your driveway. I never lied to you up until that day, and I'm so sorry you found out the way you did. It's killing me to know how much pain I put you through, and I'm sincerely sorry for my actions on that day."

Tears stream down my face as I try to hold them in. I don't want him to think I'm crying to gain his sympathy.

"You *can't* give me answers, or you *won't?*"

I pause.

"I won't."

"Why the hell not? You don't think I deserve to know?" His irritation makes me wince slightly.

"It's nothing like that, Logan, I swear. I just..." I pause again to gather my nerve. "Let's just leave it alone. It's obvious you'll never forgive me, so what's the point in rehashing it all? I regret what happened that day...more than you know, and I'd give anything to not be in that car."

He snorts.

"I've gotta go," he says acidly, and another round of pain lances through me.

"Okay," I say, but it's almost a sob.

He hangs up without saying goodbye, and I lean my forehead on my steering wheel and cry.

The next day, as I'm walking out of school, I'm running my last conversation with Logan through my mind. He sounded like he might've been in a better place in the beginning, but then his anger took hold. I can't blame him. I know he's probably trying to come to terms with all that's been disclosed, and I'm certain he was disappointed in the fact that I refused to stroll down memory lane with him. The truth is, I can't give him the details he wants. I just want to forget that day ever happened. Just then, I bump, quite literally, into someone.

"Oh, my God! I'm so sorry. I wasn't paying attention," I say as I look up.

"Hey, it's okay, Elora. I wasn't looking either," Rory chuckles as he touches my arm. "Are you done for the day?" he asks as he begins to walk with me.

"Yeah, thank God. That test was horrible."

"Oh, I know! I studied all night and day for it, but I think I failed it miserably," he says. "I'll be lucky to become a nurse's aide, let alone an RN."

I laugh for the first time in weeks.

"I know what you mean. Maybe, I should try for something in another field. I think I definitely bombed it."

"No way! Not you. You're so good under pressure. You'll do fine. You'll see," he says with a confident smile.

"Thanks," I smile back.

"Hey, to celebrate the end of the semester, do you want to get a cup of coffee with me? There's a café within walking distance from here."

My first reaction is to say *no.* I'm not really in the mood, and I probably wouldn't be great company. But then, I don't have anything to do but go home and stare at Daniel for the rest of the night, and I really need time away from *that*. I shrug.

"Sure."

"Great!" he says, and we walk the short distance it takes to get there.

We place our orders, then find a seat. The small table we've chosen is in the corner near the couches. Rory sits, and I sit across from him.

"It feels so good to know we're that much closer to graduating. I mean, I know we still have a long way to go, but every test gets us closer," he says as he leans back in his chair.

"Yeah, if someone had told me how hard nursing school would be, I probably wouldn't have done it." I snort, then look at him. He's sweating. I narrow my eyes. "Are you okay? You look a little flushed."

He wipes his brow.

"I'm fine. My heart races when I have too much caffeine," he says. "This is my millionth cup of the day."

"Ah, yes, the hazards of studying for a nursing test," I say, then laugh. "Give me your wrist. I'll check your pulse." I reach for his hand, the place my fingers on his radial artery. We sit still as I count the number of beats I feel. I frown when I notice an irregularity. "Have you ever had an EKG done?" I say, while holding onto his wrist.

"No. Why?"

"I'm not sure, but I think your heart is beating out of rhythm. It's sort of fluttering."

"Seriously?"

I nod.

"Yes. I would have that checked out before too long. It might be nothing, but I know some heart conditions, such as Supraventricular Tachycardia can be aggravated by caffeine." His brow lifts in surprise at this news.

"Oh, God. A life without caffeine? How does one survive?" He makes an expression of mock horror, and I laugh. He then smiles fondly and covers my hands with both of his. "And, *that* is why you'll make a great nurse. Thanks for being so concerned about me. I'll have it checked out."

Then, from out of nowhere, I hear a quiet gasp. Rory and I look over in the direction of the sound to see Logan standing before us. My face falls at his expression. He's horrified...but why? I glance down at Rory's hands, which still cradle both of mine, then I look back at Logan.

He clears his throat.

"Elora," he says coldly, with a chill in his expression.

"Logan. What are you doing here?"

I'm shocked, and I pull my hands back from Rory's.

"I was just in the neighborhood. I needed coffee." His shakes his head slightly. "I didn't know you'd be here with..." He stops before finishing his sentence.

I feel I owe him an explanation.

"Uh...Rory, this is Logan. Logan, I'd like you to meet Rory."

"It's nice to meet you," he says with formality. They shake hands but then suddenly, Logan looks...nervous?

"Rory is my—"

Logan holds his hand up for me to stop talking.

"No need to explain," he interrupts. "I have to go." He turns to Rory again." Take care of her," he says, as if he's just given Rory his blessing to marry me or something. I give him a puzzled look, but he leaves without a backward glance.

"What the hell was that?" Rory asks as the door to the café closes. I slouch into the back of my seat as, I blow out a long held breath.

"*That* was the one who got away."

LOGAN

I launch my fist toward the wall of my bedroom with everything I have, and end up with a nice hole in the wall. When I draw my fist back, I see blood forming across my knuckles. That's going to leave a mark. I walk over to my bed and sit. Then, covering my face, I fall backward, eventually fixing my stare at the ceiling. I hear a soft knock at the door.

"Can I come in?" Michael says as he enters anyway. I scoff at his manners.

"You're already in, aren't you?" My voice is laced with sarcasm.

"Nice hole in the wall. You wanna talk about it?" he asks, as he falls on his back next to me and laces his fingers behind his head.

"Not really."

"Can I guess?"

I shrug.

"Can I stop you?" I say, and he laughs.

"Nope."

"Go ahead then."

"Does it have to do with Elora?" I nod. "Did you call her again?" I shake my head. "Did you *see* her?" I nod, reluctantly. "Ah. I see why you felt like you needed a new window in your room." He's referring to my tantrum just now.

"You have no idea."

"Tell me about it then."

I sigh and muster up the strength to talk about what I saw today at the coffee shop.

"I saw her at a café. I stopped in to pick up some coffee, and I saw her. She wasn't alone." I hear him groan slightly. "Some guy named Rory was with her. They were holding hands."

"Are you sure they were *together* together?"

I glance over at his ignorance.

"They were holding hands. What else could I assume from that?" He shrugs.

"I don't know. Did you ask her if he was her boyfriend?"

"*No.* Don't be ridiculous. Why would I?"

"Um...so you'd know. Jeez, bro, you suck at this stuff," he says and shakes his head. "If you want to know something, you have to ask. How else will you know for sure?" I shrug this time. "You have to ask yourself a question."

"What's that?"

"How did seeing her with someone else make you feel?"

I look back up at the ceiling. I don't want to think about it.

"Like shit."

"Good," he says, and I look at him like he's an idiot...because he is sometimes. He elaborates. "If you felt nothing at all, it would mean that you're over her, and you could move on. But the fact that you felt like shit, as you put it, well, that's a sign that you need to get over this little relationship hump and go claim what's yours."

"This *little relationship hump?* She fucking ran me off the road and left the scene. That's not a hump, it's a damned mountain. How am I supposed to overlook that?"

"I don't know. That's something you have to look inside yourself to find the answer to. I'm just saying that I don't think you're done with her. Maybe, just maybe, your love for her is stronger than your will to hold this accident against her. Maybe your heart is trying to forgive her, but your mind is fighting it. When in doubt, go with your heart."

I take in a deep breath and exhale loudly. Since when is he such an expert on relationships? I tell myself that he's wrong, but I know, as usual, he's right, though I'd never tell him that.

"So, what are you gonna do?" he adds.

"I don't know what I *can* do. I've asked her for answers and she's refused to give me any. How can I forgive her if I'm still trying to understand why she did it?"

"Maybe it's more complicated than it needs to be. Maybe you can forgive her without all the details. There's obviously a reason she's not saying anything. Maybe you should take her at her word. She's said she's sorry. So, just believe her."

I exhale again. Can I do it? Can I just forgive her, even though I don't understand the whole situation? I hated seeing her with some other man's hands wrapped neatly around hers. Those should've been my hands. I let Michael's words sink in. *Just believe her.* Is my love for her stronger than my quest for justice? Can I simply let her keep all the whys and hows to herself? I rub my face, as I analyze everything she's said to me since we broke up. Something isn't sitting right with me. I need to see her—to talk to her. I have to know if we can get past all this.

I sit up abruptly. I'm on a mission—a decision's been made Michael follows my lead and smiles.

"Atta boy. Go get her," he says with a wink and a slap on my back.

As I approach her building, adrenaline shoots through my body, and my nerves take over. Shakily, I get out of my car and head up to her apartment. I raise my fist, and after a slight hesitation, I knock. Closing my eyes, I take one last deep breath and wait on pins and needles for her to open the door.

I don't have to wait long, as her surprised look makes my heart rate increase.

"Logan. You're…here."

"May I come in…please?"

"Of course," she says, then shifts to one side to allow me to enter. I look around. We're alone. I hear the door latch behind me, and I'm reminded of the last time she left my house. I swallow and turn to face her.

"I hope I'm not interrupting anything. I just had to see you."

"Um…no. I'm not doing anything. What can I do for you?" Her voice is apprehensive so I gesture to the couch.

"Can we sit?"

She nods and walks toward the couch. She sits at one end, and I sit at the other. I pull one leg up, so I can look at her. I need to gauge her reactions, to know if I can do this.

"These last few weeks have been very hard for me. I've not only been battling my anger over the fact that I now know who was driving the car that caused my accident, but I've been struggling to come to terms with the fact that it was caused by the one I love." She bows her head shamefully and peers down at her fingers. I clear my throat and run a nervous hand through my hair. "Look, I know you. I know you very well…and if you say there's a reason you drove off…I believe you." Her head swings up abruptly. "I know you'd never purposely do something to harm anyone, and for that reason, I'd like to extend my forgiveness."

She rubs both hands over her face. I think she's speechless.

"Logan…are you sure you can do that? For reasons of my own, I can't tell you what you need to hear. I'm not sure you can live with that."

I scoot closer to her and take her hands in mine. Those hands that some other guy was just holding.

"The pain of losing my legs was great…but not as great as the pain of watching you walk out of my life." I bring her hand up to my lips and kiss it softly. When I lower it, I search her expression for any sign of hope. "Elora, I can live without the details…what I *can't* live without…is *you*."

"She won't give you details, but I will," says a voice from behind me. I turn around to see Daniel standing just feet from us.

"Daniel, no!" Elora says, which causes me to look back at her.

"You've done enough for me. Now it's time I tell my side of the story," he tells her. He walks farther into the room and sits on the chair opposite us. I turn in my seat to listen.

"Daniel, can I see you in the other room, *please?*" Elora's face is angry as she silently scolds her brother. He shakes his head.

"No. No matter what you say, I'm going to tell him."

"*No!*"

"*Yes.* I'm not going to watch you throw your life away over something that's my fault."

I feel as though I'm watching a tennis match as I look from one to the other. I've finally had enough.

"Let him talk. I want to hear what he has to say," I demand, and she looks at me with concern. I then turn my attention to Daniel.

"Elora was wasn't lying when she said she was on the road that day in October, but she didn't exactly tell you the truth after that."

"Daniel," she warns, but a sad smile from her brother silences her. He continues.

"It was early evening as we drove home from the bar. I'd been there since early afternoon, when a call placed by the bartender, to my sister, summoned her to pick me up. I was drunk but somehow, I convinced Elora I was okay to drive home. She wouldn't give me the keys to my car, so I grabbed hers. She protested loudly, but I can be an asshole sometimes, and I ended up behind the wheel. She told me to take it slow, so I wouldn't rouse suspicion, and we were on our way. I don't remember all the details, but I can tell you what I remember." I nod, as I anxiously await the rest of his story.

"We were on the highway. I was about to miss our exit, so I quickly got over into the right lane. Elora kept telling me to slow down, but I was in a hurry and trying to avoid being seen by the cops. Suddenly, she looked back. She said she heard something. I looked in my rearview mirror, but saw nothing. I assured her there was nothing there, but she kept insisting and had me pull off to the side of the road. We both watched as a small puff of smoke began to rise from the berm.

She started saying she thought we'd hit someone. Panicked, I denied it, even though I thought it could be possible."

I close my eyes, trying not to relive that moment all over again.

"Anyway, that puff of smoke turned into a larger one, and Elora tried to open her door. She said she was going to see if someone needed her help. I knew if she did that, it would mean that I caused an accident, possibly injuring someone, and I might see jail time. I just couldn't handle that thought. I reached across and pulled her door shut. I told her we'd call the police, when we got further away, but that I wasn't going to let her near there. She begged and begged me to go back, but as she protested…loudly, I just kept driving. She then dialed 911. She kept looking back, as I kept denying I did anything wrong." I inhale sharply and close my eyes, as the image of the fleeing SUV surfaces. I remember reaching out for the retreating vehicle, pleading for it to stop. When I open my eyes, Daniel looks directly at me. "Logan, please accept my sincerest apology. I'm so sorry. I was drunk. I panicked, when I didn't know what to do. I should've gone back. I shouldn't have let Elora keep this a secret for me. I should've turned myself in. The truth is, if I had known it would come back on my sister, I would have." He glances at her as a tear streaks down her cheek. I can tell he regrets her involvement.

"Thank you," I say. "Thank you for telling me." I don't have the capacity to say anything more to him. He nods his head and stands, walking back into the hallway, presumably to his room. I turn to face her, as I know it's my turn to apologize.

"Elora—"

"Logan, I'm so sorry," she interrupts. "I didn't want this to happen, especially not to you. I should've never let him get behind the wheel. I should've made him stop at the first sign something was wrong. I should've leapt from the car. I should've done *something*. I'm so, so sorry." Tears streak down her face again, as she takes the blame for that night's events.

My brow furrows.

"You did nothing wrong, Elora. *Nothing.* Do you hear me?" At her sobs, I scoot even closer, and wrap my arms around her. She melts into my embrace and cries into my neck. "Shh. It's okay." I pull back slightly to see her face. Her eyes are pink and her cheeks wet, so I reach up and wipe away her tears. "Hey, don't cry. You have nothing to be upset about."

Her sorrow filled eyes reach mine as she sniffles.

"But, I could've stopped him."

I shake my head.

"Maybe, but what's done is done. You weren't the driver. You could only do so much. The fact that you tried to get him to do the right thing means *everything.*" I kiss her forehead, then let her head fall back onto my shoulder. "I only wish you had told me sooner. Are these the details you wouldn't tell me?" She nods, her head against me, and I nod in acknowledgement. "You let me blame you. Why did you do that?"

She sniffs again and pulls back.

"Daniel's my brother. I wanted to protect him. I didn't want him to get a DUI, and I was afraid he might go to jail because I was too weak to stop him."

I snort.

"Daniel's a big boy. Maybe, he needs to take responsibility for his actions. That's sometimes the only way people learn."

"And that's what I intend to do," Daniel says as he walks back into the room.

"*What?*" Elora says as she stands abruptly. "Daniel, you can't! They'll put you in *jail!*"

He shrugs.

"Maybe, Logan's right. Maybe, that's what it'll take to make me realize I'm not a rebellious teen anymore. I can't go on like this forever. I've been self-medicating with alcohol since the accident, but now I need to take responsibility for what I did." He looks at me directly. "Please forgive me. I'm so sorry that I was the one who caused you so much pain. If there's anything I can do to make it up to you, just name it." I nod, then give him a small smile.

Elora starts to cry at the thought of her brother owning up to his mistakes. She walks over to him and throws her arms around him.

"Please don't do this," she begs. He unwraps her arms from his neck and smiles fondly at her.

"You'll be okay, and so will I. Stop worrying so much about me. You've got someone else to take care of now." He glances over at me again and winks. I smile and walk toward him. Daniel stretches out his hand, and I glance down at it for a moment, before reaching out to shake it. He nods slightly, then turns his attention back to his sister. "I'm so sorry for letting you take the blame for this. I didn't realize that this was the reason the two of you broke up. Had I known, I would've confessed sooner." She nods and hugs him one more time. Then, after ignoring his sister's pleas, Daniel walks out the door, headed in the direction of the police station. Elora is upset, but she comes to stand next to me. I place my arm around her shoulders.

"There's just one more unanswered question I have," I say. She looks up, confused.

"What is it?"

"Are you dating Rory now? Am I gonna have to fight to get you back?"

She laughs loudly.

"No. Rory's just a friend from school. I don't think you'll have to do too much convincing to pry me away from him."

We both smile, which feels so good.

"Although I'm mad at you for lying to me, I'm relieved to find out the truth. Your brother will be fine. I'll talk to the officers and put in a good word for him. Hopefully, he won't see much jail time, maybe none at all." She nods sadly.

"I'm glad you forgave me, *before* you knew the truth about the accident. That says a lot about you. I really am sorry for my part in all this." I place my finger against her lips.

"And I'm sorry for the way I treated you. I guess none of us are innocent. The good thing is that we'll all be okay in the end." I smile at her and take her face in my hands. "I love you, Elora. I always will." I kiss her, and the feeling of her back in my arms again is like no other, and I know this is just the beginning.

EPILOGUE

As I set the table for dinner, I can't help but be nervous. After all, it's not every day we have both his parents, his brother, and Daniel over for a meal. I'm relieved, when Logan says he didn't tell his parents about Daniel being the cause of his accident. The police said that since they couldn't prove he was intoxicated, and the fact that he turned himself in, weighed heavily in his favor. He was fined and given a ticket for failure to control his vehicle. Other than that, he was given a stern lecture. He blames his sudden increase of alcohol intake on his guilt from that day, but since then, Daniel hasn't had a drop to drink. He's even got a new girlfriend who doesn't drink either, and she's sworn to keep him dry.

Logan still keeps his mother at arm's length. He claims he's fine with their relationship, but I've secretly devised a plan to hopefully fix it. I'm not sure it'll work, but if I'm going to be around the two of them, I'd like to see them grow closer.

As for Logan and me, we couldn't be happier. I've finished school and gotten my degree as an RN. I'm sure the work will be stressful, but there's something about the feeling of helping people that I just can't dismiss. It's as if I was born to do it. Logan has declared his desire to be a Physical Therapist. He's already started taking some prerequisite classes and has been accepted into PT school. And, because of his background being a Medic, it won't take him long at all. I couldn't be more proud of him.

Now, as I lay out the last plate, I feel a set of arms engulf me around the waist.

"Good evening, Mr. Turner." He smiles against my neck and kisses me there.

"It's a very good evening, when you're here, Miss Foster." I turn in his arms and stare into his beautiful eyes.

"I'll have to agree with that sentiment," I say, and I kiss him. As usual, the world falls away, as I float on a cloud.

"Ahem," a voice breaks in. "You know, you *do* have a room in this house," Michael says. We both turn to look at him.

"Go away. Can't you see we're busy?" Logan says with a smirk. Soon, a pair of arms wrap around Michael from behind.

"Leave them alone," Jenna scolds. "They've had enough of your comments for one lifetime." He smiles broadly and turns in her arms.

"How about if *we* get a room then? My room." He smirks at her, and her smile lights up as they kiss. Logan rolls his eyes at the sight, but I bring his attention back to me.

"I love you," I say, very sincerely. "Don't ever doubt that."

"Never," he says, and we kiss.

I'd like to take a moment to give a huge THANK YOU to all my readers and fans! I've gotten so much love from you, and it's very much appreciated. I love every single private message, direct message, and email I get from you. Keep them coming, *please!*

To those of you who took the time and left me an honest review, I send out a *special* thank you. It takes so little time and effort to bring a smile to my face. Leaving me your thoughts about my books in such a public way really makes my day! It also helps others discover stories they too might come to love. Good or bad, I appreciate every word.

If you enjoy reading my stories, then spread the word! Telling others about books you like, and writing reviews, means more to an author than you know. So please, join fan pages, discuss your favorite novels on social media, or by word of mouth. Whatever you do, just share. We couldn't do what we do, without you!

Sincerely,

Kate Squires <3

You can contact me directly at:
KateSquiresAuthor@gmail.com
My Website:
www.KateSquiresAuthor.com
Follow me on:
Facebook
Kate Squires-Author
Twitter
@KateSquires3
Pinterest

@KateSquires3
TSU
Kate_Squires_Author
Instagram
KateSquires_Author
Goodreads
Kate Squires
LinkedIn
Kate Squires
Google+
Kate Squires, Author

Kate Squires was born and raised in Ohio where she still resides with her husband and children. She has always loved writing but never, ever thought her life would lead to sitting in front of her laptop for hours on end creating stories other people would read some day. As a child she hated reading until a certain trilogy turned that all around for her. Now she can't get her hands on enough books. Kate has dabbled in all sorts of odd jobs ranging from dog groomer to dance instructor, but her true passion is creating characters out of thin air and making them do her bidding. Her published works so far are That Kiss, That Promise, I Will Catch You, Tracing Hearts, and When Love Breaks. Visit her website for more information about her books and upcoming events. www.KateSquiresAuthor.com

Made in the USA
Lexington, KY
29 July 2017